BLIZZARD

CAMBRIA HEBERT

Published by: Cambria Hebert
http://www.cambriahebert.com

Interior design and typesetting by Sharon Kay of Amber Leaf Publishing
Cover design by Cover Me Darling
Edited by Cassie McCown
Copyright 2018 by Cambria Hebert

ISBN: 978-1-946836-17-5

BLIZZARD

Bellamy

The days of me sleeping through everything, including a zombie apocalypse, were over. Now I could pretty much be summoned awake by a single drip of the bathroom sink. In the neighbor's house.

It wasn't a leaky sink that woke me up today. Or any other number of sounds that might be unfamiliar to me in this new house.

No, today I was awoken because I was being stared at.

Cracking open an eye, I glanced beside me and was met with a giant, furry head right beside mine. The second Charlie saw me glance in his direction, his big tail beat on the floor in greeting. I made a small sound, but didn't move. The St. Bernard was not to be put off. His head, which was already resting on the mattress, scooted closer, and he blew a giant cloud of dog breath in my face.

"That's so disrespectful," I told him.

His tail beat more rapidly against the floor, and a low whine vibrated his throat.

Sitting up, sleep still clinging to my brain, I scanned the bedroom, and a rush of warmth wrapped around me. Getting woken up by major dog breath at an early hour wasn't so bad when you got to wake up to a dream.

Imagine that. I didn't go to sleep to dream; I woke up instead.

Strands of wavy blond hair fell over my shoulder, brushing against my cheek when I looked to the side at Liam. He was sleeping soundly, his strong features relaxed, his light-brown hair tousled and falling over his forehead. One of his arms was thrown out toward me, and the other was folded over his abdomen.

The dog lumbered over to the bedroom door and stared back. I held up my finger, telling him to wait just a minute, then pulled the blankets up closer around Liam. Brushing back a lock of his hair, I smiled down. I still couldn't believe I was here. With him.

Even though life was crazy as hell, scary, and probably about to get even more complicated, I still couldn't help but feel awed by his presence. I felt lucky. Lucky to have gotten a second chance with my first love. My only love.

Brushing a barely there kiss across his brow, I left the bedroom, following closely behind Charlie until we reached the door leading out into the snow.

He burst out with a joyful bark, and I giggled, watching him romp off the deck and into the yard. I put on a pot of coffee, anticipating the fragrant scent of the brew, went back to the door, and called out for Charlie. He glanced up, a pile of snow on his nose, and shook his head, making it scatter everywhere.

Clearly, he wasn't ready to come back inside.

Briefly, I entertained the idea of making breakfast for Liam, but since it had only been two days since coming home from the hospital, and during that time we hadn't left the cabin at all, the kind of breakfast I wanted to make him wasn't an option. That would require grocery shopping.

Instead, I poured myself a mug of still-brewing coffee, adding a touch of cream and sugar to it. Carrying it to the living room, I turned on the fireplace. I'd never lived anywhere with a fireplace. There was something about it that was just so homey.

My eyes strayed from the flickering flames to the thin laptop lying on the coffee table nearby. *Curiosity killed the cat.* Wasn't that the saying? I forced my eyes away from the device and back to the crackling fire.

I'm not a cat.

And technically, wasn't my life already in limbo?

Glancing toward the hallway and back to where Liam lay sleeping, I made a frustrated sound and blew out a breath. Abruptly, I turned from the mantel, stuffed the laptop beneath my arm, and went back into the kitchen. At the island, I set down the mug and opened the computer and powered it on. As it was booting up, I opened the door, and Charlie came barreling in, skidded around the island, and plopped into a prim sitting position. His eyes were expectant, and I grinned.

Practically climbing over his giant, furry body, I grabbed the treats and handed him a large, wavy one. It was supposed to look like bacon. It actually kinda did.

I didn't have to tell him to lie down because the second I handed over the snack, he slid onto the floor to chomp away.

Once I was on the barstool, I called up the net browser and then typed in what I wanted. My stomach clenched. The entire time, my mind told me to turn back and that I knew better than this.

Okay. So yeah. I knew better. And I sort of felt bad for searching up my boyfriend on the internet. But I was also dying of curiosity.

Ha! Maybe that's why curiosity killed the cat! Maybe he didn't investigate when he should have, and he died of suspense!

See? It was just further proof that I needed to do this.

After all of Liam and Alex's conversations without words, every look they exchanged when his knee was brought up, and then hearing what the doctor said to him at the hospital… I had to know.

Hell, I felt bad I didn't.

I'd come plowing into Liam's life here at BearPaw. We'd barely had time to catch our breath. Liam took my problems on as if they weren't life and death. He coaxed out everything horrible about my past.

How did I repay him?

By knowing nothing about him and his life.

I knew he loved me. I felt it.

Was I really worthy of Liam's love?

I wanted to be. Desperately. So much so that here I was creeping around like a stalker to find out exactly what happened with his knee and how he lost his career.

True, he said we would talk. I knew he would tell me everything I wanted to know. Maybe if I knew a little, then talking about it wouldn't be so hard. It was beyond clear to me that it was going to be hard for him to open up about it.

Add that to the fact we still had to have a conversation with his parents… It just didn't seem like the time to bring up this stuff. He had enough on his plate.

Olympic Medalist Liam Mattison suffers major setback!
Record-setting Olympic snowboarder career on ice?
Liam Mattison surgery forces retirement.
The golden boy spiraling into darkness.
No More Medals!

The headlines I scrolled through were harsh. Article after article snowballed on top of the other, burying all the amazing press on everything he'd accomplished in the past eight years.

I should have been paying attention. I shouldn't have let my own life keep me from checking in on him.

My shoulders slumped as I stared at the screen. Even if I had known, what could I have done? It seemed our lives blew up around the same time. I would have wanted to be there for him, but it would have been impossible. Not only was I in hiding, but back then, I'd still thought he'd played me. I didn't know he'd missed me just as much as I missed him.

So much lost time. So many missed opportunities.

Tugging the mug across the counter, I cradled it in my palms, allowing the heat of the coffee to seep into my skin. I didn't want to read these articles. The headlines alone made my teeth clench. They were all written by someone else.

By a stranger who didn't know Liam. By a reporter just regurgitating what they'd heard or what "sources" had revealed.

I wanted the genuine truth. I wanted the words and feelings straight from Liam.

If I couldn't see how it all went down myself, then I would have *him*, the only eyewitness who could tell me.

See how it went down... The thought echoed around my brain.

My eyes flashed up to the laptop. Quickly, my fingers flew over the keyboard as I called up something else.

WATCH: The day Liam Mattison's career died.

I almost slammed the lid of the device closed when I saw the title of the video. But the thumbnail kept me captivated. It was Liam dressed in full-on boarding gear: black snow pants, bright-white jacket, a black helmet, and silver goggles. Not one inch of his skin was exposed. There was a board strapped to his feet, and he was midair.

His body was suspended above the halfpipe, the board up high, his hand gripping the edge.

Even if his name wasn't in the title, even without one inch of his body or face exposed, I knew. Liam had a way about him when he boarded. There was something almost majestic and joyful about the way he controlled a snowboard, the way he seemed to bend with the wind and become part of the mountain when he competed.

I'd never been to see him live. For years, I'd watch his competitions online from the secrecy of my own home.

Ah, he was something. Watching him cut through powder, flip his body into the air, and soar, it gave me chills. I could only imagine what it had been like to be on the mountain while he was competing.

I thought about the way he looked in the hospital when the doctor told him his ACL was stretched. About how he'd asked, stiff-lipped, about his chances for the pros.

Was Liam planning to return to snowboarding?

Had that been his plan along?

I didn't know. I loved him, and I didn't know.

I tapped on the video so it would play.

Announcer one: *"Next up, we have the current reigning king of snowboarding. Liam Mattison has held the title for the best snowboarder in the world for nearly two years now."*

Announcer two: *"I have to say, Tony, it's a wonder the snow doesn't melt beneath this guy when he boards. He's just that good. He's been on an all-time career high since coming off the Olympics last year and bringing home the gold for the second time."*

As I listened to the announcers, I stared at Liam, who was preparing for his run. The goggles were already over his eyes, the helmet securely in place. I watched him bend down to check his board, then stand back up and adjust the goggle straps. The black material covering the lower portion of his face dropped, and my belly dipped at the glimpse of familiar light-brown stubble and full lower lip.

He turned to say something to the person standing nearby, and he grinned. The camera stayed with him as he concealed his face and adjusted his gloves. In the background, the crowd cheered and roared. I imagined the cold air swirled around everyone as the bright sun shone down, making the pristine, packed snow glitter.

Before turning his body completely toward the pipe, he fist-bumped the guy standing nearby who wasn't in frame of the camera.

His shoulders rose and fell with his deep breath.

Announcer one: *"And here we go."*

Announcer two: *"The way he's been performing this week, this run will just concrete what we already know. Liam Mattison is a history-making athlete."*

My heart was pounding, the grip around my mug so tight my knuckles began to ache. The sound of his board cutting over the snow as he pushed off and the strength in his thighs and legs as he moved was captivating.

He went into this first move and nailed it perfectly. The announcers' voices began again, likely singing the praises of the jump, but I was beyond hearing them. All I heard was the pounding of my own pulse as I watched him with my heart lodged in my throat.

Cheers drowned out the announcers, and my own air expelled raggedly when he made the second turn perfectly. But just as soon as the relief and pride came, fear chased it back. I knew what was coming next…

My fingers and knuckles ached again. My shoulders gradually pulled up toward my ears as tension sank its claws into the back of my neck. Liam went airborne again, the board strapped to his feet.

Announcer: *"He's looking a little extended…"*

All the sound on the video cut off. It was as if the person who cut the footage knew this moment would have far more impact if there was no one saying anything at all.

No cries of disaster. No exclamations of injury. Not even a quiet recounting of what could have gone wrong.

In a spilt second, everything changed.

Liam was literally at the highlight of his career. At the top of his mountain.

Then all of it was ripped away.

His body dropped to the side of the pipeline, his board catching at the wrong place. He ricocheted back, but not enough. His head cracked off the edge. His body sort of hunched inward but then went taut as he fought for control.

Even after the blow to his head, he still fought for control.

His board hit the snow, and his body jolted. One side seemed to give out, and his leg buckled right under him. He went down. The board dragged behind him as he kept sliding, skidding over the snow. When it stopped, a mist of snow blew around his body.

The audio cut back in, and people were calling out frantically. Several were rushing toward him.

I watched Liam try to sit up, only to crumple back to the snow.

Tears filled my eyes. A horrible pressure sat on my windpipe, and I pressed the heel of my hand against my mouth to keep from crying.

With my free hand, I reached out and hit the screen, pausing the video.

The image frozen on the screen was Liam lying in the snow with a group of concerned people leaning over him.

After a few long moments, in which I sat there and stared watery-eyed at the screen, I pulled the hand away from my mouth and sighed. "Oh, Liam," I whispered. "I should have been there."

Movement from the hallway drew my attention, and I glanced up.

Liam pushed off the wall, uncrossed his arms, and levelled me with a steady, unreadable stare. "I'm glad you weren't."

Liam

First there was surprise. The surprise gave way to guilt.

"Liam." She turned away from the laptop, toward me, those emotions flickering behind her eyes.

Charlie got up and trotted over to see me. I spared a moment to scratch behind his ears, not once taking my eyes off Bells.

"I—" Her voice faltered, and she winced.

I went the rest of the way into the kitchen, hating the pain in my knee. Hating the pain in her eyes. Hating the footage I knew she'd just watched.

"You don't have to explain," I replied gruffly. At her side, I hooked a couple fingers around the corner of the screen and tilted it toward me, glancing down at the image frozen there.

A moment caught in time. Suspended in reality with technology. I'd relived that day in my head so many times. It was still jarring seeing it on screen. Things always looked different when you were on the outside looking in. In my memory, I was *in* that moment. I was *on* the ground. My viewpoint was from pain and panic. Looking at it this way sort of made it fresh again, as if I also needed to view it from the spectators' point of view.

The second I hit that day, I knew. Before my body crumpled onto the snow. Before I even really realized what was happening. I'd known. I'd known my life was changed forever.

"I've asked myself why about a million times since that day." I admitted, still looking at the screen. "Why did it have to happen then? At the height of my career. Why this injury, as opposed to all the others I'd come back from over the years? Why that? Why then? *Why?*"

I heard Bells swallow, and she rose from the barstool. "I'll get you some coffee."

I watched her move around the island. My shirt rode up the backs of her bare thighs as she reached to grab a mug. We'd barely left the bed in two days, and even still, just the glimpse of her creamy, naked thigh was enough to make my body respond.

The sound of the coffee pouring into the cup was soothing. As was the sound of her putting the carafe back on the burner and adding some cream, just the way I liked it. I sank down onto the stool she'd just vacated, the seat still warm from her body heat.

The mug made a light thump when she set it on the counter and pushed it right in front of me.

"Thanks, sweetheart." My voice was still rough from sleep, or maybe it was from the emotion clogging it.

Finding her watching this, hearing it play from the hallway, brought it all back. The anxiety, the frustration… the sense of loss. It all pummeled me for a few endless seconds as I watched the emotions play over her face as she lived it for the very first time. I felt as if it were just yesterday instead of last year.

The way I had to limp over to this counter was a bitter reminder that nothing had changed.

Drawing back, I held out my arm, inviting her into my lap. She stepped forward, then faltered, her eyes slipping to my knee. I made a bad-mannered sound and gently towed her close. She climbed into my lap, balancing most of her weight on my "good" leg.

I wrapped my arms around her from behind and dropped my chin to her shoulder. "That the only thing you watched this morning?" I spoke quietly beside her ear.

The length of her blond hair brushed across my bare chest with her nod, bringing a rush of emotion into my heart.

"There's more videos like that?" She seemed horrified.

I chuckled a little. "I've been hurt a few times. Some of them were a lot worse than this one." I recalled the past, then turned somber. "But that was the one that took me out of the game."

I couldn't help but feel acrimonious about it. In my mind, it truly wasn't the worst of my falls in my pro career. But if you asked anyone else, this one would be the one they named because this one was the one that kept me down.

It wasn't supposed to keep me down.

"Sometimes I get this feeling…" she whispered, her finger tracing the handle of the mug.

"What kind of feeling?"

The admission came out like a secret rush. As though she expelled the entire sentence with a single held breath. "Like I don't know you."

I jolted beneath her. Everything inside me withdrew from the confession. I wanted to make a joke. I had one on the tip of my tongue.

I couldn't.

I couldn't make light of that. I couldn't smile and make those words go away. If I did, they would haunt me. Hell, it seemed they were already haunting her.

I pushed up, taking her with me. She squeaked with surprise, but I kept going. Her feet hit the floor, and she turned, trapped between the counter and my body. My hands slid beneath her arms and lifted so she was sitting on the counter in front of me. Her knees fell open, and I stepped between them, anchoring my hands flat on the counter on either side of her hips.

Leaning close, I studied her blue eyes intently. "That's not true."

"If it wasn't true, I would have seen that before." She pointed to the laptop. "I would know about all your past injuries and everything you had to overcome to get those medals. I would have understood exactly what that conversation you had with the doctor was about, and I would be able to have secret conversations with you with only our eyes."

My chest tightened, and a ripple of denial moved down my spine. "None of that shit matters," I replied darkly.

"Yes, Liam, it does." Her eyes stayed intent on mine. "Details matter. Everything about you, down to how many cavities you have in your mouth, matters!"

I made a face and sniffed with an air of superiority. "*I* don't have any cavities."

Bellamy rolled her big, beautiful blue eyes. "Of course *you* wouldn't."

I grinned, showing her my pearly, cavity-free teeth.

She shook her head, but the humor died far too soon.

I sighed. "I get what you're saying."

She gave me a *yeah right* look.

I drew back just slightly (I wasn't willing to put that much space between us). "Don't you think it drives me insane that I didn't know about your dad? That you love to cook? About everything you've been through? I watched the trial coverage and read articles about the secret star witness who would be lucky to make it through her testimony alive, and I didn't know that was you."

"I'm glad you weren't there," she whispered.

The second the words left her mouth, her eyes flew to mine. I nodded, knowing what she was thinking. I'd said the exact same thing just moments ago.

Living with that injury, losing so much, had been hard enough. The last thing I wanted was for her to suffer through it all, too.

Her shoulders slumped. I felt the defeat wave off her, and I wanted it gone. Wrapping my hand around hers, I shifted so a lot of my weight was pressing into the counter between her legs.

"You might not know all the details of my career, all the places I've traveled, or even what I'd been hoping for in the future. But what you *do* know is far more important than any of that."

"And what is it I know?" she asked dubiously.

I gestured to my mouth. "Duh. About my dental hygiene."

She tried to act like she wasn't amused. Too bad the lift to the corners of her mouth betrayed her. I winked, and she shook her head.

Lifting the hand I held, I pressed her palm against my chest. Her fingers were cool compared to my skin. Her hand was small compared to mine when I pressed her palm flat over my heart. "You know places inside my heart no one else has ever met. You know how hard it is to breathe when we look into each other's eyes. And I'm betting you feel a gentle tug right about here"—I poked my finger into the center of her chest—"when I walk into a room."

Her eyes scoured mine. "You feel that, too?"

"Ah, sweetheart, I definitely feel it, too."

Our foreheads met, and we both smiled. Too soon, Bells pulled back, her brow knitting. "It doesn't make sense that I could love you so very much and not know the details."

"You think knowing my favorite color or the state of my teeth means you love me more?"

"Your favorite color is blue," she said, mildly affronted.

"'Cause that's the color of your eyes." I kissed the tip of her nose.

"I want the details, Liam. I want everything about you."

"You already have the most important parts, Bells."

A stubborn glint came into her eyes, and I chuckled even as my stomach clenched. This entire conversation made me nervous. What if once she knew about everything, she decided she didn't love me as much? I was no longer a seventeen-year-old without baggage and big dreams. I was midtwenties with experiences, failures... with—

"Liam." Bellamy interrupted my internal debate.

I sighed. She deserved everything. And I couldn't keep worrying she might find out and walk away. "Everything is want you want? Then everything is what you will get."

I lifted her off the counter and gestured for her to grab her mug. "C'mon, then." Taking the laptop and my coffee, I went into the living room, dropped down on the sofa, and propped my feet up on the coffee table.

Bellamy sat down beside me, tucking her legs beneath her. I snagged a thick, plaid blanket off the side and tossed it over her, pulling some of it over my lap.

"What are we doing?" she asked, watching me.

"Getting comfortable. Everything takes a long time."

She made a face. "How about you just tell me about snowboarding?"

"I think everything might be easier to talk about." I admitted, sipping at the coffee. When she didn't say anything, I glanced over at her. "You make good coffee, sweetheart."

"I know it's hard for you, but will you try?" The soft understanding in her voice was almost my ruin.

I'd tell her anything she wanted to know, even if it ripped open all the wounds I'd been working so hard to heal. I nodded and kissed the back of her hand before threading our fingers together. "For you? Anything."

"When I first came here, you said you came back to BearPaw because of an injury. It was always kinda implied that you weren't going back, that you couldn't."

"I did leave the pros because of my ACL. I had no choice. It was a bad tear. I had surgery, physical therapy… the works. But something like that takes a long time to heal. And even once it's healed, there's no guarantee it will hold up to the kind of boarding I do. Or that after everything I'd even be as good."

Fuck. Just saying that out loud was hard. That was always my biggest fear. That I wouldn't be as good.

I glanced down at the coffee in the mug. "From the time I was six years old, I lived with a snowboard strapped to my feet. Nothing else mattered to me. I was a junkie. Hell, the only friend that stuck around was Alex. Everyone else got sick of me always being feet deep in powder."

"Everyone here loves you," Bellamy rebuked.

I smiled. "Yeah. People love the idea of me. My celebrity. My family name. The medals and titles. That's not real friendship. That's not real love."

"You gave up a lot," she murmured.

"Even you," I echoed. Regret did not mix well with coffee. I sat up, plunked the mug down on the table, then sank back into the cushions. "My whole identity was wrapped up in being a snowboarder. In being a pro athlete. And then…" I gestured to the laptop. "It was gone."

Bellamy's free hand settled around the base of my neck, her fingers playing in the short strands of my hair. Goose bumps lifted over my arms because her touch felt that good. "It was difficult."

I made a sound. Difficult was a massive understatement. "I spiraled into this place… into this dark abyss that seemed to open up inside me and swallow me whole. I was so fucking angry. So lost. The doctors tried to tell me I might be able to return, but I was beyond hearing it. All I heard was the voice inside my head, telling me everything I worked so hard for was gone."

"What happened?"

"I was a hostile patient. I hated anything that tried to pull me back to reality."

She made a sound, and I glanced over at her. "I'm glad you weren't there, Bells. I hurt everyone around me. I never want you to see me like that. I never want to be that again."

"I would have loved you anyway," she whispered, her fingers still brushing through my hair.

I made a soft sound and closed my eyes. "I'm not so sure you would have." I kept my eyes averted toward my lap even when I heard her indrawn breath and felt her physical reaction.

"You actually think that you being hostile and angry is enough to make me stop loving you?"

My chin lifted, eyes boring into hers. "How do you know?" I challenged. "How could you possibly be so sure?"

She didn't even have to think about her answer. She was absolute. "Because even after I thought you played me, I loved you."

Leaning up, I kissed her fiercely. My heart ached with love, with the fear of loss. And from all the years we missed with each other. She tasted like coffee and comfort. When I deepened the kiss further, the fingers against the back of my neck tightened, and she sighed softly.

Too soon, she pulled away. "Are you trying to distract me?"

I lifted one brow. "Is it working?"

"No." She confirmed but then sucked her lower lip into her mouth. "Maybe."

Growling, I forced my eyes away from her seductive lips. "Alex came home from the army and showed up at the facility I was staying at."

I was totally skirting around what I needed to spill. I was being a chicken shit. I ought to be embarrassed.

Better embarrassed than watching her walk away.

Bellamy made a small surprised noise. "You weren't here at home?"

I shook my head. "Not at first. At first, I was in some state of the art facility in Denver, with trainers and doctors that specialized in sports medicine. I ate, slept, and breathed my injury… I know being there helped the recovery of my injury, and I was a lucky bastard to have access to that kind of care, but…" Faltering, I shook my head and leaned it back against the couch.

Bells withdrew her hand from my neck and brushed at the long strands of hair on top of my head. "It was good for your body, but not your mind. And when those two things are working together, it makes you feel like you're falling apart."

I rolled my face in her direction. I don't know why, but the fact that she could verbally communicate what I was feeling left me a little awed. "Yeah."

Lifting our clasped hands, she kissed the back of mine. Her lips made a crack in the darkness that still lived deep inside me, the same darkness this conversation was making swell. Like a ray of sunlight, she burst through that crack, and a little bit of relief brought me a sense of peace.

"Alex took one look at me and recognized the dark in me…"

"He has it, too," Bellamy echoed.

"Yeah. His time in the army hardened him in a lot of ways." I made an amused sound. "He told me to stop being a damn Nancy and suck it up."

She drew in a breath.

I smirked. "I punched him in the face."

"Oh my God! Why do you look proud of yourself for that?" she demanded.

I shrugged. "It made me feel better."

Bells made a disgusted sound, and I chuckled.

The laugh was short lived because I knew this conversation couldn't go further until I confessed. "He's the one that figured it out. I couldn't hide from him."

Bellamy sat forward, leaning her body into my side. Her face was intent, perplexed. "Figured out what?"

My shoulder brushed against her when I inhaled. Turning my head, our eyes collided. I prayed to God that soft, worried… yet loving look in her eyes didn't change once I spoke the truth.

Swallowing, I tucked a strand of hair behind her ear, letting the softness of it soothe my ache.

"I was abusing pills." I confessed.

Then, because I wanted to be very clear about what I was telling her, I went at it balls to the wall.

"I'm an addict."

Bellamy

Just like that, Liam's darkness stepped into the light.

Of all the words he could have spoken. Of all the secrets those silver eyes could conceal, him being an addict was something I didn't expect.

Yet it made perfect sense.

Liam was a man of commitment. He committed himself so hard to what he loved, almost to the point it was detrimental to his own health. He committed to me full throttle all those years ago, to the point of wanting to give up his dreams. He committed to boarding to the point of becoming the greatest boarder in the world.

And now?

Now he was recommitted to me, despite the mob. Despite the danger I brought into his life.

When Liam did something, it wasn't halfhearted. So in a twisted way, it made sense that he became an addict.

"Bells," Liam rasped.

I glanced up, realizing my silence was probably hard for him to bear.

"This is why you've been so reluctant to talk to me. To tell me about what happened after your accident." It was also why Alex seemed to watch Liam carefully when talk of his reinjured knee came up.

"I wanted to be the guy you remember, Bells. Not some half-assed, broken version that you thought you might have to pick up off the floor from beside a bottle of empty pills."

I sucked in a breath. "It got that bad?"

I never should have stayed away for eight years. I never should have let that little girl scare me off.

He shook his head. "No. But it could have."

Relief washed through me. Not for myself, but for him. These last few weeks, he'd been taking care of me. Sheltering me. He hid it so well, the fact that he needed it just as much.

"I'm sorry I didn't tell you sooner." The apology rumbled out. "I just..." He reached for the front of my shirt, bunching the fabric in his hand, tugging me even closer. "It was just so good to finally have you back. I didn't want to lose you twice."

A strangled sound vibrated my throat and chest. "Oh, baby," I whispered, cupping his face and staring nowhere else but into his silvery, stormy eyes. "When I said I wanted everything, I meant it. Everything isn't just the good... It's the difficult, the dark, and sometimes the scary."

A sense of awe came into his face, lighting up the storm in his stare like lightning on the darkest night. He was absolutely stunning. Flawed. Strong.

Mine.

"I don't think you understand. I'm off the pills now, but I'll be an addict the rest of my life. There will always be that chance that I could slip back into that darkness that lives in here." He tapped his chest.

"And there's a chance—a really good on—some scary men are going to come here and try and kill us." I shrugged a shoulder. "We both have some baggage."

Liam made a sound. "That's out of your control. But this? *Addiction?* That is something with the ability to control *me.*"

I tilted my head to the side, regarding him. "I don't care."

He blinked.

I smiled.

His lips parted, and though I loved the sound of his voice, I cut off his words with my fingers. "You aren't the boy I remember from eight years ago. You're more. You're better." I smiled, then whispered, "No longer a boy… but a man."

His throat worked. "I lost my career. I fell to the bottom of a pill bottle…"

"Even still, I've never met anyone who compares to you."

The back of his head hit the couch. "You mean it."

I smiled. I'd barely—if ever—seen him vulnerable before. Not like this.

It was adorable.

Smiling, I climbed into his lap, my thighs falling to either side of his hips. "I love you, Liam, and nothing will ever change that."

The sound of him inhaling as his lips met mine set my heart to a fluttering pace. It felt he was somehow sucking out a piece of my soul and keeping it for himself.

I let him take all he wanted.

When finally our lips pulled apart, I smiled. "Maybe now it will be easier for you to tell me the rest."

He smiled, a new ease surrounding him, and it made me feel guilty for not giving it to him sooner. "I'm an open book, sweetheart."

"All right then," I mused. "Read me another page."

Liam

I shouldn't have doubted her.

Staring at her now, into her earnest blue gaze, and physically feeling the unwavering support she boasted, I should have known.

It was hella hard, you know?

To realize someone could possibly love you as much as you love them.

Now I knew. It was undeniable.

I didn't have to hide that darkness in me. That deep change addiction had caused. I was more jaded as a man than I'd been at seventeen.

Bellamy was still here. Still in my lap.

Just wait until she sees that darkness up close. Knowing it's there and seeing it are two completely different things…

Shut. The. Fuck. Up. I told the taunting voice inside me.

In my lap, Bellamy turned and reached for her coffee, which she'd abandoned on the table. Once it was in her palm, she turned back and took a sip, still focusing those blue orbs on me from over the rim.

"You gonna share that?" I rumbled.

She smiled and, instead of offering the cup, she pulled it to the side, leaned in, and kissed me. I sucked the coffee flavor off her tongue.

"Best coffee I've ever had," I murmured when she drew back.

"I love you," she told me.

Those words seemed overused these days. Three words that had been spoken so much by everyone you would think people would become desensitized to them.

It was different when she said it.

Almost as if she spoke in another language, but it was still perfectly clear.

"Now talk." She demanded.

I obliged.

"It was after my surgery. I started taking too many pain pills. They were meant to dull the pain in my knee, but they also seemed to dull everything else around me. It made it easier not to think."

"What about your parents? Didn't they realize?"

I swallowed, the remnants of some old feelings rising. "My parents weren't in Denver with me. They, ah, weren't there."

Bellamy's forehead creased. I watched her try and reconcile what I'd just said with what she knew about my parents. It didn't match up, something I was all too aware of. "I don't understand."

"They had pressing commitments here," I answered.

"But you're more important."

I'd thought so, too. *Yet another reason you fell into the bottom of a bottle.*

Clearing my throat, I moved on. Rehashing the way it cut when my parents weren't as present when my life imploded wasn't something I wanted to do. Besides, it didn't matter now. I'd come home, and it was like that time hadn't even happened. My parents treated me as they always did.

Which made their absence all the more confusing.

Still, I wasn't going to dwell.

"Alex came to visit. He figured out real fast the doctors there were letting me have too many pills—perks of being a star athlete, you know."

Bellamy's face pinched. "Those doctors knew you were abusing pain pills and did nothing!" The fire in her eyes and the way her small hands fisted at the mug was endearing. She had a lot of intensity in her for someone half my size.

"I can be very convincing." I wagged my eyebrows.

"That is not funny, Liam Mattison!"

It was kinda funny. "Well, I was a lot easier to deal with drugged up. Like I said, I was a beast of a patient."

"You couldn't have been that bad." She doubted.

"Yes," I intoned, allowing just a touch of the darkness in me to show. "I can."

Crossing her arms over her chest, she huffed. "You don't scare me."

"That's because I would never hurt you, baby," I told her gently. "But not everyone is you."

Her eyes widened a bit, hearing the underlying steel in the words.

"Anyway, Alex cut off the supply of pills, sat his ass beside my bed until I was discharged, then convinced me to come home."

"The doctors listened to him?" Bells questioned.

I chuckled.

She grimaced.

"Alex can be very persuasive, too."

Her eyes went wide. "Did he punch someone, too?"

I smiled, nice and toothy.

She groaned. Then she surprised me. "Whoever he punched deserved it. They weren't supporting you; they were hurting you. I wish I could punch them, too."

My heart tumbled. I kissed the backs of her knuckles. "No punching people, sweetheart."

"Could you walk?" she asked, going back to the subject. "When they released you?"

"By that point, yeah. I still wore a brace. I still used crutches, which I fucking hated." My voice turned growly at the thought of those damn wooden chopsticks. "I sat in this cabin for a few weeks, surly and pissed off." I blinked, trying to clear the old emotions that still felt so fresh, and smiled at my girl. It was hard not to smile when she was looking at me so innocently with those cerulean eyes.

"That's when Sharon brought me Charlie."

She sat up a little straighter, interested. "Sharon gave you Charlie?"

"His owner died in a car accident. He was lonely. I was lonely… Sharon knew we needed each other."

Charlie knew we were talking about him and lumbered into the room with a giant string of drool hanging from the side of his mouth. His tail wagged when we both looked at him.

"Oh, Charlie," Bells crooned and patted the space beside her on the couch. Needing no more invitation, the dog leapt onto the couch, making it dip, and crawled as much of his body into her lap as he could. The drool smacked into our clasped hands and slimed us both.

"Ew!" Bells shrieked.

I laughed, and Charlie tried to push closer, his hot dog breath filling the air.

"Dude," I told him.

His tail beat against the couch.

Making a face, Bellamy lifted our hands and began wiping them on the blanket. "I'll do laundry later," she murmured.

Charlie's giant tongue licked up the side of her cheek. She squealed again, and I laughed out loud.

She released my hand and used the shirt she was wearing (which was mine) to wipe her face. Then her humor-sparkling eyes turned to me. "He made you feel better."

I smiled and nodded. "After that, things seemed to get easier. I started getting out more. Alex and I spent some time together… I got back on a board and started picking up some lessons. It was good to be back in the snow. It made me feel more normal, less like my life was over."

"You were happy again," she surmised softly.

I reached out and dragged my fingers through the silky length of her hair. At the ends, I curled it around my fingers, tangling us together. "As happy as I could be without you."

She smiled and leaned forward, pressing her cheek against my chest. It took a moment of untangling, but once I was free of her hair, I tucked my arm around her and held her close.

"Was it hard? You know… to stop taking the pills."

I stared over her head at the fireplace. Kicking the addiction to pills had been brutal. "I can only imagine how much worse it would have been had I been taking them for years instead of just a couple months," I replied.

"What about your career?"

"No one brought it up for a few months. I think everyone was afraid it would send me spiraling again. I might have been putting one foot in front of the other, but it was still a huge loss for me."

Her head lifted off my shoulder, and she met my gaze. "I'm sorry, Liam. I know what it's like to feel like you've lost your entire life and to have to start over again.

I know how hard that is. And you did it all in the face of addiction."

We gazed at each other for long, charged moments.

"I'm proud of you," she told me.

The electricity and tension in the air was palpable and caused a tightness in my lungs. I honestly didn't know how I'd spent the last eight years without her. How I could ever spend another day without knowing she was mine. In that moment, I knew she understood my losses. She'd had them, too.

But in that moment, those losses paled in comparison to that morning eight years ago when she never came. In this moment, the greatest loss of my life had been her.

But she was back. She was here. "You're mine," I growled.

Surprise widened her eyes, along with a veil of confusion because we hadn't been talking about us. I moved quickly, my body leaving the back of the couch, torso twisting to face her. My hands cupped her jaw, thumbs stroking lightly over her jaws.

"Promise me you're mine. That you won't leave. No matter what."

"Liam," she breathed out. "I already promised you that."

I gave her a gentle shake. I needed to hear it again. Listing off everything I'd lost over the years and knowing… *knowing* there was more to come left me desperate. "Promise me, Bellamy. Again. Right now. I can handle anything as long as I have you."

A troubled look came into her eyes. Tears welled, threatening to spill over, but they didn't. "I'm yours."

Our mouths fused together with the sound of my breath expelling. Against my ribs, my heart hammered wildly, and the tips of my fingers sank a little deeper into her skin. Bellamy tilted her head back and opened up. My tongue plunged into her mouth and twisted around hers.

We kissed until oxygen became essential and the demand of my own body made me mad. Ripping free, I gulped in great breaths even as I yanked the neck of the T-shirt down to expose her collarbone and shoulder. Dragging my lips across her skin, deep satisfaction teased inside me.

I wanted more.

Needed more.

"Liam." Bellamy gasped.

Her hands palmed the sides of my face and forced it up. My stare slammed into hers, and her breath caught. I let her see the bold desperation in my eyes, just how bad the need was.

She didn't say whatever it was she'd planned.

Bellamy didn't say anything at all.

Instead, she lowered her mouth to mine once more.

Bellamy

I couldn't have everything. Not unless I gave it.

Right now, Liam didn't want words. Or explanations. It was clear he would talk and confess anything I ever asked. It was also clear a man with his kind of demons needed far more than just a listening ear.

Kissing Liam was what I imagined free-falling would feel like. Thrilling, breathtaking, so intense that thoughts couldn't even form in your head. There was no fear, though, because I knew when I landed, it would be in his arms.

A rough sound vibrated his throat, and his body pushed closer. Flattening a palm against his warm shoulder, I pushed. He went because I went with him, not once breaking the contact of our mouths. His back hit the couch, and I rocked instantly against the rock-hard erection between us.

I pushed off of his chest, forcing our mouths free. Liam's eyes shot to mine, his stare like a silver lightning storm in a summer night sky. His chest heaved. His lips were glossy and plump from the kiss.

With gentle hands and flashing eyes, he pushed the length of my hair behind my shoulders. I couldn't stop the shiver wracking through me as his hands brushed over the bare skin of my shoulder.

The second my hair was out of the way, Liam hooked a single finger into the neckline of the T-shirt I'd stolen from his drawer. In a sudden and seductive move, the sound of it tearing filled the room.

I glanced down, surprised, as the morning air brushed over my bare chest. My nipples turned erect instantly, from the breeze or the way he looked at me.

I was possessed. Completely. Totally. It was almost as if I were no longer my own… but solely his.

The shirt hung tattered around me. His large hands made such easy work of the soft material. I wanted to speak, but his stare held me speechless. I wanted to smile, but the intent on his face left me anticipating.

Pushing the shirt off, I allowed it to fall onto the floor behind us. Liam made a sound and surged forward, his hands cradling my back as his mouth latched onto one of my breasts. I arched into him, fisting my hands in the long, messy locks on his head. He sucked deeply, so deliciously that my center began to ache and throb. Rocking into his erection, I arched forward, riding his rigid cock while he sucked and rubbed my chest.

His nails dragged down my back when his face finally lifted, and I continued to ride him, wishing there was a lot less clothes between our bodies.

Liam surged up, hugged me to him, and latched onto my neck. He sucked deep and hard. I cried out, and he started to pull away. The tension in his body changed and spiked.

I pushed his head back down and gasped. "No." I tilted my chin up. "You didn't hurt me. I liked it. I want more."

He growled. The sound vibrated my throat when he went back for more. I sighed deep, bearing down on his middle as tension knotted within me.

Liam's hand tangled in the hair hanging to my waist. He wrapped his hand around it and held my head back while he assaulted my throat and neck and sucked until I knew without a doubt there would be a mark.

Shoving my hands between us, I rocked back enough for me to work my fingers down into the waistband of his shorts, beneath the boxers, to brush against his head. Breath hissed out from my lips when I felt the dampness on the tip and exactly how rigid he was.

Liam moved so fast I didn't register the movement until my back hit the couch and he was over me, all bare skin, wild eyes, and straining muscles.

Charlie retreated somewhere in the house. I heard his nails clicking over the floor, but then Liam ripped the panties off my body and threw them over his shoulder.

I was breathing heavily when he rose onto his knee (the good one) and scorched me with the heat in his stare. I watched him shove down the shorts and boxers, his proud, thick dick jutting out from his body and literally quivering with need.

He lifted my ankle, draped it over the back of the couch, and then placed his palm against the opposite thigh and pushed wide.

Completely spread out beneath him, his eyes raked over my body and his fingers dipped into my dripping core. He groaned, and the tendons stood out in his neck.

"I'm yours." I reminded him, almost a taunt.

In one single motion, his body came over mine and pushed deep with a single stroke.

Both of us moaned. My body sank deeper into the couch as some of his weight pushed against me. Both of us had gone still with that first rush of blissful contact, but then Liam started to move.

Our stares caught and held as he thrust into me over and over again. The sound of our skin smacking together and the way his hair fell over his forehead as he drove was incredible.

"Liam," I whispered, reaching up.

He dropped down, bringing our chests together, grabbing the end of the couch over my head and using it as an anchor to pull himself even deeper inside me.

My mouth fell open and my head rocked to the side as pleasure unlike anything I'd previously felt before vibrated through me. He was so deep I knew he had discovered a part of me no one else had. It was almost as though he were taking my virginity all over again.

He was my first for the second time... my only forever.

Breath hitched in my chest. Liam rocked, and his head rubbed against my walls. I felt his hand on my chin. My face was tilted up, and I knew he was looking at me. I tried to look back, but everything was blurry.

His voice was gruff. "You're crying." I felt his thumbs brush over the wetness on my cheeks I hadn't even known was there.

I sensed his retreat before he actually moved. I reacted fast, locking my legs around his ass and holding tight. "Don't," I whispered. "Stay."

Liam pushed deeper. My eyes rolled back in my head, and I began to move against him. I felt every single inch of him, and every time I rocked, his head rubbed the perfect secret spot.

He held himself deep and let me fuck him, my breath coming in shorter and shorter gasps the closer I got to the edge.

Suddenly, I felt his lips at my hairline, drifting softly over my forehead. The gentle sensation of such a tender kiss combined with the unyielding steel literally filling me up was my undoing.

My legs fell open as I rocked down on him one last time. A cry tore from my throat as an orgasm ripped through my entire body, taking over and robbing me of every single sense but pleasure.

When my body went slack, Liam began to move. He mimicked the way I'd been fucking him just moments before, rotating his hips and rubbing that spot over and over again.

My body quivered and shook beneath his. The amount of force behind the orgasm that ripped through me lingered even after it started to fade.

Liam drew back just slightly, and I looked up, but I still couldn't see. His warm chuckle made my eyes slide closed, and I arched into him with a moan. Even after that soul-shattering orgasm, he felt so incredibly good.

"Can you handle more?" he asked, his voice gravely and restrained.

I smiled. "Can you?"

His body rose, his dick retreated from my body until it was almost gone, and then he plunged back in. Over and over, he thrust into me, fast and hard, bringing my satiated and spent body back to the edge again.

As he plunged in me again and again, he reached down and pushed my legs even wider. Suddenly, he was gone. His cock that had filled me perfectly left me empty. I started to sit up to follow, but he pushed me back down.

His tongue licked up my core, and I shuddered. Lips closed around my clit, and he began sucking gently, making my hips rock to his rhythm. His fingertips played along my opening, caressing the fine skin, playing in the slippery silk, and occasionally dipping into my body.

I called out his name, and he bit the inside of my thigh playfully and rose back up. His dick was still painfully hard, the head swollen. I watched with heavy eyes when he wrapped his hand around the base and stroked up. A bead of pearly white appeared on the tip, and I licked my lips.

I didn't get the chance to taste him, though. He plunged back inside me like a stallion and pumped his hips until we strained against each other.

"You're mine," he growled, his mouth falling right against my ear.

I grabbed his face and pulled him down for an ardent kiss.

I knew the instant he was ready to explode because he shoved deep again, so deep a strangled sound left his mouth and floated into mine.

Liam lifted just enough so our eyes could collide. "I'm staying," he insisted, a renewed fire lit his stare. It was almost a challenge.

Liam would never have to challenge me, though. I would give him anything he wanted.

"Always," I whispered, lifting up far enough so I could press a kiss to the corner of his lips.

Liam's arms wound around me, clutching me against his sweat-slick chest. I hugged him back as the release flowed over him, making him quake and moan until we were lying in a heap, gasping for breath. Every few seconds, his stomach muscles would contract and he would thrust lightly into my core.

His lips latched onto the top of my shoulder and sucked gently. I dragged my fingertips up the length of his spine. He was heavy and hot, but I didn't care. I lay there completely spread eagle beneath him, but I had never felt so secure.

"Baby," he murmured, releasing my shoulder and pushing up enough to look down. His lips were pouty and full, his eyes relaxed and their usual shade of gray.

Whatever it was he'd been so desperately seeking before, he'd gotten, and I felt the deepest gratification knowing it was with me he'd found it.

I swept the hair away from his face and cupped his jaw. "I love you."

The pupils of his eyes dilated. I watched them expand with my whisper. His chest swelled, pressing against mine once more. "There's love. And then there's the way I feel about you," he murmured, nuzzling the underside of my jaw.

My heart tumbled. When it recovered, it felt heavy in the center of my chest. It beat slowly, thudding along as his words found a place to settle inside me.

After another moment, Liam pushed up. His body towered over mine, blocking out the rest of the world as if he were the only one who existed.

I could live in that world. Hell, I would volunteer.

"I'm sorry."

That snapped me out of the post-sex stupor I'd been so happy to wallow in. "Sorry?"

His eyes closed briefly, as if he were guilty.

"Hey," I crooned, reaching for him. "What's the matter?"

"After that?" he mused, shaking his head. "The entire world could blow up around us and I would burn a happy, blissful man."

I smiled at the image he painted. Then I asked, "So?"

He moved inside me. "I didn't wear a rubber, Bells."

My mouth formed a little O.

The guilt from his features cleared, and his dark brow arched. "You didn't notice?"

"I noticed that it felt... *so* good. Like I was so close to you." I rubbed my hand up his chest.

His arm muscle flexed when his body lowered so he could kiss me softly. He didn't linger, though. Instead, he pushed up, his body leaving mine. I made a sound of protest, but he sat down on the couch and kicked off the shorts and boxers still around his ankles.

I sat up, and he reached for me, tugging me right into his lap. The evidence that he definitely did not wear a condom was between my legs, a sensation I was most definitely not accustomed to.

Liam wrapped the red plaid blanket around my shoulders and met my eyes intently. "I took advantage of you."

I laughed. He didn't join in.

Oh. He was serious.

"Liam."

He shook his head like he wasn't going to let me explain it away. "I was half out of my mind, just talking about what it was like after that fall… thinking about my father. Having you here in my arms."

"You were thinking about your father?"

He made a sound. "Not during."

I pressed my lips together, trying not to laugh at the look on his face. "I meant before, when we were talking." I kept my voice patient. Liam was so much alpha. So much in control. But there was this other part of him… almost like a little boy who sometimes needed a little bit of reassurance. I didn't think I quite realized that until this morning.

"Yeah," he replied, rubbing his palms up and down my blanket-covered arms. "I'm a possessive bastard." He concluded.

"Possessive, definitely." I agreed. Then I touched him softly. "But I don't mind."

His eyes flashed to mine.

I smiled. "That means I can be a possessive bitch with you."

He threw back his head and laughed. "I don't want anyone but you, sweetheart."

"Neither do I."

"I'm not gonna change." He warned. His hands flexed against my arms.

I covered one of his hands with mine, calming the agitated gesture. "I don't want you to change, Liam. I love every part of you. Even the possessive part."

"What about the part who made love to you without a condom?"

"You act like you have some nefarious plan to either infect me or impregnate me." I teased.

His jaw muscles flexed. "If I had anything wrong with me at all, I never would have put my dick inside you, even wrapped." He jabbed his finger in the direction of my, um, lady parts.

I grabbed his wrist and stroked the inside of it. "I know that," I told him gently. My, he was a prickly bear this morning. I paused, still rubbing the sensitive skin below his palm. "Do you ever... still want pills?"

His brow furrowed. "What?"

"The darkness you mentioned before. It's not just what happened with your career that caused it. It's the addiction. It never fully went away." I saw remnants of it in his eyes.

He rubbed a hand over his face and blew out a breath. "Me being an addict will never fully go away, sweetheart," he replied, gentle. "Do you understand that?"

I nodded. "I know. I can handle it." I started to say more, then stopped.

"Don't do that." He took my hand. "Tell me. Tell me everything."

"I'm kinda relieved to know. To know where that dark in you comes from. I've felt it before, so to finally understand..."

"I'm usually better at keeping it at bay." His shoulders left the back of the couch, and both arms slipped around my waist. "It's been hard lately... with you and all the shit going on."

"I know. It's okay."

He shook his head once. "Don't do that."

"Do what?"

"Give me a free pass to take advantage of you and act like an asshole."

I grabbed his face. "You didn't take advantage of me, Liam. I loved it. I just said I'd never felt closer to you."

"Yeah, well, there was nothing between us." His voice was rueful. "Once I realized what the hell I was doing, I couldn't convince myself to pull out."

"I wouldn't have let you," I whispered. It was why he'd told me he was staying right before he came. Liam came inside me. I shivered.

He tightened his arms around me, rubbing a palm up and down my back.

"You came inside me," I whispered against his neck. My voice was sort of awed.

He must have thought I was upset, because he pulled back. My stare found his, bouncing between his beautiful eyes. "You're inside me still."

"Yes, sweetheart, I am."

Ah, the knowledge of that was overwhelming. An instant aphrodisiac. Perhaps I hadn't only been kidding when I told Liam I would be possessive, too. The idea of him inside me, with nothing between us… It was just as delicious as it had felt.

Knowing he'd left something of himself behind… That was even better. Without thinking about it, I put my hand over my middle. I knew I wasn't pregnant. The odds of that after only once without protection were pretty slim.

Still. That slimmest chance caused a feeling inside me. It wasn't panic. Or even dread. It was something else.

A soft sound left Liam, and I glanced up. His stare was focused on where I touched my belly. "I like the way that looks, Bells," he intoned, still staring. "A whole fucking lot."

"You do?"

He made a rude sound. "Are you kidding? Just the idea of you walking around with my baby growing inside you is enough to make me want to go at you again."

I smiled. A wistful feeling moved through me, and I sighed, letting my hand drop from my middle. "Now wouldn't be a good time for that, you know, since I'm a target of the mob and all."

A look so deadly passed over his features. I shivered again. After a moment of me not saying anything, he expelled a breath. "I won't do it again until you're on the pill. Rubbers from here on out."

I didn't like the idea, especially since I just had a taste of what he was like without anything at all. But I knew it was necessary. Yes, the idea of having Liam's baby was wonderful, but the reality was less than. At least right now, when people were trying to murder me and Liam had an injury… plus his father. Something he just admitted was weighing heavily on him.

"I'll call and make an appointment for birth control as soon as I can, okay? Then we can ditch the condoms."

He grabbed my face, pressing our foreheads together. "Only if that's what you really want."

"Oh, I want." I assured him. Then, feeling sort of shy, I confessed. "No one's ever been inside me like that before."

A rumble filled the space around us. "You have no idea how happy that makes me."

I smiled.

"I've never been bare in any woman before, either."

I sat up. "Really?"

"I'm not a dog, sweetheart," he replied dryly.

I launched forward, hugging his neck. I felt his chuckle vibrate his chest. "That makes me happy."

He chuckled quietly against my ear, slowly dragging his fingers through the length of my hair. I lay against him for a while, reveling in being here with him. Refusing to go back into witness protection was a big decision. One the Feds literally called irrational and unsafe.

They were right. At least about it being unsafe.

I was a sitting duck now. Crone, Spidey, and any other people within Crone's organization knew exactly where I was. They were coming back. It wasn't a matter of if. It was just a matter of when.

Feeling Liam's heart beat against mine, guilt over my decision flooded over me. It wasn't the fact I was putting my own life on the line, but his. At this point, though, it wouldn't matter if I left. Liam would be a target regardless, just because I loved him.

And you know what?

Maybe I was irrational, too. It wasn't something I liked to admit to myself… but yeah, maybe they were right about that as well. Maybe I loved Liam so fiercely, so fanatically that it made being rational impossible. Especially when it came to leaving. I couldn't leave. Not now. Not ever again.

I was afraid, though. So incredibly afraid.

Not of dying.

Of losing this. Of the way I felt right in this moment.

Liam needed me. More than I knew. He was so strong, so utterly stubborn in protecting me, shielding me… making absolutely sure I knew just how much he loved me. There was another side to him, though, one I had only caught glimpses of until this morning.

A darkness lurked in Liam. A sleeping beast. And though he wouldn't admit it and I never would voice it, I think that beast scared even him sometimes.

Liam was incredibly blessed in his life, yet he'd still suffered loss. Perhaps being so blessed made that loss even harder to endure because he knew what it was like to have so much and watch it be ripped away.

I might need protecting. But I wasn't the only one. Liam did, too.

Not just from the men coming for me, whatever was happening with his father, and the state of his knee. There was something else he needed shielded from… something bigger than all those things combined.

Himself.

Liam

I couldn't get it out of my mind.

Of all the things going on right now, of all the heaps of shit I had to deal with and worry about, it all suddenly took a backseat.

I'd been inside Bellamy bare. The kind of raw, intense sex we'd just had on this couch made every single manly instinct inside me roar with pride.

Oh God, the way she felt. Silky-smooth heat that clenched around my hard dick in literally just the right places. I couldn't get deep enough. I fucking tried, though. The way she moaned and moved against me was sinful, as if she too just couldn't get enough.

I was an ass for staying inside her even after I realized what I was doing. I didn't feel bad for it, though. It was a fucked-up thing to know you were acting like a jerk, but not feel any kind of remorse.

Maybe I would if she did.

Fucking A, the way she pressed her small hand against her flat belly. I knew there wasn't a baby inside her, but the rush of pride and pure fucking want at the thought?

Yes.

Hell yes.

I could practically feel my boys scrambling around in my sack with the urge to get up in her and do their job.

A baby. Having kids was literally something I never thought of until I saw her hand on her belly. Until she looked at me with soft, focused eyes that brimmed with awe. Until I slid inside her without anything between us. How primal the urge was to do it again, to plant a life inside her and watch it grow.

"Liam?"

"What, sweetheart?" I murmured, letting the silk of her hair cascade through my fingers.

"What changed?"

The stubble on my jaw caught in her hair when I titled my head down toward her. "What?"

Bellamy sat up, and though she was still in my lap, she was no longer pressed against me. A moment of sorrow whipped through me. Hair slipped over her shoulders, and the blanket fell around her back. Her cheeks were pink, her lips still swollen from kissing. Her perky breasts were on full display, the pink nipples at attention.

"God. You are so fucking beautiful," I told her, rubbing my thumb over her lower lip.

She smiled, the light-colored lashes around her eyes sweeping downward. Tenderness surged inside me, piercing my heart and once again making it difficult to breathe. If this shit kept up, I was going to need an inhaler to live in this house with her.

Loving her body but knowing it was chilly, I tugged the blanket back up around her, pulling the ends closer together beneath her chin. Her eyes lifted to mine, and I smiled.

"Ask me."

I watched it dawn on her that she had been about to ask me a question. No wonder she and I were so slow at learning about the details of each other. We could barely have a conversation without becoming distracted.

Bellamy is the ultimate distraction. Something about that thought pierced me, and I didn't like it. *Maybe your eight years apart were meant to be. So you could become a pro boarder.*

I gave that thought a violent shove. I didn't know where the fuck it went, but I hoped it never came back. That felt a whole hell of a lot like me having to choose. Choose between her and my career.

Not today, Satan, I thought darkly. *Not today.*

"You said before no one ever brought up you returning to snowboarding. But it's obvious that idea was there."

"My coach called me. A few weeks before you came home actually," I answered. "The Olympics are next year, and my sponsors called… They want me to come back."

"They didn't replace you after your accident?" she questioned.

I smirked. "I'm irreplaceable."

Her finger jolted out between the blanket edges and poked me in the stomach. "Modest, too."

"Just stating the facts, sweetheart."

She rolled her eyes, but then the finger that was previously poking me was joined by the other three, and the poke turned into a caress over my chest. "I can't say I disagree. No one was ever able to replace you in my heart."

I caught her hand and narrowed my eyes. "Nor will they."

"Never," she whispered.

Well, that was a satisfying response.

Entwining our fingers, I relaxed into the couch. "I hadn't wanted to retire. Hell, I planned to stay pro for as long as possible," My jaw tightened a bit, and I glanced across the room toward the fire. "When I did finally go out. I wanted to do it on my own terms. My own choice." An angry sound ripped from me. "Not because of some twist of bad luck, something I couldn't even control."

"You were going to go back."

"I was definitely entertaining the idea. I'd been boarding between lessons. Alex and I would go to the back part of the mountain, one that wasn't part of the resort. I was working on some stuff… seeing if my knee could take it."

Her blue eyes implored me for more information. "And could it?"

"Yeah." I admitted. "With some conditioning and dedication, I could have gone back."

"Could have?" She puzzled. Then her eyes widened, looking down at my knee and the brace strapped around it. Her gasp filled the entire house. "I ruined it for you."

"No," I insisted immediately. I'd known the second her eyes drifted to my knee she'd blame herself.

Bellamy shook her head and scrambled backward, trying to get off me. The blanket was tangled around her, and she fell backward. With a curse I shot forward and caught her just before she hit the coffee table.

She didn't stay still, though. The near fall barely registered. She used my arm to steady herself and finish moving away from me.

A surly feeling bubbled up inside me as I watched her step backward, clutching the blanket around her. "You were about to head back to the pros, to the Olympics!" She fretted. "Then I showed up and you got involved with me… and now look!" she exclaimed, pointing at my knee. "Just look at what I did to you! I took the one thing you wanted most away from you!"

Shoving up, I stalked across the distance between us, my angry strides eating up the space like it was crumbs. Taking her shoulders, I stared down at her face, which was beginning to pinch as if she were going to cry. "That's enough of that," I growled. "Stop."

"Stop what? Telling the truth?"

"What happened on that mountain is *not* your fault."

"Well, you wouldn't have been involved if I hadn't come here!"

I went calm. Deadly still. "You saying you regret coming here?"

Her shoulders slumped. I felt guilty for a fraction of a second, but I couldn't allow this. I *wouldn't* allow her to blame herself.

"No." Her voice was weak. "I just—"

Tightening my fingers around her shoulders, I cut off whatever she was going to say. "Snowboarding isn't the thing I want most."

Her eyes shot up, surprised. "It's not?"

I shook my head. "No. It's you."

She made a sound and pulled away from me. I watched her clutch the blanket around her as though it would somehow protect her. I didn't like it. Not the fact that she pulled away or that she acted like she needed protection.

"That's not true, Liam."

My eyes widened. "Excuse me?"

She made a rude sound, and it was cute as hell. I ducked my head to try and cover up the fact that her angry exasperation didn't make me want to kiss the shit out of her.

"You just sat here and told me about how hard it was to deal with your injury, how out of control you spiraled when you thought you'd lost your career. You just said you planned to go back."

"I said they wanted me to come back. I said I was thinking about it."

She made another rude sound. If she didn't stop it, I was going to have her naked and beneath me again.

"Don't be cute with me." She shook her finger in my direction.

I laughed.

Her eyes flared into blue flames.

"Are you laughing at me?" she intoned.

"Now, sweetheart…" I tried to placate her.

She gasped.

I guess that was the wrong thing to say…

I admit, for a split second, I thought about letting her go off on a tangent about whatever it was that was pissing her off. Angry Bellamy turned me on. She was like a little firecracker that had the fuse of a thousand suns. But then I realized she was angry because of what I was saying, that my words could cause hurt in her heart.

No amount of being turned on was worth that. Not ever.

Closing my arms around her from behind, I held her firmly when she tried to wriggle away. "Listen to me," I demanded beside her ear.

She stopped fighting with a little huff, and I kissed her earlobe.

"Yes, I was considering going back to boarding. In all truth, I wanted to. But I hadn't agreed to anything yet. Around the same time my coach and sponsors were calling, my dad called me into his office. He brought up the subject of taking over the resort."

Bellamy relaxed into my chest. My arms went from holding her still to cradling her. The amount of rightness I knew when she was in my embrace was unparalleled. And that was something that spoke more words than the English dictionary held.

"He's always wanted me to take over the resort, you know. He never pressured me. He never made me feel bad for going off and becoming a snowboarder. Hell, him and mom were the ones that made it possible for me to even go pro."

"You don't want to disappoint him."

"No," I replied quietly. "I don't."

"I think if you went back to boarding, he would understand."

I made a sound of agreement and gently rocked us as I held her. "Yes, he would. He would be proud and he would come to my competitions and he would be front row at the Olympics, just like he was before."

"I wish I'd been there," she mused. "I'm so proud of you, Liam. Of everything you've done."

My eyes closed. I didn't need those words from her, but goddamn, they meant so much to me. "In the back of my mind, I always kinda hoped you were watching." I admitted.

"I did. I watched the Olympics on TV. I saw you win those medals. I cried. I followed your career up until I couldn't anymore..."

Leaning over her shoulder, I pressed my lips against her cheek. "Literally right before you walked into the resort, I had another meeting with my dad. I still wasn't able to give him an answer for sure about taking over the resort. I was going to tell him about going back to my career, but something kept holding me back."

She tilted her head, glancing up at me out of the corner of her eye.

"Then he asked if I could start my training this spring. You know, to take over BearPaw. I was shocked. My father has been a hard worker all his life. My mother, too. They built this entire place. Hell, they put the entire town of Caribou on the map."

My stomach dipped at that because I hadn't known his idea of someday was so soon. And now I wondered if it was so soon because it had to be and not because it was what he wanted.

I thought back to just two days ago when he'd walked into our hospital room dressed like a patient.

Bellamy's hands slid over my arms. "We should call them, Liam. Everyone's avoiding everything. I think we needed these couple days to just... breathe. We only have a small window of time before Perry's men come back. It's time. I think now, more than anything, we need to get you some answers."

I was afraid of what they would say. Maybe because, deep down, I already had an idea. The reason I'd been holding off on going back to pro.

My voice was hoarse when I finally spoke. "I'll call them."

I felt her nod, then turn in my arms. I released her long enough to slip beneath the blanket and pull her close so I could feel her skin on mine. "Before I do, though..." I began. "There is still something I need to make very clear."

She lifted her head off my chest, a question in her eyes.

"For a long time, my career was the most important thing to me. It's what I wanted more than anything." She nodded. I kissed the tip of her nose. "But you, Bells. *You* are more important to me than anything else. Do you understand me?"

"But—"

"No buts." I insisted. "I'd been ready to give it all up before it even started eight years ago. And the second I saw you standing in the resort just a couple weeks ago, I was willing to never go back."

"I don't want to hold you back, Liam. I want you to have everything you ever wanted. It's not me *or* snowboarding. You can have both. I want you to have both." She glanced down at my knee, sinking her teeth into her lower lip. "If that's even possible now."

I tipped her chin back up. "What happened is not your fault. I don't regret following you up that mountain for one second."

"Really?"

I smiled. "Swear."

Bellamy burrowed back into my chest. I rested my chin atop her head. My thoughts turned back to my parents. Specifically, my dad.

The urge to forgo the phone call and just drive over to my parents' house was strong. To walk inside and demand answers. The image of my father in a hospital gown haunted me. The look in my mother's eyes compacted the sense of dread that slammed into me the second I saw him like that.

Deep down in my gut, I knew it was bad.

So bad they were putting off telling me. So bad I was letting them.

It had been two days since Bells and I were in the hospital. Two days since someone tried to kill us. Two days since we met with the FBI and local police. Two days since my parents and I promised each other we'd explain our presence at the hospital.

Two days of avoidance.

Though, if I was being truthful, I'd been avoiding this conversation with my parents since before Bells came back to my life.

Bellamy was right. I couldn't avoid this anymore. I wanted all the information. Like my girl, I wanted everything.

I just wondered how badly everything was going to hurt.

Bellamy

The sound of a door opening and closing, plus the sudden outburst of Charlie's barking, made the blood in my veins turn to ice water.

The dog's deep timbre echoed through the entire cabin, reaching into the bedroom. Grabbing the T-shirt I'd just retrieved to replace the one Liam had ripped off my body, I held it up against my chest like a shield. The spike in my heartrate left me feeling erratic, and the nervous tremor in my hands was unmistakable.

Charlie stopped barking almost instantly, and the sound of voices carried down the hall.

Everything is fine. I assured myself. Myself didn't care to believe me.

Standing stock still with the shirt gripped tightly, I forced myself to relax enough to creep over to the open bedroom door. I moved like a ninja (a very untrained, less-quiet ninja) to the side of the wooden doorframe and peeked out to see who was there.

I was being ridiculous. I knew. If it was someone who had come to kill me, the dog would still be barking. Liam would be yelling or fighting... There certainly wouldn't be a normal conversation going on.

Still. It was difficult to stop clutching the shirt. It was hard to calm the tremble in my knees and the sudden chill over my naked back and arms.

A shadow moved across the wall, and I jolted back, then peeked out again. Liam was in the hallway now, gazing at me, a frown on his face.

"Everything okay?" I whispered.

How he managed to move so gracefully down the hallway, even with a limp, I would never comprehend. Maybe he didn't look as steady as I thought. Maybe the muscles in his upper body were distracting me since he had yet to put on a shirt.

Liam stopped on the other side of the doorframe, leaning down so we were eye to eye. "It's just Alex, sweetheart."

I blew out a shaky breath and smiled. "I figured."

His eyes called me a liar, but wisely, he kept his lips shut. Instead, he brushed a strand of hair off my cheek and smiled tenderly. "You want me to get rid of him?"

"Yo!" Alex called down the hallway, almost as if on cue. "Girl who got away, you back there? I brought you something!"

Interest piqued, I shook my head at Liam. "He brought me something!"

I started to push past him, but Liam's broad, naked chest got in my way. "Hey!"

"You aren't wearing any clothes, Bells," he growled.

I glanced down. I was still holding the shirt, not wearing it. Wincing, I quickly pulled on the new shirt with the BearPaw Resort logo and glanced back at Liam. "Better?"

"Pants," he said patiently.

"I don't have any." We hadn't left this cabin in two days. And though I technically lived here now, I hadn't moved in. That meant the only pants I had were the ones I'd been wearing the night Spidey and friend tried to kill me.

Liam made a grumbly sound that kinda turned me on and wrapped his arm around my middle as I walked by. My feet left the floor even though they kept moving as if I were walking.

"You ain't walking around in front of Alex with no pants on, woman."

A disgusted sound ripped out of me, and I glanced up. "I'm not putting on my murder pants!"

"What the fuck are murder pants?" Liam intoned.

Alex cackled from the end of the hallway.

I sniffed. "Pants that I almost got dead in!"

Liam laughed.

I objected to that. My near demise was no laughing matter!

"Definitely can't be wearing those," he said, humor still in his tone.

I smacked his arm, and he put me down. I marched down the hallway, pantless.

"I just want you to know that it doesn't need to be awkward. Not at all," Alex said when I stepped into the living room.

Charlie lumbered over and pushed his drool-dampened mouth against my hand. I glanced around at Liam with a "look" and then wiped the drool on the side of his shirt.

He grinned widely. "Don't be like that, sweetheart."

With a little huff, I turned back to Alex. "What doesn't need to be awkward?"

"You know… that I had to touch some of your *unmentionables*."

I blinked. "My what?"

Alex pointed to several bags all piled near the couch.

I gasped in surprise. "You brought all my stuff?"

"Figured I wouldn't be allowed to hang out if you didn't have any clothes on," Alex quipped.

Behind us, Liam made a sound of agreement.

I jolted forward and hugged Alex around the waist. "Thank you!" I exclaimed.

"Why can't all bunnies be this excited when I touch their bras?" Alex wondered.

I laughed, but Liam wasn't amused.

"You touched her bras?" he hollered.

"Not all of them," Alex argued. "But there was one hanging in the bathroom." He glanced at me and winced. "Some panties, too," he whispered loudly.

Liam made an aggressive sound and stepped farther into the room.

"What was I supposed to do? Leave them there?" He defended himself. "I was bringing everything else. But like I said, it doesn't have to be awkward. I used a hanger... didn't actually touch them... just sort of flung them in the bag." Alex made a gesture of what he must have done when "flinging" my "unmentionables" into a bag.

I laughed.

"Dude," Liam rumbled. I could hear the amusement underneath his possessive ways.

"Thank you for getting my things, Alex. I could definitely use them." Going over to the bags, I peeked into a few with the new clothes I'd just bought. It felt like it had weeks since we'd gone into town, not just days. My eyes slid to the duffle I'd brought with me when I fled to BearPaw. My emergency bag.

Lots of people might have *in case of emergency* bags or even just plans. No one ever thinks they'll need them.

But I did.

Just looking at that bag—the sum of pretty much everything I owned, the symbol of everything I'd left behind in Chicago—my stomach clenched, and I glanced away. The life I had in Chicago definitely wasn't my choice. It wasn't exactly the kind of life that made me happy, but it was mine, you know?

And for a while, I'd been safe. Safety was something I would never take for granted.

It was also something I might never assume was for me ever again.

You're safe in Liam's arms. My heart reminded me. It left a sorrowful echo through my chest. In that moment, it felt as if taking that safety he so unselfishly offered was putting his own at great risk.

His feet appeared before me. Liam even had good-looking feet. The guy was an anomaly. I glanced up from my things. My eyes went up his legs, lingering a bit on the knee brace.

"Bells." Liam spoke above me. His voice brought my stare all the way up. His mouth crooked up at one side, and some of the tension at the back of my neck eased. "You okay?" he asked softly. Knowingly.

I'd never met anyone who could read me the way he could. Not even my own mother.

"Yeah, I was just making sure everything was here."

"It's all there." Alex confirmed. "I even looked under the bed."

I smiled, glancing over my shoulder. Alex was standing there with his hands shoved into the pockets of his dark jeans. A red hoodie with black-and-white striped strings hugged his upper body. His hair was curly but controlled on top of his head, the style going from longer on top to closely cropped around his ears and at the back of his head. The black wraparound sunglasses were on the back of his head as if he had eyes back there, too. Really, I had no idea how he kept the glasses from falling off when he wore them like that, but they stayed, not even slipping.

"Want some coffee?" I asked him.

"Hell yeah," he drawled. "Liam never asks me that."

Liam grunted. "You know where everything is."

"Sometimes a guy just likes to be asked." Alex informed him rather haughtily.

Liam gave him the finger. "Screw you."

"Liam!" I gasped.

"Please." Liam defended. "He was just going on about touching your underwear, and you want me to make him coffee? Not gonna happen, sweetheart."

I shook my head and poured some coffee into a mug. When I turned from the machine, Alex pointed to something rectangular, wrapped in foil. "Sharon asked me to bring this by."

"What is it?" I asked, sliding the coffee toward him, along with some cream and sugar.

"Banana bread," Liam replied, reaching around Alex to grab the loaf. "Sharon makes the best banana bread."

"It's true." Alex agreed.

"That was sweet of her, especially since I haven't had a chance to get groceries."

"Liam is Sharon's favorite." Alex informed me.

"Am not," Liam rebuked.

"When we both moved back here, she used to show up at your place a couple times a week with food. She never did that for me."

I turned to get some plates and a knife from the cupboards behind me.

"That's because the first time she tried, you answered the door with a gun," Liam cracked.

I glanced around, forgetting about the plates. "What?"

Alex's mouth flattened. "It was the crack of dawn. I wasn't even awake yet."

"Awake enough to get a gun before going to the door," I pointed out.

"Whose side are you on?" Alex accused.

Liam laughed. Then he glanced at me. "Don't let him fool you. Sharon spoils him, too. She just gives it all to me to bring to his house because he doesn't scare me."

"I don't scare anyone," Alex muttered, dark.

I couldn't really imagine Alex scaring anyone. Not considering how snarky and easygoing he always seemed. But then I thought back to the hospital, about how that ominous look came into his eyes and how Liam mentioned he'd been in the army.

Liam slapped Alex on the back and smiled. I turned back to get the plates.

"Speaking of guns. We need to hit the range."

I whirled around, plates in hand.

"I was thinking the same," Alex said.

Neither of them seemed to notice me standing there gaping. "What are you talking about?"

Liam glanced at me. The edges of his lips turned down. "Alex and I go shoot at the range sometimes. Never know when you might need shooting skills."

Alex guffawed. "Should have seen our boy when we first started going. He couldn't hit a target from three feet away."

Liam's eyes narrowed.

Alex held up his hands, surrendering. "It's true. You sucked."

"I don't suck anymore." The absolute confidence he spoke with made me squirm a little.

"True dat." Alex flung his arm around Liam's shoulder. "I taught him everything I learned in the army." An ornery look lit his blue eyes. "Though, you still can't outshoot me."

Liam pushed Alex away, which made him laugh.

"You have a gun?" I asked, wishing my voice didn't sound so hollow. "In this house?"

Both guys glanced at me, their expressions changing from fun to concern. I swallowed, waiting for Liam to reply. He set down the bread, which was partly unwrapped, something I hadn't noticed until just then.

"I have a few guns, sweetheart."

A hollow feeling punched into my stomach. When I breathed, it felt as though my middle were caving in on itself.

Liam's hands closed around my arms. "Bellamy."

"I—ah, I'll just head out," Alex said, bringing me fully back to the present.

"No!" I said, jolting out of the moment I'd just had. "Stay. Have breakfast and coffee. You can keep Liam company while I take a shower and get dressed." I stepped around Liam to pick up the loaf of bread to unwrap it completely so I could slice some.

There was a huge bite taken out of the end.

"Who did this?" I said, pointing at it.

Alex widened his eyes and pointed at Liam. Liam pointed at Alex.

I couldn't help it. I laughed. They were like a pair of little boys!

"Liam!" I turned my eyes on him. "Did you take a bite out of this? I was getting plates!"

"Why do you just assume it was me?" he demanded.

"You have crumbs on your lip."

He brushed them off quickly as he mumbled, "You were taking a long time."

I laughed. Alex seemed to think it was very funny Liam got caught. I turned to him. "Oh, please. Like you weren't gonna take the next bite."

That wiped the smile off his face.

I sighed and set down the bread to slice off the end with the bite in it. "You're like animals," I muttered.

Charlie looked up at me from the floor and licked his lips. I broke off a piece of the bitten slice and tossed it to him. "Good boy," I crooned.

"Hey!" Liam exclaimed. "That's good eats!"

I broke off another piece and fed it to him. The way he smiled at me as his lips brushed over my fingertips made my legs go all wobbly.

The next slice I cut Alex snatched off the island before I could even move it to a plate. "I give up," I declared, cutting a few more pieces. "You two are manner-less."

A piece of the bread Liam snatched appeared in front of my lips. "I think you might be hangry," he told me solemnly. I gave him a deadly look. He nodded. "Bite."

I took a bite. The scent of it right beneath my nose was too hard to pass up. It was moist and sweet, with the perfect amount of banana. "That is good," I said, chewing. "I need the recipe."

"It's a secret," Alex said, snatching another piece.

"*You* asked her for her bread recipe?" I said, dubious. I could not picture Alex in the kitchen, cooking anything.

"My moms did. Sharon won't give it up."

"Your moms," I repeated. Why in the world did he have to add an s to the end of her name? Why in the heck did it make it sound more charming that way?

"Hmm." I turned thoughtful. "Maybe if I take her a loaf of pumpkin bread, she will trade recipes with me."

Liam's hand clamped around my wrist. "You make pumpkin bread?"

I nodded, a little flurry of butterflies sounding off in my belly.

"Pumpkin is Liam's kryptonite," Alex said. "Pumpkin and tacos." He amended.

"I know," I said softly, glancing up into my lover's gray eyes. His stare went soft and then beyond just a look. His eyes felt more like a caress.

"You remember I like pumpkin?"

"Just like you remember I don't like mayo." I'd spent a long time perfecting my pumpkin bread recipe, trying to make something he would like. I never thought he'd actually eat it, but making something I knew he would like… It made me feel closer to him even though we were so very far apart.

Our stares bounced between each other for a few charged moments before I finished up what I was doing, then stepped away from the island. "I'd tell you not to eat it all, but I know you will," I said, gathering up some of the bags Alex brought over.

Chewing loudly, Liam appeared and took the entire load out of my arms. "I got this," he said, still chomping.

I picked up the duffle and followed him back to the bedroom, where he tossed all the bags on the bed. I put the duffle on the floor and then moved to dump out a few of the shopping bags of new clothes so I could find something to put on. "Thanks," I told him, reaching for a soft, loose sweater.

"Bells."

My shoulders slumped a little. "I'm fine, Liam."

He sat on the end of the bed and pulled me between his legs. Taking the sweater I was holding, he tossed it aside and threaded his fingers through mine.

"You don't like that I have a gun."

I shrugged. "This is your house. You can have whatever you want."

His body went rigid, and his hands left mine, settling on my hips to give me a shake. "No. This is *our* house now. Yours and mine."

I looked into his eyes. My heart squeezed. "I'm not against guns. I just—" my sentence ended there, my voice fading away.

"You don't like them." He finished.

"I watched my father get shot to death. I've been held at gunpoint more than once. Shot at…" My lips clamped together.

Liam stood, gathering me against his chest. I sighed and sank into him. He smelled so good. Like a new winter day. But he was warm, and his body easily surrounded mine. I buried my face in his chest, using him to blur out the images I'd just described.

I didn't like guns. I never would. To me, they represented death and finality. Still, I understood why having them here wasn't a bad idea.

His palm cradled the back of my head as he rocked me back and forth slowly. After a minute, he kissed the top of my hair.

"If I could take away all the shit you've been through, I would do it in a heartbeat. I know I was only a kid eight years ago, but if I had known what your dad was all about back then, I would have done something. I would have kept you away from it all."

"I didn't want away from him," I said, turning my cheek so he could hear my voice. "He was my father, and I loved him."

I felt Liam digest my words. I knew he didn't like them. He probably felt the way my mother had, felt I was better off not knowing him. I couldn't say if they were right. Maybe they were. It didn't really matter though, did it?

I'd made my choice, and even after everything, I couldn't regret getting to know the little bit I did about my father.

Liam pulled back, taking my face in his hands to gaze into my eyes. "I want to give you everything, sweetheart. Hell, I will make it my life's work. But please don't ask me to get rid of the guns. I can't. I won't. Getting rid of them is getting rid of a source of protection I have for you. With everything going on, with the men after you, I have to do everything I can to keep you safe."

Emotion welled up inside me. "I know."

He blew out a breath, relief shining in his eyes. "Yeah?"

I nodded. "I understand. I guess I just hadn't really expected you would have them…"

He made a low sound. "We live on a mountain, sweetheart. There's wildlife. There's a resort full of strangers very close by. I don't hunt, and I don't take them out for sport or even fun. Alex and I do take them to the range because part of having them in the house is knowing how to use them responsibly."

"You don't have to explain. I trust you."

"Your trust isn't something I take for granted. I just want you know where I'm coming from."

Rising onto tiptoes, I pressed a lingering, soft kiss to his mouth. The whiskers against his chin and above his lip tickled. "I understand." I promised.

"Love you," he murmured, still kissing me.

I smiled.

"Need some help in the shower?" His hand slid up the back of my thigh, dipping under the shirt.

"Alex is waiting for you." I reminded him.

"Eating all my bread," he grumped.

"I'll make you more."

Liam drew away slowly. "Don't take too long."

"I won't." I promised.

When he was gone, the sense of foreboding I'd felt when they were talking about guns returned. It wasn't just the guns, though. It was having my stuff officially here. Having Alex over… Life moving on.

The two days of alone time we'd had just weren't enough. That was ending, though. Real life and all the problems that came with it wasn't something anyone could put off.

8

Liam

I did it.

I made the call to my parents.

Since I'd hung up the phone—*hell*—ever since I'd dialed their number, a heavy rock settled in my stomach, weighing me down, leaving me with that overfull, uncomfortable feeling.

Bellamy came out of the bathroom, a brush in her hand and a frown on her face.

"What's wrong, sweetheart?" I asked, unable to not peruse her body with my eyes as she walked closer. It was the first time in days she'd been dressed in anything other than one of my shirts. The jeans she wore were more fitted than the ones she'd arrived at BearPaw in. The dark color molded to her ass in a way I frankly found sinful. I'd almost said something about it when she came into the kitchen earlier after her shower, but I figured me telling her I didn't want other people appreciating the view wouldn't go over very well.

The sweater she had on was loose. The gray fabric was soft and slid off her one shoulder, exposing some of her creamy skin.

"My hair is a mess," she declared, tossing the brush onto the bed.

"Looks good to me."

She gave me a look. "I have total bed head because that's exactly where I've been for two days. I should have washed it again this morning, but it's too much work with only one arm."

I glanced at her shoulder, the one she'd separated in the avalanche. It was easy to forget it was injured, especially when she wasn't wearing the sling. "Are you hurting?" I asked, concerned.

Before she even replied, I went to the dresser and retrieved the sling off the top. "I should have made you wear this."

"I've been in bed. It's not like we've been doing that much," she rebutted. Her voice grew softer the closer I got. Her blue gaze dropped to my chest, then slid back up.

Not doing much = sex. But even so, I'd been careful with her. Of her.

"Did I hurt you this morning?" I kept my voice soft like a caress and brushed the back of my knuckles lightly over the injured shoulder. "I was rough. I wasn't thinking about your shoulder."

A ghost of a smile appeared on her face. "I don't think either of us were thinking at all."

I was thinking now, though. Thinking about a repeat of this morning. I shook the thought off. It didn't go far, clinging to the back of my thoughts like an itch that needed scratched. "Put this on." I pulled the sling over her head and positioned it.

The look on her face was adorably grumpy, and I chuckled. I guided her arm into the sling, noting the slight drawn look around her eyes. I sighed. "I was too rough."

"No." The word came fast. "You were perfect. I'm just sore. Probably best I wear this today."

I frowned. "I'll call the PT place I used when I moved back here. See if they can get you in. I'll come with and see what all they are recommending. Then I'll work with you here at home, too."

"You will?" Her voice was small, almost shy.

I kissed her quickly. "Anything for you, sweetheart."

"What about your knee?"

I made a sound. "I'll do PT after that thermal shrinkage procedure."

"That's next week, right? In Denver?"

"Yeah." I could barely think about that right now, though. Funny how the last time I hurt my knee, it took over my whole life. Right after the avalanche, I'd been worried. Hell, in the hospital, I'd been worried. I saw my hopes of returning to snowboarding circling the drain for a second time.

The bitterness and anger still swirled inside me. Even Bells saw it. But right now? Right now, it was the last thing on my mind. Right now, that darkness was being fed by more than just my injury.

I was too concerned with what my father would tell me when we got to their house. I was worried about Bells and the look in her eyes when we talked a while ago about guns.

How much shit could be heaped on a man before he snapped? How severe of a blizzard could hammer a mountain before we all got buried?

Small fingers touched my chest. I glanced down, drawn away from my turbulent thoughts to be soothed by troubled sapphire eyes. "Are you worried?"

I rested my hand over hers. "About my knee?" I shook my head once. "Not right now."

Her brows drew down.

I smiled. "It's all about perspective, I guess. I have more important things to be worried about right now."

Understanding dawned in her eyes. "Your family."

I nodded, noticing the way her very long hair was trapped beneath the straps of the sling. Carefully, I went about freeing it.

"I tried to braid it, but holding my arm up that long hurt." She made a face. "I'm going to look a mess when I meet your parents."

"You met them at the hospital," I pointed out.

She made a rude sound. She tossed her free arm up in the air. "And I looked even worse then!"

I thought it was kinda cute the way she was worried about what my parents thought. I knew they couldn't give a rat's ass. Hell, this was the girl who literally managed to hold my heart for eight years *without* even being around.

"I know they won't care." Bellamy sighed. "It's silly to even think about considering…" She swallowed and glanced up at me. She expected bad news, too.

I picked up the brush and smiled. "First world problems are still allowed even when we have the worst world problems going down, too."

She stared blankly.

I grinned. "You don't know what first world problems are?"

"I'm kinda surprised you do."

I laughed. "I have a TV."

She giggled.

I gestured for her to turn around. "I have work to do, woman."

"You're going to brush my hair?" She was highly doubtful but clearly also intrigued.

"Just helping my girl out," I said, beginning to brush through the very long golden strands. I loved her hair. It was like a waterfall of sunshine down her back.

I didn't realize I'd professed my love for it out loud until she answered, "They wanted me to cut it."

I paused. "Who?"

Even though she was facing away, I heard the smile in her voice. "Witness protection."

I grunted and started brushing again. "The Feds are assholes."

"They did keep me alive during the trial and for a year after."

Begrudgingly, I relented. "Well, there is that."

"They wanted me to cut it and dye it dark." She went on. "But I couldn't do it. I flat out refused. They were quite sour about it."

"Assholes," I muttered, still stroking her now tangle-free stands with the brush.

"I remembered how much you liked it," she whispered, shy. "You told me once you liked it long."

"I still do," I told her, hoarse. It still got me, knowing how much she thought of me all that time we were apart. How much we were still part of each other's lives even in absence. "It's even longer now."

"Leaving it long made me think of you." She paused. "It's silly."

I stopped brushing, gently pulling her around. "It's not. It's fucking music to my ears." My stare pierced hers. The regret I sometimes felt for not going after her all those years ago was so heavy. Almost crushing.

I reached out for the length again and gave her a rueful smile. "I'll braid it."

Surprise covered her face. "You know how to braid?"

"Ye of little faith," I said, guiding her back around. "I'm an excellent braider."

I was a lying liar.

But it was okay to be a lying liar if it made your girl smile, right? Besides, how hard could it be to braid?

My girl wanted braids. I would make it happen.

"Whose hair do you braid?" she asked, clearly doubtful.

"You know, people with long hair." I hedged.

She paused. It was a poignant sound. "Past girlfriends?"

"No!" I said swiftly, not even wanting that idea in her brain. I leaned around so I could stare into her eyes. "You're the only girlfriend whose hair I've ever braided."

"I'm your girlfriend?"

My entire face softened. "You're so much more to me than that."

"Does that mean I get to call you my boyfriend?"

God, she was so sweet. And innocent. And genuine.

I fucking loved her so hard.

I smiled, moving around and sitting on the bed in front of her. "I just moved you into my house. I literally am so lost around you I forgot to wrap it before I made love to you. I'm about to show you my mad braiding skills..."

She giggled. My heart tumbled.

"*Yes*, Bells. Yes, you can call me your boyfriend. Hell—"

Her fingers pressed over my lips, stopping my words. "You're so much more than that," she whispered.

I kissed her. I mean, how the hell could I not?

I drank her in. The sunshine in her soul, the love in her heart... I swallowed down every part of her I could.

When I pulled back, her cheeks were rosy. Satisfaction puffed my chest, and I reached for the hair on the right side of her shoulder, gathering it up. "You're about to be amazed."

She was laughing when I stood suddenly. I had to seriously braid her hair.

"Just let me get it into the four sections here..." I began, sticking my fingers into it.

"You mean three." She corrected.

"Of course. I was just seeing if you were paying attention."

"Mm-hmm," she drawled.

I got it into three sections and then tried to remember what the hell I was supposed to do. I'd seen girls do this before. It couldn't be *that* hard.

After two failed attempts, I dropped it and sectioned it into three.

"How's it going?" Bells asked, amused.

"Perfection," I told her as I weaved the strands into a braid.

Ah-ha! I was totally doing it. Farther down her hair, it started looking more like a twist, so I figured that meant it was done. "What, ah…" I started glancing around.

She held up a thin black band. "Need this?"

I snatched it and looped it around the end of the braid.

I repeated the same process on the other side, only having to restart once. Okay, fine. Twice.

When that was done, my fingers were kinda cramping and I was growing grouchy.

"No wonder your shoulder hurt. This shit takes forever," I muttered.

"I could just put it in a ponytail," she offered.

I glanced down at her. *Now she tells me.* A ponytail. That would have been a lot fucking easier.

I took the second offered black band and tied it around her hair.

"Done!" I declared and stepped back to admire my handiwork.

I did a damn good job.

"I want to see," Bells said and took off for the bathroom.

I blanched.

Her light giggling trailed out from the bathroom. I scowled and marched to the doorway. Bells was standing in front of the mirror with her hand pressed against her mouth, muffling the sound of her laughter. Her bright eyes danced with humor.

The braids were lopsided. One was longer than the other, and yeah… maybe the braids ended halfway down, leaving a lumpy-looking weave and then a ponytail.

And yeah, maybe a strand (or two) had come loose and stuck out.

Ah hell.

I grinned. "Points for trying?"

She twirled around and looped her one arm around my neck. "All the points."

"I'll put it in a ponytail." I offered.

She gasped and drew back. "You will not! I'm wearing it like this!"

My face screwed up, horrified. "You've been through enough, sweetheart. You shouldn't have to walk around with that crime on your head."

Bellamy collapsed in laughter against my chest. I laughed, too. I couldn't help it. That shit was terrible.

"I think it's beautiful," she said with a surprising straight face, looking in the mirror once more. "Because you did it."

As we stared, one of the bands at the end slid down, and the "braid" unraveled.

Both of us burst out laughing again.

I pulled both bands free and set them on the counter. Once I had the brush, I pulled it all back into a ponytail at the back of her head, making sure I actually made the band tight enough to hold her hair this time.

"The fact you even thought about wearing that mess says love."

She smiled. "Well, you are definitely better at a ponytail."

I grunted and set aside the brush.

"What time did you tell them we'd be over?" she asked, looping her finger through one of the belt loops in my jeans.

"Soon."

"It's going to be okay," Bellamy told me, nudging close until she was in my arms. I took care to not squeeze her too tight, though my instincts urged me to crush her close.

"I don't know, Bells," I murmured, stroking the ponytail. "We both know this probably isn't going to be good."

She lifted her head. "No matter what it is, I'm here for you. We'll deal with it. Together."

And maybe that was why.

Even though that familiar darkness was rising up inside me. Even though it seemed I was faced with more than I had been a year ago, I was still holding it back. I was still holding everything together.

Because I wasn't alone. Because I had Bells.

"I'll get a shirt. Then we should go," I said, my voice slightly hoarse.

She nodded and released me.

Before I left the bathroom, I kissed her. Her lips fortified me—something I needed in that moment because I knew the minute I stepped into my parents' house, everything could potentially change.

Forever.

Bellamy

Liam's parents lived in a stone and log cabin located at an elevation that seemed to look over BearPaw resort. There were large, full-grown trees capped with snow and simple mountainous landscaping surrounding the property.

His parents didn't have a huge plot of land, though they likely could have. I would say it was closer to only one acre, but the way it was perched on the mountainside made it feel as though it sat much more privately away from the neighbors.

The house appeared smaller from the front, but I knew it probably only seemed that way as we approached because all the houses here were more impressive in the back where all the views were.

The driveway was paved and surprisingly clean of snow. It pulled around to the side, leading to a three-car garage that was built right into the house. Liam parked the Extreme in front of one of the doors, and I gazed up at the large deck that wrapped around the back of the house. I knew there would be stunning views from up there, and part of me was looking forward to gazing out over the resort.

"Your father must be really proud," I said. "To be able to sit up there on that deck and stare down at a resort town that he basically built himself."

"I actually said that to him once. When I was younger. Told him it was like he was the king gazing out over his kingdom." The smile in Liam's voice drew my eyes.

The smile on his face was wistful and looked even better than it had sounded.

"What did he say?"

"He said he didn't create BearPaw to be a king. He created it because this is where he wanted to be."

"He has amazing vision, because everyone else wants to be here, too," I replied, thinking what a humble man Liam's father must be.

"He's well liked." Liam allowed, his voice turning inward.

I reached for his hand. "Just like you."

"It's not hard, you know? You just have to treat people like they're your equal. Like we're all on the same playing field. In reality, we are."

I didn't think Liam was on the same level as anyone I knew, but I didn't point that out because I understood what he meant. Besides, I think part of his charm was that he didn't actually realize just how amazing he was.

"Are you ready to go in?"

He stared at the house, then hit one of the buttons on his visor overhead. The garage door to the right began opening, slowly revealing the back end of a Chevy truck.

I smiled. "Your dad drives one, too?"

Liam tugged his hand from under mine and grinned. "Of course. He supports the businesses that support me."

When his feet were on the ground, he leaned back in the cab and winked. "Mine's the only exclusive model, though."

I waited for Liam to come around, thinking that even though the driveway appeared to have no ice, it didn't mean there wasn't any. It was a long drop from the interior of this truck, and with one arm already in a sling, the last thing I needed or wanted was to slip, fall, and bust my butt.

Plus, I liked when he palmed my waist and lifted me down. It was just another excuse to have his hands on me. And to feel those inevitable butterflies that always fluttered around sporadically when he was close.

"Breathe," he murmured as he slid me down his body and onto the driveway.

I inhaled.

"Thanks."

He kissed the tip of my nose. Those butterflies got all wound up again. When he stepped back and I could think again, I noted how well my boots stood atop the driveway. "There is no ice at all."

He smiled. "Driveway is heated."

I felt my eyes bug out. "That's a thing?"

Liam chuckled. "Apparently. Sure cuts down on shoveling."

I pointed to the stone beneath me. "This driveway doesn't need shoveling!"

Liam's chuckle turned into a full-blown laugh. "When there are really bad storms or a lot of snow, obviously it still needs shoveled. There isn't enough heat under those rocks to melt a blizzard."

I continued to stare at it as if it were magic.

"Dad usually has a plow come out here for snow removal. Then the heat melts the rest, keeps it clean."

"That's amazing."

"What would have been amazing is if we'd had that when I was growing up. Apparently, he didn't see a need for a heated driveway or a plow company when he had a teenage son to do all the work for free."

I chortled.

"Builds character," he said in a voice I knew was meant to mimic his father.

"So the heated driveway is new." I surmised.

"A few years now." He caught my hand and pulled me toward the open garage door. "He had it installed because he didn't want my mom slipping on the ice and falling."

"That's sweet."

Liam made a noncommittal sound.

The garage was large, open, and organized. Beside the Chevy truck, there was a Chevy SUV, and then on down in the last spot was a vintage Camaro. "That's gorgeous!" I said, letting go of his hand so I could beeline for the old car that didn't look old at all.

Liam's low laugh followed behind me. "You like?"

"It's gorgeous!" I said, running my palm lightly over the cranberry-colored hood with silver racing stripes. "What year is it?"

"Sixty-seven," he said, fondness in his tone. "I helped Dad restore it."

"You guys built this?"

"Not built. We aren't that good. We bought it years back, right after Chevy signed me. It was in rough shape. We fixed it up, and the stuff we couldn't do we hired out. Then we had it painted."

"Do you ever drive it?"

Liam nodded. "'Course. But only in the summer when everything around here thaws out."

"It's definitely too nice for all this ice and snow."

"It was a fun project. Dad and I worked on it in my off seasons."

I noted the BearPaw emblem that hung from the rearview mirror inside the car. "You and your dad are really close. Aren't you?" I asked softly.

Liam swallowed, then nodded.

My stomach clenched. I didn't even want to think about what was waiting for us inside the house. I knew how I felt when my father died. It was terrible. Liam was ten times closer to his father, so...

Don't go there. Stop acting like he's dying when he hasn't even said if anything is wrong.

I lifted my chin. "Maybe you can take me for a ride this summer?"

A slow, seductive smile spread over the lower half of Liam's face. Did I mention the trimmed beard he rocked was like the sexiest thing ever?

I shivered a little, remembering what it felt like between my thighs.

"Cold?" Liam asked. His eyes weren't concerned, though. They were molten silver. He knew what he was doing to me. He knew the power of a sly smile.

The door leading into the house opened. Overhead, the open garage door shuddered a little.

"Liam?"

"Mom," Liam replied instantly. "We're over here. I was showing Bells the Camaro."

Liam's mother stepped out of the house. When her eyes found us, she smiled. "Ah, yes. The apple of the boys' eyes." She walked forward, her feet and lower legs covered by a pair of boot slippers. They looked like a sweater. You know, the kind with the reindeer print and sweater pattern? They had drawstring cords on the back that bobbed when she stepped.

She was dressed in a pair of thick-looking black leggings and a long-sleeved velvet blouse that looked like an oversized shirt. It was tailored well, though, because it didn't appear frumpy or boxy. Just loose and stylish.

Her hair was brown, cut into a chin-length bob, with bangs that slashed across her forehead. The hairstyle framed her face very well, drawing attention to eyes that looked very much like Liam's.

"How are you, Bellamy?" his mom asked, glancing at my arm. She couldn't see the sling, because my coat was wrapped around me, yet I was sure she noted how the one arm wasn't being used.

"I'm fine, thank you. How are you?"

"I'd be better if we got out of this drafty garage." She motioned for us to follow her in the house.

I took Liam's hand as we went. He hit a button near the door as we entered the house, the closing of the garage door sounding.

The lower level of their home was very open with large windows on the back that offered those sweeping mountain views I knew there would be. It looked mainly like a family room and entertainment space with a pool table, wet bar, and huge TV displayed in front of a sectional. It wasn't anything ostentatious or austere. In fact, it looked like a setting you would find in any family home. Of course, it was just a little bigger and had a better view.

Coming up the stairs made it feel as if you were literally materializing out of the lower floor and onto the main level. The light was spectacular. Almost the entire back of the home was made of windows. My eyes went there instantly, the view having its own gravitational pull.

I stared out over the resort, watching the mountains rising up around it with ski runs and lifts stretching vertically up the hills.

I knew in just a few hours, the sun would dip low and all the buildings and cabins would be lit up, as would the slopes and snow.

"Hard not to look at, huh?" Liam said, coming to stand beside me.

"I feel small standing here," I whispered.

"Keeps a man humble," Renshaw Mattison said, coming up behind us. "Looking out at that every day is a good reminder that there are much greater things at work than just you."

I turned. Liam's father wasn't a huge man, but he had a definitive presence about him. One that commanded attention and respect. Confidence was like a cloak around him, and I knew those qualities were what made him so successful at what he did. Those qualities had also been passed down to Liam. It was likely what gave him the drive to become an Olympian.

He was dressed casually in a pair of jeans and a ribbed sweater with a half zipper near the neck. His short hair was brown, not quite as light as Liam's. Except around the temples and ears where it appeared to be lightening to what looked to be a striking silver.

His eyes were not gray like Liam's. They were brown. Liam got his eyes from his mother.

"Hey, Dad," Liam said.

"Good to see you, son," he said, smiling. He had a note of formality about him. Not stuffiness or even reserve. Just formal, as if he didn't know how not to be professional.

"Your home is gorgeous." I confessed.

It was all honey-colored wood tones with pitched ceilings and massive beams that soared overhead.

"I'm glad you approve," he said warmly and then came forward, offering his hand. "It's nice to finally meet you, Bellamy. I have heard about you a bit from Liam."

I felt my cheeks heat, but I smiled and shook his hand. "I've heard a lot about you."

He held a glass that was half full of what I was sure was beer. "Let's get you both a drink," he said, putting his hand at my waist and guiding me across the large open living area, past the staircase opening, and toward the kitchen.

It was a chef's dream. Granite, high-end appliances, a built-in cutting board, vegetable sink, and a grill built right into the gas stovetop.

I stood there kind of in awe, anticipation tingling my fingers as I thought about all the meals I could cook and how much space there was to work with.

"You look like Liam did every Christmas morning!" his mother exclaimed.

I blinked and then laughed. "I'm sorry, Mrs. Mattison. I just love this room." I grinned, rueful. "I think I like it better than the view."

"Ah, she likes to cook! And as I said at the hospital, call me Holly."

"I used to be a chef," I replied. "Well, I was working up to be one."

"Well, I'm a terrible cook," she said. "So anytime you want to come over and use this space is fine with me."

"That's a generous offer," I said, practically salivating over the possibility.

"Not so," Liam's father said from behind. "'Cause if you come here to cook, then I'll get to eat it."

"I'm still trying to get her to cook for me," Liam muttered. "So get in line."

I grinned. "We've been a little busy."

"Yes." Holly's face turned cloudy. "I've been worrying about you." She glanced away from Liam to me. "Both of you."

My chest squeezed a little. She sounded so genuine. It brought a rush of emotion through me because it had been so long since anyone had worried about me. It had been so long since I had any kind of family or support around me at all.

The touch of Liam's hand at the small of my back startled me, and I jumped. "Do you want a beer, sweetheart?" he asked, holding up the bottle in his hand. I hadn't even heard him get one.

"No, thanks." I shook my head.

"Wine?" Holly offered, holding up a bottle. It was a red and a good label.

I nodded. "Thank you."

She poured us each a fairly generous glass. I wondered if perhaps we were all liquoring up because of the conversation we were about to have.

"I'm anxious to know what's been going on." His father began. "I don't like shady happenings going on at my resort. I especially don't like not knowing about them when they involve my son."

"I'm very sorry for the trouble I've brought here," I said, looking down into the wine glass. I was embarrassed. Ashamed. These were wonderful people who worked hard all their lives. They built something that mattered, something that elevated an entire town.

And what had I done?

Brought the mob down on all of them.

God, it was laughable, wasn't it? Or sounded like some bad TV movie. *The mob*. This wasn't the fifties. This was modern day. How could this even happen?

"Bells," Liam intoned. His bottle hit the top of the large wooden dining table stretched out in front of a window offering a view of snow-covered trees. "We've talked about this."

"I can still be sorry." I reminded him. I glanced at both his parents. "I am."

"I'm pretty sure that whatever is going on here isn't something you want," Holly said, reaching out to pat my hand. Her smile was genuine and understanding.

I hoped it stayed that way even after we'd told her everything.

"Liam told me that you might be in some trouble." Renshaw prodded.

I nodded. "And I'm sorry to say that now Liam is involved. Along with the police and the FBI."

Both his parents frowned, and I knew my likability just went down a few notches. Or a lot.

Probably better I hadn't worn those awful braids Liam so skillfully did up for me. I needed all the parental points I could get right now, and bad hair wouldn't offer much credibility.

"And this is why you were at the hospital the other day?" Holly pressed. She turned to Liam. "How is your knee?"

He made a face, took a pull on his beer, and then began picking at the label on the dark-colored bottle. "I stretched the ACL out. I need a procedure and some more PT."

Both his parents seemed to forget I was in the room. It gave me a sense of relief but also one of loneliness. It also made me homesick for my mother.

"Oh, Liam!" Holly exclaimed. "It's not torn is it? Are you sure?"

"I'm sure," he said confidently. "We're going to Denver in a few days." He went on telling them about the thermal shrinkage he was set to have done.

"How long?" his father asked. I could see in his eyes he knew exactly what this could mean for Liam. It made me wonder… Were Liam's parents in the dark about his desires to return to snowboarding?

"I'm hoping just six weeks."

"And the knee will be good as new?" Holly implored.

"I don't think my knee will ever be good as new, Mom." He sounded accepting, but I knew better. I recalled the look in his eyes when he told me about losing his career. I felt the way he'd desperately reached for me.

Beneath the table, my hand slipped over Liam's thigh, gliding down where the tips of my fingers settled between his leg and the chair. Without being inconspicuous at all, Liam let go of his beer and put his hand over mine.

He definitely was not a man who was shy about public displays of affection. Even in front of his parents. Even when my hand was between his thighs.

Granted, it was a gesture of comfort and not sexiness, but still. He made a private gesture public but still held the ability to make it feel secret.

Both his parents turned their attention back to me. Remembering I was there. Maybe realizing it was me Liam looked to for comfort. How awkward did it feel to them? To watch Liam with me, to know we were so much together, barely knowing me at all.

I smiled tentatively. I felt I was skating on thin ice. I didn't want it to appear I was somehow gloating or taking advantage of him. But at the same time, I wanted them to know he was it for me. That in all honesty, their approval meant so much.

Having a family would mean so much.

The mob ripped apart my family nearly two years ago. Actually, no. My father's connections with the mob ripped apart my family before I was even born.

And now here I was… hoping for a second chance at a shot on a family. Wanting people to love me despite the massive luggage I came with. It was selfish. It was probably wrong.

I sat here with my hand in Liam's anyway.

Did that make me a bad person?

I really wasn't sure.

"Bellamy," Liam's father said, sitting forward. "How hurt are you?"

"Looks worse than it is," I replied, glancing down at the sling.

Liam's free hand came up, the pad of his thumb grazing lightly over the giant bruise on the side of my face. Who needed makeup when you had your own personal color wheel already spread over your skin?

"She almost died," Liam replied, slightly hoarse.

Holly gasped. "I think we've danced around this enough," she said firmly. "I want to know what's going on." She divided her gaze between the two of us. Her eyes flashed like Liam's sometimes did. "I want to know everything."

And so I told them.

Everything.

The entire time I talked, I prayed they wouldn't throw me out of this house. And if by some grace they didn't… I prayed the mob wouldn't rip everything away from me again.

10

Liam

The silence that reigned through my parents' house when Bellamy's voice went quiet was astounding.

It was a lot to absorb. I mean, I knew that.

But damn. Did they have to sit there and gape at her as though their throats were full of raw sushi that just wouldn't go down?

The sound Bells's chair made when I grabbed it by the seat and dragged it so close it smacked against mine seemed to shake through the silence. Bellamy glanced at me, her eyes panicked because they were saying nothing at all.

I anchored an arm around her waist, sliding her body along mine. It was a silent message to everyone in this room, including Bellamy, that I just didn't give a damn about all this shit.

I only cared about her.

Dad recovered first, clearing his throat. "You'll have to forgive us, dear. This is definitely not what we were expecting to hear."

She nodded, her blue eyes wide. "It's a lot to process."

"A murder trial, the mob, and an avalanche…" Mom murmured and took a sip of her wine. Actually, it was more than a sip. She drained the glass. "I think I'll get a refill," she said and excused herself to go into the kitchen.

"And the FBI can't do anything? Protect you?" Dad pressed.

Bellamy opened her mouth, but I glanced at her and she closed her lips. "The FBI are assholes," I announced.

"Liam!" Bellamy gasped and yanked her hand from my lap to smack me in the chest. "That is not an answer!"

I made a rude sound, grabbed her hand, and pushed it back into my lap with mine. I liked it there. "It damn well is," I muttered.

"The FBI is doing everything they can. I'm in contact with them on a daily basis."

"And witness protection?" Mom asked.

I made a sound. She'd already told them about her first go in the dumb program.

"They offered to put me back in." Bellamy hedged I almost heard her buckle.

Oh, hell no. "If she goes back into witness protection, her entire identity will be wiped out. Again. I won't ever see her again."

"It's very clear you love her," Mom said to me.

"I wouldn't finish that thought," I intoned. I knew she was about to suggest that sending Bells away might be better. For everyone involved.

"Don't you talk to your mother like that!" Bellamy snapped. She yanked her hand away from me. Again.

Before I could snatch it back, she reached for her wine. "I realize staying here is selfish. I do. I also realize what kind of target I'm putting on Liam. On all of you. That's why I will understand if you ask me to leave your home."

I sat upright. The sudden jolt made my knee sting with pain. "I'm a grown-ass man sitting right here. Bellamy isn't making me do anything I don't want to do. I'm in love with her just like I was all those years ago. She's staying here." I glanced at her. "And if she leaves, I'm going with her."

"No one is asking anyone to leave," my father said, calm. He was always so calm. It was probably why he was so successful in business. He never let them see him sweat. Hell, I really didn't think he ever did. "We're just trying to understand."

"Sometimes even I have a hard time with that." Bellamy confessed.

My father smiled at her. "It's a complicated situation."

"What will you do when they come back here?" Mom asked, frowning.

"I'm not sure yet," I replied.

"I'm still hopeful the FBI will resolve this," Bellamy added.

I wanted to debunk that, but I wouldn't take away her hope. Hell, for all I knew, that's what helped her sleep at night.

Besides me, of course.

"Well, I can double the security around the resort. We have cameras and security measures in place already, obviously. But I'm sure there is more I can do. I'll call Bill in the morning. See what he suggests."

"I wouldn't tell him the exact situation," I put in. "The less people that know about the mob connection, the better."

Renshaw agreed. "Bad for business."

Bellamy's mouth dropped open. It was kinda adorable. Reaching over, I pushed her chin up. "Bill is the guy we use for security here at the resort."

"I don't understand,"

"Sweetheart, this place is too big for us to run security ourselves."

She made a sound and scowled. "I know that."

"Then…?" I was messing with her. It was an asshole thing to do. How was I supposed to resist those little dents between her eyes and the way she wrinkled her nose, though?

"I—" She glanced away from me at my mom, then Dad. "Aren't you going to ask me to leave? It's too dangerous for me to be here around you. Around your son."

I was done messing around. It was fun for about thirty seconds. Was she expecting my parents to toss her fine ass out on the heated driveway? Like for real?

What the hell kind of people did she think we were?

I sat forward, ready to set her straight, but Mom spoke up first.

"Do you love my son?"

Bells looked across the table sharply. Without an ounce of hesitation, she replied, "More than anything."

"Then why on earth would we ask you to leave?" she implored.

"Because," she started, but then words failed her.

"Liam came to me eight years ago and told me he wanted to give up the pros so he could be with a girl he was in love with," Dad told her.

Bells's eyes rounded. "He did?"

"I already told you that." I reminded her.

"No one ever told me that," Mom interjected. "Ren?"

Dad smiled. "Never had to mention it because it didn't work out."

My hand dropped into Bellamy's lap, palm up, fingers spread wide. Her hand slid into mine, and when our fingers linked, it was like an unspoken promise to never let that happen again.

"This time is different," I told my parents.

"Yes, it is," Dad replied. Then he looked at Bellamy. "And life is far too short to not do everything you can to stay together."

Suddenly, this conversation wasn't about Bells and me. It wasn't about the mob, my injury, her injury, or how crazy it was we were sticking to each other like glue.

This was about everything he didn't say but everything I definitely heard in his words.

"Why were you at the hospital, Dad?"

The silence permeating the room when Bellamy told them about her troubles was back. I watched my mother reach across the wooden tabletop, and my father met her halfway. Their hands linked, staying that way while my father picked up the glass of beer and took a sip. I waited as though I were standing on the street level beside a tall building, staring up, watching a heavy object plummet from the roof... clearly intent on crushing me.

When he was finished, the sound of the glass being replaced on the table was background noise for his voice.

"I have cancer."

No. I dropped back against the chair as if I'd been kicked. Three words. That's all it took to change my life forever.

I cleared my throat, but my voice was still raspy and low. "What?"

Bellamy's hand squeezed mine. Her body leaned into me just a little bit farther, silently offering support. My heart thudded heavily, slowly against my ribs as my brain, equal parts glazed over in shock, raced with questions.

"It's kidney cancer. I—" He visibly swallowed. "I'm so sorry to have to tell you."

"No," I told the room. "You can't. You're the picture of health. There's no way you have cancer. You need a second opinion."

"I've had a second opinion," Dad said, patient.

"Then a third." I insisted.

"I—ah…" He glanced at my mother. The look they shared didn't help erase the feelings of disbelief and dread. "We"—he corrected and looked back—"were hoping we wouldn't need to say anything. That it would be treated and taken care of quickly."

"But that didn't happen," I said, my tone monotone and dull.

"Unfortunately, no." Dad's voice cut out, and he glanced at Mom.

"I'm sorry, honey," she said, tears threatening to spill over.

Averting my gaze, I glanced at the sweat forming on my beer glass. "How bad is it?"

There was a brief pause. A pause long enough to break my heart.

"It's spread. To more than one organ."

I opened my mouth to say something. Words failed me. There were none. Nothing I could say. Or ask. Nothing at all that would make this okay. Or even bearable.

I was a grown man. A man who battled his own share of challenges and hurdles. I was strong. Capable. Able to overcome.

I was also reduced.

Reduced to a boy, to a son who worshipped his father, to a human suddenly overflowing with fear. We all know life is fragile. Every day could be our last.

However, it isn't every day you are shown a reminder, given irrefutable proof. It isn't every day that someone you couldn't imagine living without tells you there might be no other choice.

I was having too many of these moments lately. Too many close calls with the people I loved.

"How long have you known?" The soft steadiness of Bellamy's voice elevated me, if only a little. It brought me out of my own churning feelings just enough to be present for this conversation. Gazing at her profile, noting the strength in her posture, the resolve in the set of her jaw. She was speaking for me because right now I wasn't able to do it for myself.

I loved her.

More than I thought possible.

"Close to a year," Dad replied.

Shock crashed over me like a tsunami. I jerked upright, sliding onto the very edge of the seat. My shoe tapped on the floor rapidly, my body's way of expelling some of the anxious, angry energy consuming me.

"A year!" I bellowed. Unable to sit another second, I bolted up. My hand ripped free of Bellamy's, and I moved behind our chairs to pace. "You've had cancer for an entire year, and you haven't said shit to me!"

"As I said, we were hoping the treatment would work and we wouldn't need to burden you with this at all," Dad replied.

I nearly choked. "You are *not* a burden!"

"I don't want to become one, either," he retorted.

I began pacing twice as fast.

Bellamy rotated in her seat, her back to my parents so she was fully focused on me. I avoided her gaze. If I looked at her right now, I'd break.

"The timing wasn't good." Mom jumped in. "You just had surgery. You were angry and lost, facing the reality that you might never be able to pro board again. Adding this to your plate…" Her voice faltered, then hardened. "You're still our child. You always will be. We will always try to protect you."

"Protecting me from the truth is called a lie." I seethed.

How could they not tell me about this? This was literally life and death. I felt robbed. Robbed of choices. Knowing this would have changed everything. I could have done more, been more… *Not been so fucking selfish.*

"You were in the hospital, Liam." I could tell Dad was barely holding on to his patience.

That made two of us.

"You should have told me."

"Why?" Dad's voice rose. "To give you even more reason to swallow more pills?"

I jerked to a stop. Slowly, I rotated and stared at him in disbelief. Was he really using that against me? Using my reliance on pills back then as an excuse to justify not telling me he was goddamn dying!

Holy shit. Is he dying?

I laughed, a hollow, humorless sound. Rubbing my hand over the back of my neck, I noted how hot my face felt. How the tips of my ears burned and how my skin felt tight, uncomfortably tight. My lips parted. Words and sentences spilled across my tongue, fighting for the right to tumble out first.

Cool, soothing hands slid over my heated cheeks. Bellamy's palms were silk against the roughness of my short beard. "Look at me," she whispered.

I tilted up my chin enough so she could see my eyes and read my need to lash out.

"Let's get some air," she murmured. Then without waiting for a reply, she turned to my parents. "He just needs a minute. It's a lot to process."

The soothing, cool hands turned much more controlling. Her arm slipped around my waist and pushed me toward the large glass doors leading out onto the deck with a view fit for a king.

I laughed a bitter sound. Not even kings were immune to cancer.

Blustering wind blew, plastering my shirt to my chest and whirling the hair on my head all around. Lifting my cheeks, I let winter take a bite out of me. My hands gripped the railing. I stood with my back to the house, staring out over the grand resort my father had built.

"It's not fair," I whispered. "It's not fucking fair."

"No. It's not." Regardless of my mood, Bellamy ducked beneath my arm, positioning herself between my body and the railing. She didn't face the view, instead looking solely toward me.

I sucked in a ragged breath and avoided her eyes.

"Hey," she demanded, grabbing my cheeks and pulling my head down. "Go ahead."

Confusion pierced the haze of turmoil. "What?"

"You want to yell at someone, yell at me."

I made a sound.

She gave me a shake. "I mean it, Liam. Fighting with your parents is the last thing you want to do right now. Yell at me."

All the fight drained out of me. Truth was I didn't want to yell at anyone. Except maybe myself. "Cancer, Bells. He has fucking cancer."

Before I realized what she was doing, the sling was ripped off over her head and tossed at our feet. Both her arms came around my waist, enclosing me in a bear hug, a bear that was half my size.

But damn. It was the most encompassing hug I'd ever felt.

One of her hands smoothed up and down my back as her cheek rubbed lightly over my chest. My body remained rigid for the first few moments. I took the comfort, but it was all I was able to do. I stared out across the snow, allowing the frosty wind to blow everything out of focus. Bellamy didn't let go or loosen her grip.

She remained.

Eventually, despite that frost around us and inside me, I began to thaw. Enclosing her in my arms, I hugged her back, rubbing my beard over the top of her head.

"It's why they weren't in Denver as much." I realized. "At the time, I'd just been pissed off that they weren't. I was selfish. I couldn't see past my own surgery. Past my own life."

"You aren't selfish. Your entire world had been flipped upside down."

"So had theirs. And I wasn't fucking there." The guilt of that might eat away at me forever.

Bells pulled back. Strands of her long hair caught in my beard, creating a visible tether between us. "You're here now." Her cerulean eyes searched mine. "Maybe he wasn't ready to tell you, to tell anyone. But you know now. You're here now."

My mind was going a mile a minute. So many thoughts and feelings. So many questions. I took a deep breath and blew it out slow. My palms settled against Bells's face. "You're right."

I didn't know before, but now I did. Now I could be there for them. I could be the strong one like they'd been for me all my life.

Her hands fisted in the front of my shirt and tugged. "I'm not going to tell you it's all going to be okay, because I don't know if it will be. But I'll be here for you. Whatever you need."

I pulled her in, briefly closing my eyes and just feeling her and the calmness she brought to me. "I love you," I whispered.

"I love you," she whispered back.

I bent down and picked up the sling. "You took this off." I gave her a disapproving look.

"You needed both my arms."

My stomach flipped. She was right.

After pulling it back over her and making sure it was in place, I turned back to the house. My parents were still at the table. They looked up when I approached.

"I'm sorry about that. I shouldn't have gotten so pissed."

My father half smiled. "I understand better than you think."

A hollow cavern opened up inside me. I couldn't imagine what he was going through. From here on out, I was going to be strong for him and Mom. What I felt didn't matter. This was about them.

I cleared my throat and pulled the chair back out to sit down. "So you said the treatments didn't work?"

"No," Dad replied. "The cancer is more aggressive than they originally believed."

"Okay, so we'll try something else. What's the next step?"

"Chemotherapy and radiation," Mom replied.

Bellamy sort of teetered behind us, part of the conversation, but not really. Without turning around, I held my hand out to her.

So much for a nice meet-the-parents dinner. Or brunch. Hell, at this point, any kind of meeting that didn't involve some sort of dire circumstance would have been welcome.

Her fingers slid across my palm. I pulled her around into the chair beside me.

"And they think that will beat this?" I asked.

Mom and Dad shared a look.

"What?" I demanded.

Mom answered, her voice shaky. "It's not good, Liam. The prognosis. Even with the heavy treatments."

"How could they possibly know that?" I stressed. "They can't. I'll make some calls. We'll see a few specialists. I'll—"

"Liam," Dad said. "I've seen specialists. Here and in Denver. I even flew to California to see someone. We haven't just accepted what we were told. It's been an entire year of doctor visits and medication and tests."

"So what?" I said, absorbing what he was telling me. "You want me to just accept it now?"

"There's not much left to do."

Mom produced a tissue from somewhere and dabbed at her eyes, then her nose. "Your father isn't certain he wants the heavy treatments."

My eyes rounded. "Why the hell not?"

"Because it will greatly decline the quality of life I have left. And they might not even work."

The life I have left.

Bellamy's hand fisted in the shirt against my lower back. "It's hard to live like you're already dead," she whispered.

I stiffened.

Dad's eyes swung to her, and an inkling of what looked like relief shone through. "That's exactly how I feel. I want to be present for as much as I can. I don't want to be hooked up to machines, enduring the many side effects of the chemo and radiation. I want to *live,* not buy time to waste away."

There was that anger again. It rose so fast, like bile from an acidic upset stomach. I wanted to rage so badly. To demand that he do everything humanly possible to save his own life. That he fight. That he not lie down and accept his fate.

"You can't just give up," I said.

"I'm not. I won't. I'm still working with my doctors. There are alternatives I haven't tried yet. Ones that won't have such severe effects."

"There's still hope," Mom said. I heard in her voice just how much she clung to that hope.

My parents had been together nearly thirty years. What was it like for her to look into the future and not know if her other half would be there?

My stomach clenched and ached. "I want to come to your next appointment. I want to talk to your doctors."

He nodded. "Of course."

"As soon as possible." Prickles of panic began eating at the rage inside me. Along with it, the sound of a ticking clock whispered that time might be running out.

Mom nodded. "I'll call and set something up."

"I really wish you told me about this sooner," I rasped.

"We were doing everything that needed to be done," Mom replied. "We didn't want you to worry."

I glanced at Dad. "This is why you wanted to start training this spring, isn't it?"

He swallowed. "Partly."

Not partly. Totally. My father wanted to train me in running the resort as soon as possible because he didn't know how much longer he would be here.

Jesus.

And I dragged my feet.

"We'll start tomorrow," I declared.

Dad shook his head. "That's not necessary."

"No better time to start."

"Your knee, Liam." Mom reminded me.

I made a sound. My damned knee was always getting in the way. "After the procedure, then. It's a same day thing. I can be up and moving around the day after."

"Liam," my father said in that fatherly tone he always used when he wanted to have a serious conversation.

Like we weren't already having one.

"I don't want you to commit to taking over BearPaw if it's not what you truly want."

"I do want to."

"Then why have you been wavering until now?"

I glanced at Bells. She offered me a supportive smile and nodded.

"I'd been considering going back to the pros."

Mom gasped. "You are! I didn't think that was possible."

"My trainer called about a month or so ago. A few sponsors were hoping I'd come back. I was considering it… you know, for the Olympics next year."

"They are in our back yard." Dad agreed.

They were. It was the first time in a decade that the winter Olympics were going to be held here in the States. In Colorado, no less. What a rush it would be to win another medal in my home state, where it all began for me.

It would be like coming full circle. It would be a chance for me to leave the sport on my own terms, on a high note. And not forever have my career ended by a bad run.

That was before.

"It doesn't matter now," I said. "Going back isn't going to happen."

"Because of your knee," Bellamy said, guilt creeping into her tone.

I snatched her hand and kissed the back. "I told you that's not your fault."

"What about the thermal shrinkage? What's the recovery time on that?" Mom asked.

"Recovery time is minimal, but there's no way to know if it will even work well enough to make me pro ready," I replied. "It doesn't matter. I'm staying here. Taking over BearPaw."

"This is exactly what I didn't want," Dad said, becoming agitated. "You giving up your life because mine is ending."

His blunt words hit me in the face, knocking me a little sideways. I didn't want to ask. Dear God, what the hell kind of question was it? But I had to. Sort of like a queer fascination or a bad movie you couldn't look away from.

"How long?"

Everyone looked at me.

"Liam…" Mom implored.

I shook my head, my stomach caving in. "They told you, didn't they?"

"There's no way to really know. The body—" Dad danced around the question. Which meant I wasn't going to like the answer.

"How long did they give you to live?" Beneath the table, I reached for Bellamy's hand.

"A year."

And suddenly, my father's life, our moments, memories, and everything left unsaid, was on a timeline. A very short timeline.

"You're terminal?" I rasped.

Is that what they'd been trying to tell me this whole time and I just hadn't grasped it? My mind had just refused to go there.

"I'm afraid so," Dad answered, sullen.

Bellamy slipped out of her chair and went around the table. The next thing I knew, she had her arms around my father, hugging him.

He glanced at me, surprised, but then he hugged her back.

Mom got up from the table and left the room. Part of me wanted to go after her; the other part of me knew it wouldn't matter if I did or not. Nothing I could do would make this better.

When Bellamy pulled away, my father cleared his throat. She slipped back beside me and put her hand in my lap. I clutched it, grateful for the lifeline.

"I don't want you to give up on your life so you can finish mine," Dad said. He was almost stoic about this. Accepting.

Or maybe in the last year, he'd had a lot of time to digest. To come to terms with this.

Was that even possible?

"Running BearPaw is what I want," I told him. It was the truth. "I always planned on coming back here. You know that. I just ended up home sooner than planned."

Was it fate?

Was a higher power at work here? Was my injury the best thing because it brought me back to find Bellamy again and to have this time with my father?

"If you can go to the Olympics next year, then you have to go."

I felt like an overcooked steak. Done. I was tired, too many emotions coming at me at once. I didn't want to debate this. I didn't want to argue.

"How about we plan to start training as soon as possible? *If* the thermal shrinkage goes well, then I will consider returning just for one last season. But I still plan on running BearPaw, Dad. I still plan on following in your footsteps."

What's going to happen when his footsteps disappear?

My time as a pro snowboarder was over.

As important as that had been in my life, there were now more important things.

11

Bellamy

I went to the store and bought a suitcase. The duffle I came here with wasn't for travel. It was for escape. I couldn't look at that dark bag and not think of the reason I kept it all these years, its purpose.

For emergency only.

That's the way I saw it. And though I guess a large portion of my life was an emergency, I was trying not to live as though it was.

Or maybe I was just in denial.

Or stupid.

I preferred to think of it as trying to move on.

That's what this trip was about. Moving on. Moving forward. Merging my life with Liam's just a little bit more.

This wasn't an emergency. The clothes I packed in this suitcase weren't necessity only. I wasn't shoving an envelope full of cash in the pocket to get me by.

I was still nervous, though. Even as I neatly tucked my clothes inside, adrenaline made my heart beat more rapidly, and a funny, queasy feeling took over my middle. Going back to Chicago wasn't going to be easy.

Stepping foot into my apartment would likely bring back vivid memories of the last time I was there. You know, that fun night when a fake UPS driver broke in and pointed a gun at my face.

Mmm. Good times.

Not.

It was time. Time to face the past so I could move into the future. I wished I could say I would be leaving it all behind, but I wasn't. The past was coming with me to BearPaw. Hell, it had already followed.

I made my choice. Liam and I both did. There would be no sitting holed up in the cabin, though, jumping at every noise and creak. Life was far too short, something fate reminded us of again and again.

And again.

I glanced over my shoulder. Liam was standing motionless in the doorway of the closet. Forgetting about my suitcase and my own internal struggle, I went to him.

As I went, I tossed the sling over my head, letting it slap against the wood floor. Both my arms went around his waist from behind, and my cheek rested in the center of his back.

Liam made a sound, covering my arms with his.

Funny how I was the one hugging him, but he made it feel as if it was me in his arms.

"I can fly to Chicago by myself." I began.

Before I could say another word, he made an angry sound and turned.

"No way in hell," he intoned, voice hard and cool.

I persisted, tugging on the front of his shirt. "We can meet in Denver, then fly home together."

"No."

"It's only—"

Liam grabbed my hands, folding them in his. "The answer is no. You are not going alone back to the place where someone tried to kill you. Even if there weren't still men out there plotting against you, the answer would still be no."

"You're stupid."

His lips twitched. "That the best you got?"

I slid my hand down his abs, over the front of his jeans, and cupped his manhood.

He smirked. "Sweetheart, not even your sweet little seduction and those naughty hands of yours could convince me to let you go to Chicago alone."

I made a frustrated sound and dropped my hand.

He laughed.

"I just wanted to give you more time with your dad." I confessed. "I know you don't want to leave right now."

Hooking an arm around me, Liam pulled me against his body with a groan. He kissed the top of my head and angled closer. "I fucking love you."

"I love you, too. Which is why—"

He growled. "Don't fucking say it again, Bells. You are not going alone."

"Maybe Alex..." I suggested.

His body stiffened instantly. "I'm not sending my best friend to take care of my girl. That's my job. A job I happen to like."

I wound my arms around his waist again. "What am I going to do with you?" I wondered.

"For starters, you can put your hand back on my dick."

I gasped. "Liam!"

"You're teasing me, baby." His eyes twinkled when I glanced up.

Ridiculous. He was utterly ridiculous. And charming. And protective. And the keeper of my heart.

Holding his eyes, I slipped my hand back down to the front of his jeans.

"That's better," he rumbled. "Now. What was I saying?"

I rubbed against him. "You were being stupid." I reminded him.

He chuckled. "Right." With a deep inhale, he cupped my face and searched my eyes.

"You aren't any less important than my father," he said quietly. "Yes, I want to be here with him, and yes, I plan to spend as much time with him as I can." A broken, haunted look passed behind his stare. "Especially since our time is limited…"

"Liam," I whispered and leaned up to kiss him softly.

After I pulled away, he shook his head once. "You're important, too, Bells. Just as important. I'm coming to Chicago. I'm going to help you pack up your stuff, make sure your landlord doesn't give you a hard time, and see the place you lived before you came home to me."

He had a way with words, didn't he?

"I'm also going to make sure you're safe. I'm losing my father." He paused, a steely note coming into his voice. "I sure as fuck will not lose you."

The finality in his tone, his absolute resolve, sank into my bones, and I was insanely glad I wasn't on the receiving end of that part of Liam.

He loved fiercely. Completely. He held nothing back. It was the strongest thing I'd ever felt in my entire life. So when a man like him took that kind of intensity and applied it to protecting what it was he loved… God help anyone who dared get in his way.

"I just want you to know that it's okay if you want to stay."

"Thanks, sweetheart. The fact you are even willing to go back there alone is proof enough."

"I won't be alone." I reminded him. "The FBI will be there."

He made a rude sound, telling me everything I needed to know about his opinion of that.

I stroked his cock, which was hard beneath his jeans. "You're teasing me again."

"It's only teasing if I don't plan to do anything about it," I replied, salacious. My fingers made easy work of the button at his waist and eased down the zipper. A breath hissed between his lips when I ducked beneath his boxer briefs and freed his rigid length.

His skin was silky and smooth under my hands. His hips jutted out toward me with every stoke. Liam moaned in satisfaction, which made my tongue dart out to wet my lips.

Slowly, I worked the jeans and pants down his body, abandoning them when they were around his knees. I sank onto my knees in front of him, and he moaned again.

His dick was pulsating when I wrapped my hand around it again and pulled it away from his body toward my lips. I moistened his head first, licking around and sucking just the tip.

Liam slapped his hand onto the doorframe and widened his stance a little. His free hand went to the back of my head, delving into my hair.

I sucked him deep. His head hit the back of my throat, and he moaned. I loved making him moan. Knowing I had the power to make a man as strong as Liam weak.

I pulled back slowly, my lips hugging his thick length, and then sucked deep again. His fingers tightened against my head, and I began bobbing up and down.

A few incoherent words floated above my head, and I grabbed his hips, pulling them into me and settling his body into a gentle thrusting motion. Liam held the doorframe and fucked my mouth. The feel of him slipping in and then gliding out made my body tremble and moisture slick my panties.

After a few minutes, I pulled back, gazing up the length of his body. He gazed down, silvery eyes nothing but slits. I licked across his tip, staring straight into his eyes.

His flared, no longer slits, but wide, unfocused orbs. Liam moved fast, slipping his hands beneath my arms and lifting. My legs wound around his waist at the same time my back hit the doorframe.

Liam's mouth descended onto mine fiercely. I barely had time to breathe, but when his tongue stroked mine, oxygen was the furthest thing from my mind.

His hips moved, pushing his body into mine and teasing my core with his firm cock.

Pulling away from the doorway, Liam carried me across the room and laid me on the bed. My pants were ripped away. The sound of a packet tearing was brief, and then he was inside me.

Liam still stood at the side of the bed, my legs wrapped around his hips. Half of me was draped on the bed; the other half was suspended in the air while he pushed into me again and again.

A sound ripped from Liam's throat. His hand went between my legs to stroke my swollen clit. My body arched up off the bed, an orgasm instantly cleaving through me.

Liam shoved deep as his body jerked, his own pleasure spilling out.

My legs turned to Jell-O and slid from around his hips. He caught the backs of my thighs and held me up so I wouldn't slip right off the bed. Liam scooted my body up onto the mattress, then slowly eased out of me.

"We need to leave for the airport in an hour." I liked the way he stroked the inside of my thigh as he spoke.

"I'll finish packing."

"I'm gonna take a quick shower."

I nodded and then lay across the bed and watched his naked, tight ass waltz into the bathroom.

"I saw you looking," he called out when he was in the bathroom.

"Damn right I was!" I called back.

His muffled laughter floated out through the open door.

When the sound of the shower reached me, I sighed and pushed up off the bed. That had been a nice little distraction, but it was over too soon.

My eyes strayed to my suitcase and Liam's open duffle. Then I glanced around the bedroom and marveled at how quickly this place had become my home. How the place I was flying to in Chicago felt like a stranger's apartment where I'd left some of my clothes.

Anxiety and fear trickled in, drowning out some of my own thoughts and replacing them with ones I hated. With a dry mouth, I gazed toward the bathroom where Liam was singing horribly in the shower.

My heart seized, and an overwhelming urge to run came over me.

It was stupid. I didn't want to run. Hell, I didn't *want* to go anywhere.

You didn't want to come to BearPaw at first either. The wicked voice in my head reminded me.

Screw you! I answered.

I swear the echo of a laugh bounced around the back of my skull. I had a sudden thought of the giant spider tattoo on the back of Spidey's neck.

My movements were quick and wooden. I hated what I was doing, but I had to do something to try and calm the panic rising inside me. In the corner of the room, I stood over the "emergency" duffle that had remained in my closet, packed and ready to go for so long.

Many of my emergency supplies were still in there because I'd bought myself other items. Almost on autopilot I added a few more things, including a change of clothes. Next, I lifted out the wrinkled old envelope my father had given me and glanced at the cash inside. There wasn't as much as there used to be.

But it would be enough.

At least until I could close out my accounts in Chicago.

I pulled out a few bills for the travel we were about to embark on and then zipped the rest up with the rest of my supplies inside that awful old bag.

In the bathroom, Liam stopped singing, and the absence of his voice haunted me. Seconds later, the shower shut off.

I picked up the duffle and carried it out of the bedroom, padding down the hall and toward the coat closet near the kitchen. I tucked it on the top shelf near the corner, then stood staring up at it. I resented that bag and everything in it. Everything it represented.

Still, life's hard lessons had taught me to be prepared.

This might be my home now. It might even be next week.

But I wasn't naive enough to think it might be forever.

Liam

When we landed in Chicago, the police were waiting. I didn't need to be told the seriousness of the situation, but getting a police escort to Bellamy's old apartment definitely hammered it home. This wasn't just any ordinary *help your girlfriend move into your place* scenario.

Nope.

My girl had to go the extra mile to set herself apart from every other woman on this planet.

Part of me wondered if having the police drive us around was just shining a light on the target already on our backs. Just because it was an unmarked car and the detectives were wearing suits, not badges, didn't make them any less inconspicuous. At least to the mob. I kept those thoughts to myself, though, because I didn't want to make her any more nervous than she clearly already was.

I'd been to Chicago before, but being here now was sort of like seeing it for the first time. Knowing this was where Bellamy had spent the past year of her life had me looking at everything we passed and wondering if she'd been there and where I'd been when she had. For the first time, I had an inkling of understanding about how she confessed sometimes she felt she didn't know me. I sort of felt like a ghost rattling around in her past, looking for details I didn't know.

"That's where I used to work," she said, her voice subdued, and pointed out the window to a tall building with mirrored windows.

"Yeah?" I said, staring at the cold structure. I couldn't imagine her trudging into that place every morning in a pair of heels and a suit. It wasn't her. Not at all.

I felt her nod. "On the second floor." As we continued past, she said, "I should probably tell them I won't be coming back."

"It's taken care of," the detective in the front seat commented.

My jaw tightened. I didn't like having them here. I didn't want to experience any of this with strangers and prying eyes watching us like hawks. I didn't want Bells to feel she had to contain any personal thoughts or feelings because we weren't alone.

The detective who wasn't driving extended a white envelope into the back of the car.

Bells took it, and asked, "What is this?"

"It's your final paycheck. They added it to the box of your things we had the officers go and pick up."

"Oh," she said, tucking the envelope into her lap without bothering to open it. The law firm's name was stamped in the corner.

"The rest of your stuff is at your apartment. I didn't want that just lying around."

"Thank you," Bellamy replied. Her gaze turned back to the window. "That market has good ingredients," she murmured.

I grabbed her hand, lacing our fingers together. "What's your favorite thing to make, Bells?"

She glanced around. "What?"

"I've never asked you. What's your favorite thing to cook?"

"Alfredo," she responded almost instantly. Then she smiled. It was the first smile I'd seen since we got off the plane. "White pepper is my secret."

Impressed, I asked, "You make the pasta, too?"

"With the right appliances, I can."

I tapped the side of my head. "I'm making a list up here, sweetheart. Of all the stuff I expect you to make me when we get home."

Ducking her head, she smiled. I gave her fingers a little squeeze. I'd do anything to make her smile. Anything to give her a moment of relief.

I just hoped she really was a good cook. Otherwise, I was going to be eating a lot of shit I didn't like.

And I wouldn't complain about one bite.

We turned into a parking garage, and the interior of the car became dim and shadowed. Bellamy stiffened instantly. The car slowed to roll through the garage carefully. My eyes searched every inch we passed. Just because we were with the cops didn't mean I trusted them to protect us.

A real man didn't allow someone else to protect what was his. A real man did it himself.

The detective parked near the elevators.

I got out of the car, once again scanning the area around us. Once I knew it was safe, I leaned back into the open door and held out my hand. "Come here."

Bellamy slid across the seat and put her hand in mine. I didn't leave much room for her, so when she unfolded from the car, her body was pressed close, and I crowded around her, using my own body as a shield.

We went with the two detectives to the elevator. Inside, Bells hit a button for her floor, and we all rode in silence.

The men stepped off first, and when they nodded everything was clear, we moved into the hallway. Even though I walked ahead, I knew which apartment was hers because there was a uniformed officer standing outside the door.

Bellamy's feet stuttered. "I don't have my keys." Her eyes were a little too wide for my liking. "I ran out without them."

I smoothed a hand down the back of her head. "It's okay."

Without saying anything, one of the detectives pulled out a cell and hit the screen a few times before holding it up to his ear. "It's Detective James. We're upstairs. We need you to come let us in the apartment." He listened a moment, then ended the call.

"The building manager will be right up," he told us.

We all stood there awkwardly, not speaking. Bellamy's eyes were fixed on the yellow crime scene tape covering her door. A minute later, a man with thinning hair entered from the stairwell, stepping into the hall. He had on dark-brown khaki pants and a striped sweater. He gazed at me, clearly not expecting to see Bellamy with a man. But then his eyes went to her and narrowed.

"How nice of you to come back." His voice was annoyed and sort of haughty.

"I'm sorry for the trouble, Mr. Ray," Bellamy replied quietly.

"You're behind on your rent," he snapped, moving toward the door.

The keys in his hand jingled when my hand shot out and gripped his shoulder. He made a surprised sound, wide eyes shooting to my face. "Wha—"

"I don't like your tone." I warned him. "You're going to need to show a hell of a lot more respect the next time you even look in her direction."

The man blustered and looked at the officer standing close by. "You're going to let him threaten me?"

I smiled, a nice toothy grin. "No threat," I said, releasing his shoulder and brushing some invisible lint off his sleeve. "Just letting you know a little bit of understanding toward a woman who fled *your* building to avoid being murdered would go a long way."

The man glanced at the officers again. Red spots bloomed over his cheeks.

"Open the door." The detective pointed at it.

Mr. Ray cleared his throat and did as he was told.

Bellamy started forward when the door swung in, but I put a palm against her chest and shook my head. Then I gestured for the detectives to go.

They drew their guns and moved in to sweep the place.

A few minutes later, they came back. "All clear."

I went ahead of her, holding my arm out to keep her behind me.

"They just checked the place." She reminded me. Her voice wasn't nearly as sturdy as it should be.

I made a rude sound. "I'm still going to be careful with you." I glanced over my shoulder and gave her a look. "You should already know that, sweetheart."

Once I was down the short hall, past the kitchen, and standing near the small island that looked over the living room, I turned. The detectives and the landlord were all standing inside.

"Think we could have a minute?" I asked.

"We'll be right outside." The officers nodded and left.

I settled my gaze on the landlord, who was standing there like a lump. "This really isn't her apartment anymore."

I stalked over to him. He slunk back because he was easily intimidated. "How much?" I barked.

He jumped. "What?"

"How much is the rent?"

"Twelve hundred."

A disgusted sound ripped out of me. "For this box? That's highway robbery."

He stiffened. "It's Chicago. And I'll have you—"

I held up my hand. "Stop talking."

His mouth slammed shut.

Reaching into my jeans, I pulled out a money clip stuffed with cash. Retrieving two five hundred-dollar bills and a pair of hundreds, I held out the cash.

He glanced between me and the money.

"Take it," I said, impatient. Once it was in his hand, I pointed at the door. "Now get out."

He rose to his full height, which was still shorter than mine. "I'll be in the hall."

I folded my arms over my chest and glared. He left.

The second the door clicked shut, I turned and nearly collided with Bellamy. "Shit," I swore, grabbing her shoulders to steady myself. Instantly, I pulled back from the injured arm. "Did I hurt you?"

"My arm is fine." She promised.

She had more range of motion now. I wanted her to wear the sling on the plane, but she refused. Little did she know I stuffed it in her suitcase.

"What's wrong?" My gaze narrowed on her face.

"You just paid my rent."

I blinked. "So?"

"So that's my responsibility."

"You can pay me back." I lied.

She gave me a look that called me out on said lie.

I took her face, stroking my thumbs lightly over her cheeks. "You can be mad at me if it makes it easier to be here," I said gently. "I'm man enough to take it."

Her body slumped. "I'm not mad at you."

"I know." Pulling her into my body, I hugged her.

She was rigid at first, but then she began to relax. A moment later, she pulled back, visibly fortifying herself.

"The last time I was here, someone tried to shoot me." She pointed into the kitchen, near the stove. "Right there."

Bellamy moved past, went to the stove, and dropped down on hands and knees. Delving her fingers under the appliance, she pulled out a phone.

"Right where I left it." She held it up. Bellamy set the phone on the counter and gazed around.

There was a pan on the floor, partly propped against the lower cabinet. Dried food (looked like vegetables) were scattered around, and an oily substance dotted difference places on the floor, counter... everywhere. When her eyes landed on the island, she frowned.

"What?"

"Those bastards took my wine!" she said. "That was good wine, too."

I tried not to smile. "I'll get you a new bottle of wine."

She made a sound and left the kitchen, avoiding the food scattered about. "So this is my place." She motioned to the living room. "Bedroom and bathroom are through there."

It was small, kind of impersonal. Not at all the way I would expect her home to look. The furniture was basic, but there were a few throw pillows in different colors around the room. And a fuzzy blanket.

"The apartment came furnished. I added the pillows to try and make it feel like home."

"Did it work?" I asked.

"No."

I watched her grab her purse off the island and look inside. "They left my ID and cash. How nice of them," she murmured, setting it aside.

She looked out of place standing there looking around like a stranger to her own things. Her arms wrapped around her middle. I went to her immediately, enclosing my body around hers from behind.

"This is harder than I thought it would be." She confessed.

"You thought coming here would be easy?"

She shook her head. "No. It's strange, though," she muttered. "I thought the hardest part would be seeing the kitchen, remembering that night that man was here with a gun."

I closed my eyes against the images her words produced. Closing my eyes didn't make them harder to see, though. If anything, the darkness just removed all other distractions, making those vivid, unwanted pictures more prominent.

"But that's not the worse part."

The trembling in her voice made my eyes pop open. Tenderness and the need to shield her came over me. I moved around so I could look into her sorrowful eyes.

"Ah, baby. Tell me." I urged.

"It's the emptiness of this place. The loneliness," she whispered, glancing around. Her eyes found mine again. "Can you feel it, too?"

I felt as though someone had just kicked my puppy. "I feel it."

"I didn't realize that night I ran out of here, I wasn't just fleeing from a man with a gun. I was fleeing from my own life. I was so lonely here, Liam. So lost. I had to be someone I wasn't just so I could be someone at all."

Her chin lifted, and a single tear tracked over her cheek. "I had no idea just how miserable I was until I spent a few weeks with you. Coming back here, it's…" Her words fell off, and she shook her head. "It almost shocks me."

I gathered her close, holding her more tightly than I had since the avalanche. I'd been too worried about her shoulder, but now I realized her shoulder wasn't the worst of her wounds.

No. The worst was the fracture inside her, the one that still seemed to be slowly pulling apart. The nights and days of solitude. The day in and day out fear. Of being someone she wasn't because it was better than being dead.

She lifted her head. Her expression was helpless when she asked, "Do you think it's better to live like you're dead just for the sake of living? Or die because you refused to stop existing?"

I made a sound of torment and strife. "I can't answer that, baby," I rasped, pushing her back into my body. I couldn't look in her eyes right now. I couldn't see the look on her face while the words she just spoke lingered in the air, clinging to my skin like damp fog on a rainy night.

Keeping my arms crushed around her, feeling her breath on my neck, I spoke close to her head. "It's over now." I soothed. "You aren't going to be alone ever again. You have me, and we're going to build a family. You can go back to being a chef. You can be whoever and whatever it is you want. I'm going to make you happy again, Bells."

She pulled back enough to look into my face. "Liam," she whispered. "You've already made me happy. So happy."

"You ain't seen nothing yet." I vowed.

She rubbed her damp cheek with the back of her hand and sighed. "You paint a beautiful picture."

My brows drew together. "It's not a picture. It's a promise."

Bellamy stretched up and kissed me. I wasn't a man who would turn down some sugar, not from his favorite girl anyway. Even if she was trying to distract me.

When her lips left mine, the rest of her pulled away, too. "I'll pack up my clothes. Then we can leave. I don't like it here."

I wasn't a fan of this place either. *Fuck.*

As she stepped away, our hands slipped apart. I started after her, then backtracked to the coffee table where there were some boxes stacked and ready to be packed.

I made a face. The sweater-wearing douchebag of a landlord left them for us. According to the cops, he wanted to pack up her crap, take it to the local dump, and then get the place rented again.

Frankly, I thought I deserved an award for not decking him in the face already. That was some serious control I was emitting.

The thought of him going through her things, deciding everything she had was trash, royally pissed me off. The cops stopped him, though. This was a crime scene after all. Bells might not like this place, but she had a right to pack up anything she wanted to keep.

"How many boxes do you think you need, sweetheart?"

She stopped just shy of entering the bedroom and gazed back. "Just a few. I don't have very much."

Those words kicked me in the nads, too. Fuck, she was slaying me today. I knew everything she'd been through, and it sucked. But seeing it? *Feeling* it?

I picked up the boxes and shook my head. I could spend the rest of my life trying to make this up to her, but it still wouldn't be enough.

I couldn't help but ask myself, *repeatedly*, if this would have happened if I'd just fought for her eight years ago.

Bellamy walked into her room and stood in the beam of sunlight let in from what I assumed was a window. The light turned her hair a golden shade, which made her look like a living, breathing angel when she turned to smile at me from over her shoulder.

"There's something I want to show you."

The worst of the storm battering my insides subsided. Her smile could do that. Her smile had the ability to quiet my greatest demons.

"Oh yeah?" I grinned. "You got something sexy—"

Something glinted through the light, flickering off her hair and disrupting the whole angel look she had going on.

My instincts literally screamed. They screamed so hard a yell erupted out of my mouth. Everything morphed into slow motion, seeming to take an excruciating amount of time.

"Get down!" I roared, throwing the boxes into the room and leaping across the distance separating us.

I watched her face change from a teasing smile to one of confusion, then fear. The sound of shattering glass exploded in the room. I knocked into Bellamy, wrapping my arms around her and taking us both to the floor.

We hit the carpet with a hard thud as a bullet plowed into the wall behind us.

Confusion and chaos broke out around us. In the other room, the door to the apartment burst in. Officers were shouting. Cold winter wind rushed the room, the curtains flapped against the wall, and the sound of my breathing threatened to drown out everything else.

Under me, Bellamy struggled, but I used my weight to keep her prone. Keeping my body on top of hers, I lifted my head and shielded hers with my arms as I looked at the bullet embedded in the wall. It was right where she'd been standing.

"Stay down!" One of the officers warned from the doorway, his gun drawn.

"Liam?" Bellamy's voice was muffled against the carpet.

"Stay still," I told her. "You're okay. Everything's okay."

"What about you?" She fretted.

Someone just tried to snipe her, and she was worried about me?

"I'm fine, sweetheart. Stay still."

"Clear!" the officers yelled, and then the three of them swarmed the interior of the room.

From the doorway, the landlord was being super helpful. "Was that a gunshot?" he exclaimed. "What the hell is going on here? I thought this apartment was secure! I'll never be able to rent it out now."

I pushed up, twisting around to glare at him.

He shut up and slunk backward.

Bellamy rolled so she was staring up at me. "They shot through the window."

I glanced over the mattress at the shattered window, then back down. "Yes."

"You shoved me out of the way."

"Of course I did." I smoothed some hair back off her face.

"You could have gotten shot!"

"I didn't."

"That doesn't make this okay!" she cried, her voice verging on hysteric.

"We need to get you out of here," an officer said from above us. "We have units dispatched to the building across the street, but the shooter probably will be long gone."

I nodded once and pushed up off Bellamy. The officers covered me when I pulled Bells to her feet. I wrapped my arm around her, putting my body in front of hers.

If the shooter was still there, he would have to shoot through the cops and me to get to her.

"'C'mon. Away from the window."

All of us moved as a unit out into the main living area, making sure to stand away from the window, which had a curtain drawn over it. Why the curtain wasn't drawn over the bedroom window, I would like to fucking know.

My heart was still pounding and my hands shook from the rush of adrenaline. I wanted to pace, to rush across the street and find this assassin, wrap my hands around his neck, and squeeze until the light of life left his eyes.

Brutal?

Hell yeah.

Regretful?

Fuck no.

Bellamy's shaking hand gripped the front of my shirt. "Liam?"

"Hmm?" I gazed down, trying to bank the murderous feelings.

"How'd you know?"

"Know?"

She nodded, her eyes wide, pupils dilated. She was in shock. "Know there was a gun."

"I'd like to know that, too," one of the detectives said, holding his gun down at his side. The other detective was across the room, speaking rapidly into a phone.

"It glinted off her hair. I just… I had this feeling." More like I almost pissed my pants in panic. I wasn't going to tell anyone that. Thank fuck I'd just moved on instinct instead of trying to find some logic first.

Jesus. She almost got shot right in front of me.

"Well, you probably just saved her life," the officer said, as if he was telling me the weather outside.

I swung around, anger getting the better of me. "Isn't that what you're here for? What the fuck was that? Shouldn't you have known this was going to happen?" I stabbed my finger in his direction. "You should never have told her she could come here."

"Liam." Bellamy soothed, putting a palm against my middle. My breath heaved and my eyes stayed focused on the man. But my hand settled over hers. "They can't know everything."

I barked a laugh. "We're getting the hell out of Chicago, and we aren't coming back."

"They'll follow you," the officer said. "Witness protection—"

"No!" Bellamy cried, stepping a little in front of me. "I won't do it. I'll be in danger either way. I need to be in control of my own life."

"You're putting everyone around you in danger, too," the officer told her, his eyes sliding to me, then back.

She jolted as though he'd slapped her. I growled and moved, parking myself totally in front to block her from view. "Don't you dare put that shit on her. If you'd done your fucking job, none of this would be happening in the first place!"

The apartment door opened, and I swung around, making sure she moved with me. Everyone lifted their guns.

Something I didn't have.

I need to fix that.

"Stand down," Agent Frost said, striding into the room.

My back teeth came together. *Oh, goodie,* backup was here.

"Ms. Lane, are you harmed?"

I felt her peek out from around me. "No."

"Good," he replied, then gestured for the other officers. They all went to the side of the room to fill him in.

I spun around to face Bellamy. "Did I hurt your shoulder when you fell? I wasn't gentle."

"It was a lot gentler than a bullet." She giggled.

I frowned and took her hands. "Bells."

She looked up. "Sorry, I—" Tears flooded her eyes.

I cursed and pulled her against me. Her hands fisted in the shirt against my back.

"It's okay. Everything is okay," I murmured. They were stupid, untrue words. Everything was *not* okay.

But it would be. I would make those words true.

How the fuck was I going to make this okay?

"Our guys found the room where the sniper was camping out. He's gone, along with the gun he used. We're having forensics go over everything, and we have officers out speaking to people in the building,"

"But you won't find shit." I surmised.

"We will follow up on every possible lead." Frost assured me.

This guy was as bland as a slice of white bread. Untoasted.

"Have you found Spidey?" Bellamy questioned.

I glanced at her, noting the tears from before had vanished, her chin was high, and she was staring straight at Frost and company.

That was my girl. *Strong.* Strong enough to stay alive.

"We believe the assassin with the spider tattoo on his neck—" He began.

"Spidey," Bells interjected.

He cleared his throat. "Yes, ah, Spidey."

I smirked. Dude did not want to call him that. Too bad for him.

"That's what his partner called him." Bellamy tried to explain.

"Right." Frost agreed. I smiled. "We do believe he's still alive. However, we have found no trace of his whereabouts."

"He said they have a sort of witness protection for assassins." Bellamy reminded him.

"Yes, we are looking into that, too. As well as trying to place him at the scene a few moments ago."

Bellamy shook her head definitively. "It wasn't him."

Frost seemed surprised. "How do you know?"

"I just know. That's not his style. He's too angry with me. This is personal now. He wouldn't shoot me from that far away. He wants to be…" Her voice faltered. "Up close."

I swallowed. Just the sound of it made my skin crawl.

Over my dead body.

"Well, everything you've told us about him definitely lines up with that theory."

"Face it," I told him. "She knows more about this guy than you."

Frost slanted his head. "Since you have seen him more than once, I am inclined to believe that."

So glad he was *inclined* to believe her.

"That means Crone has more than one man after me."

"Affirmative." Frost agreed.

"How many?" I asked.

"We don't know. He has a few men who work for him who exclusively contract kill, one of them being Spidey. But there could be a few more rogue men in his organization that are hoping to score and get into his good graces."

"Score meaning murdering me," Bellamy echoed.

"Is there anything you *do* know?" I spat.

"You aren't safe here. I can have a few officers pack up your things, and I'll ship them to an address you provide. I think it's best that you leave from here. I'll have my men escort you directly to the airport."

Bellamy glanced around and then back to Frost. "I don't want anything here," she announced. "Just get rid of it all. Donate it. Whatever. I don't care."

"Bells," I said, touching the small of her back.

She shook her head. "They're just things. None of it means anything to me. I'll just buy whatever I need."

I nodded once. "Good enough for me."

"Can I at least stop at the bank on the way to the airport? I need to close out my accounts."

"I wouldn't advise it," Frost replied. "I assume you're transferring the funds to a new account? If you give me the routing information, I'll have it done for you. The funds will be available to you by the end of this week."

Her teeth sank into her lower lip, and her body leaned toward me just slightly. I angled, pushing closer so she could lean more firmly into me.

"I was just going to get the cash and open an account when I got home."

Home.

I liked the sound of that. I liked knowing that place was with me.

"I wouldn't advise carrying that much cash," Frost stated.

I reached into my pocket, pulling out the money clip. "Anyone got a piece of paper and a pen?"

The uniformed officer produced both and held them out. I pulled out a paper card with all my bank information on it and scrawled out what he needed. When I was done, I handed it to Frost. "Have it all transferred to this account."

"To *your* account?" His haughty voice pissed me off.

"It's fine," Bellamy injected instantly. Her hand clasped around mine. "That will work for me."

"You want me to transfer *your* money into *his* accounts?"

"I trust him," she replied simply. Shyly, she glanced up at me. "It's okay, right?"

The center of my chest burned with emotion. With love. "Yes. It's good." I cleared my throat, trying to make it sound less raspy. "I'll add you to the accounts. You'll have total access."

Surprise flickered in her eyes. "I don't—"

"I trust you."

"You two are either the dumbest people I've ever met, or you deserve some kind of Hallmark movie," Frost commented. "That is if you live."

A couple of the other officers in the room chuckled.

"That's not funny," Bellamy snapped.

"I wasn't making a joke," Frost replied coolly. "I'd like to remind you that witness protection is the only way the FBI can make any kind of promise to your safety."

A harsh reply bubbled up, but Bellamy laid her hand on my chest and stepped forward. "You mean like that last promise you made me?"

He blanched.

"C'mon, Bells. Let's go." The longer we stayed here, the higher chance someone else decided to shoot up the place.

"Drive them," Frost told some men at the door. "You sure you don't want anything in this place? There's nothing here of value?"

"You wouldn't let me keep anything from my old life." Bellamy sounded bitter. I couldn't blame her.

As soon as the words left her mouth, she gasped. Abruptly, she stopped, turned, and took off into the bedroom.

Right back into the place where someone had just tried to kill her.

13

Bellamy

"Bellamy!"

The sound of Liam practically roaring my name as I ran into the bedroom almost made me stop. But I couldn't.

There was something here that meant so very much to me.

The only thing I'd brought from my old life into this new one. I didn't leave it behind before, and I wasn't going to leave it behind now.

The sound of pounding feet behind me was unmistakable, as well as some shouted orders from Frost, but I ignored that, too.

I went through the bedroom, my eyes automatically going to the shattered window. Shivers rolled up my spine, but they weren't from the wintry wind blowing around the room. I couldn't keep my shoulders from bunching up around my neck as I turned my back to the window and raced into the small walk-in closet.

I half expected another shot to ring out. I half expected the feeling of a bullet to slam into me. Oh, you knew your life was a shit circus when you were prepared for the feeling of a bullet plowing into your flesh.

I flipped on the light, blinking against it, and scanned the space overhead. There was a single box on the shelf.

It only had the one item in it.

Liam plowed into the doorway, his eyes glittering angrily. "What the hell are you doing?"

"I remembered something I wanted to bring."

He let out a string of *very* rude curses.

"What's a mangy-ass taxi?" I asked, wide-eyed.

He dropped his hands from the doorframe. "You just ran into a room where someone was shooting at you," he growled. "*Without me.*"

I batted my eyes. "So next time, you would prefer if I held your hand while running in the direction of my killer?"

"Yes!" he roared.

I winced.

Liam came forward and grabbed me up. "Don't ever do that again, Bellamy. I mean it. I go first. Always."

He was really angry. Like for realsies.

"I'm sorry." I relented, feeling bad. "I didn't mean to scare you. I just remembered—"

His lips crushed against mine, cutting off all words. My arms wrapped around his neck as his tongue licked into my mouth. Hunching around me, Liam lifted me, holding me so we were on the same level and he could kiss me more intensely.

My feet dangled over the floor, but I barely noticed because he invaded my senses.

A long moment later, he ripped his mouth free and sucked in a deep breath. His eyes were still flashing silver when they found mine again. "Don't scare me like that again."

"I'm sorry," I repeated, still breathless from his kiss but nearly speechless from his intensity.

He hugged me close another minute, then finally set me back on my own two feet.

"What did you just risk your life for?" He grumped. He was grouchy.

And seriously, what was a mangy-ass taxi?

I pointed to the lone box overhead. "Can you get that down for me?"

He lifted the box down and held it so I could open the top and reach inside. My hand closed around the soft item, and I pulled it free.

He dumped the box at his feet and stared incredulously. "You came running in here to get a stuffed animal?"

I glanced down at the small white teddy bear with a red ribbon around its neck. He was a little worn from age, but otherwise, he was as perfect as the day I got him.

"It's not just any stuffed animal," I said, tucking it into my chest and glancing up at him.

I wondered if he would remember…

A flash of recognition moved through his eyes as his stare lingered on me and the bear. "Is that…?" he whispered.

I nodded. "You remember?"

All the anger drained from his face, leaving behind a tender, faraway look. "You kept it? After all this time?"

I nodded again. "It was the only thing I kept from my past." I tilted my head. "Besides my memories."

Eight years ago when I was at BearPaw, Liam took me to a winter carnival outside in the snow. Lights had been strung up, and there were actual igloos, snowball tosses, hot chocolate, fresh donuts, and games.

He spent twenty dollars trying to win me this bear from a rigged game of ring toss. He never gave up, though. And eventually, he won it. I would never forget the way my stomach almost fluttered right out of my body when he handed it to me.

A soft sound vibrated his throat, and he pulled me into him. The bear squished between us when he hugged me tight. "Just when I think I couldn't love you more… I do."

I pulled back, hopeful. "Does this mean you forgive me?"

"No."

I frowned.

He chuckled and fingered the ear of my bear. "Knowing you held on to this all these years, that you kept something I'd given you, makes me kinda high."

"Not high enough," I muttered.

Liam threw back his head and laughed, but then he turned serious. "But even so, it's not worth your life."

"I'm keeping it," I said, stubborn.

"I wouldn't dream of ripping it out of those beautiful hands."

Exhaustion wafted over me. This had been a really long day, and unfortunately, it wasn't over. "I'm ready to go now."

Liam swept his eyes over me, head to toe, then turned to exit the closet. I think it goes without saying that he body-blocked me the entire way across the bedroom and back into the living room.

"Ms. Lane." Frost addressed me. "I'll keep in touch."

I nodded. On the way out, I grabbed my purse off the counter. It would be smart to have ID. "Oh, Agent Frost?" I said.

"Yes?"

"I want my old identity back."

"That's not possible."

I frowned. "Why not?"

"Because we made it disappear. Legally, you are Bella Lane."

"Then legally change it back." I insisted.

"You were given all new documents. Birth certificate, social security number, etc. Your previous details are not available."

"Then my name. Change my name back."

He began to shake his head, and I sighed. "Fine."

"Seriously?" Liam put in. I could feel him standing just behind me. "You can't even give her that?"

"I'll see what I can do," Frost replied effortlessly.

I rolled my eyes and turned away. That was the equivalent of when a mother said, *I'll think about it.* That meant no.

We left my old apartment, two officers leading the way. Liam tucked an arm around me, and I surrendered just a little bit of my weight as we walked.

Mr. Ray came rushing out into the hall behind us. "What about all these damages?" he yelled. "And the mess in the kitchen?"

"Hire a cleaning crew," Liam called back.

"This is a violation of your lease! I'll sue."

Liam made a sound. The tendons in his body rippled.

"I feel sorry for his next tenant," I muttered as we continued on.

"You little bitch," he snarled partly under his breath, but not quiet enough.

Before anyone could say or do anything, Liam wrenched away from me, stalked back down the hallway, and decked my old landlord in the face. The man crumpled right to the floor in a heap of khaki and bad sweater.

"I warned you," Liam spat, towering over where he lay.

I rushed over and stepped in front of Liam, pushing him back. "Come on."

Mr. Ray put a hand over his eye. He looked like a poor excuse for a pirate. "Me eye!" he yelled.

He sounded like one, too.

"Did you see that?" he wailed at the officers at the end of the hall.

"What happened, sir?" one of the officers said.

"He just punched me. I know you saw!"

"We were facing the other direction," he replied. He turned to Liam. "Is this true?"

"Don't know what he's talking about," Liam responded smoothly. "I heard him fall and was going to offer him a hand."

He outstretched his hand to Mr. Ray.

"This is insane!" the man roared.

"We really need to leave." I reminded Liam.

He put his arm around me and led me away from the scene he'd created.

In the elevator, the two officers snickered. "That man impeded this investigation the whole time. What a giant pain in the ass."

"It was a pleasure," Liam said, proud of himself.

I shook my head.

In the backseat of the unmarked car, I watched the streets of Chicago go by, knowing it was probably the last time I would ever be here.

I wasn't sorry. At all.

"You didn't need us to come to the station or give any kind of statement?" I asked as we turned onto the ramp for the airport.

"No," the man driving answered. "There was enough law enforcement there. They can give statements. It's probably best if you just get out of town."

I glanced at Liam and frowned. "I'm sorry we came. It was a waste of time. Time we could have been home with your dad."

He shook his head. "It wasn't a waste. I got to see where you've been living. I got some of those details you love so much."

"Flying bullets are not details."

A dark look passed over his face, but then he banked it and glanced down at the bear still clutched in my arm. "We got this," he murmured, tugging its ear.

I laid my head against Liam's arm and closed my eyes. I couldn't help but wonder if there would be men waiting in Denver to kill me, too.

14

Liam

"I don't like this," I declared.

"I think you look sexy in a hospital gown."

I glanced up at my girl who was wagging her eyebrows at me salaciously. I couldn't help but chuckle. I might be in a sour mood, but Bells was all sunshine to me.

"This gown is lame, but I do make it look good." I allowed. Then I grunted. "But you know damn well I'm not talking about this getup." I gestured to the scratchy, starched, paper-thin fabric the hospital insisted I put on.

Stupid.

Bellamy sighed dramatically. When she came closer to the bed I was perched on, I spread my legs a bit and guided her between them. "You need something to keep you calm during the procedure, Liam. You can't just go in there and get lasered up cold turkey."

Resting my hands on her hips, I sighed. "Yeah, I know."

Her teeth sank into her lower lip, and she glanced back at the door. "I could find the doctor, maybe see if they could just put you to sleep? That might be less—"

"Hell no," I asserted. "Being totally out of it would be worse than partial."

She frowned. "It's just for a short time. You can tell them no strong pain pills once the procedure is over."

It dawned on me we weren't talking about the same thing. She thought I was worried about taking some pills. Of getting that kind of "high" that would dull reality.

If I were being honest with myself, I'd thought of that, too. I'd kind of looked forward to it.

But not enough. Not nearly enough to make me crave it.

"Hey," I said, catching her attention. The second our eyes collided, I tightened my palms at her hips. "I'm not worried about slipping back into the bottle. I don't want you to worry about it either. I'm solid. That darkness in here"—I rubbed a hand to my chest—"isn't taking over."

Her tongue wet her lips, then disappeared. "Then what is it?"

"Being out of reach. Away from you. Someone tried to kill you yesterday, Bells. And now I'm supposed to swallow some pills to be half out of it while I'm taken into a room for a procedure where I can't just get up and run out of if you need me."

Bellamy leaned forward, touching our foreheads together. "Today isn't about me."

"Every day is about you," I refuted.

She pulled back out of reach and shook her head at me. "No, Liam. Today is about you. About repairing your knee, about getting your career back. So stop it."

I lifted an eyebrow. "Stop it?"

"Stop being protective and perfect… and so entirely lovable."

The door to the room opened, and I yelled, "Come back in five!"

The door clapped shut instantly.

"Liam!" Bellamy gasped.

"What?"

"You just yelled at that poor nurse!"

"To be fair, sweetheart, you just told me to be an asshole."

"Oh my gosh! I did not!"

I laughed. I loved messing with her. I wasn't kidding, though. I wanted another few with her before the day became all about my damned knee.

I crooked a finger at her. "Come here."

A stubborn glint came into the blue of her eyes.

"Now, Bells."

Her feet shuffled over, and I pulled her between my legs again and slipped my arms around her waist.

"You're taking this asshole thing a little too far." She sniffed.

"You like it."

Indignance flashed over her features.

I smiled and brushed a thumb over her visibly erect nipple through her T-shirt. "Don't even try to lie."

Her chest arched ever so slightly into my caress, and the smile I was wearing widened.

Before she could comment, I leaned forward and rested my head against her middle. Instantly, the dynamic changed from heated and intense to tenderness.

"It's going to be okay," she told me, rubbing across the backs of my shoulders. "It's a fast procedure. You'll be done in no time."

The center of my chest squeezed at her words, and I couldn't deny that some of what I was feeling wasn't just anxiety about leaving her unprotected while I was in surgery. It was for the procedure, what happened yesterday... my father.

Lifting my head, I stared into her eyes. "Promise me you'll stay in the waiting room the whole time. Don't go anywhere alone. Stay here."

"I promise."

"If you need anything—" The door to the room opened again, and annoyance flashed over me. "I said..."

"Are you guys getting in to on in here? Because if you are, that is totally inappropriate."

I jolted up and stared around Bellamy at Alex strolling right into the room as though he owned the place.

"Alex!" Bells exclaimed.

"I gotta tell you, bro. I came all this way only to be yelled at and kicked out of the room before I even enter." He shook his head. "I've never felt more disrespected."

"Thank goodness it wasn't a nurse!" Bellamy rejoiced.

Alex gave her a look. "Sure. Sure. Abuse the best friend and not the staff. I see how it is."

"What are you doing here, man?" I asked as Bellamy stepped out of my embrace so I could see him.

"You think I would let you have this done and not be here?" He put a hand to his chest. "I'm offended."

"Bells is here..." I began.

Alex scoffed. "And you was just bitching and fretting like an old granny about leaving her in the waiting room alone."

"You were listening at the door!" I yelled.

"Just for a few." He sniffed. "I ain't above it."

Bellamy giggled.

I shook my head, smiling. "I can't believe you came all the way to Denver."

"It's not that far. And I didn't come alone." Backtracking to the door, Alex opened it, and my parents appeared.

My eyes widened in surprise. "Mom? Dad?"

"I assume it's safe to come in?" Mom asked, glancing at Alex.

"Everyone's decent." He confirmed.

I rolled my eyes. I was about to have surgery. What a douche. He thought I would be in here getting it on?

The thought had crossed my mind.

Clearly, he knew me well.

"What are you doing here?" I asked.

Dad stepped up to the bed. "We weren't as present the last time you went through this, and I deeply regret that. We're going to be here for this every step of the way."

I wouldn't say it out loud, but I was touched. A little bit of that leftover pain sort of eased, almost as if their presence now really did make up for their absence before.

"This is a simple procedure. It's not like last time. Not that big of a deal. I feel bad you came all this way."

"Nonsense!" Mom exclaimed.

Dad glanced at me, then away. "We just want to be here for as much as we can."

Because someday he won't be here at all.

I cleared my throat. "I really appreciate that."

The next time the door opened, it really was the nurse, and I didn't yell at her. Instead, I dutifully, if begrudgingly, swallowed the "happy pills" she handed me in a stupid paper cup.

"Those should kick in shortly," she said when I was done. "Then I'll have to ask everyone to wait out in the waiting room, and we'll take Liam back."

Bellamy sat on the bed beside me, resting her cheek on my shoulder. Her hair was so long I was able to absentmindedly play with the soft ends where it fell onto the mattress. The room settled into a comfortable silence, broken with a few jokes from Alex and a few questions from my parents.

My body began relaxing, my mind clouding over. Most people probably drifted into this peaceful sort of blankness when given this kind of meds.

It was the opposite for me. It seemed the more I began to relax, the easier it was for my mind to bring to the surface everything I was trying to keep controlled.

The subconscious was a tricky bastard. He just lay in wait until he could spring the worst of thoughts on you.

If I wasn't sure which was the deepest of my fears before… hell, now I had quite a list to choose from. Once those meds kicked in and kicked out most of my control, I was certain.

1. The permanent loss of my career.
2. Getting a laser fired into incisions in my knee.
3. My father dying.
4. Someone trying to kill me.
5. Someone trying to kill Bells.
6. Falling prey to my addiction again.

See?

That was an accomplished list.

When I did anything, I didn't do it half-assed. I was an overachiever.

So which one was it?

I jolted upright, my body having begun to slump.

"Hey," Bellamy spoke softly, her hands guiding me up onto the bed. "Here, lie down."

I reclined against the mattress because it was pretty comfortable. I felt Bells tug the gown around me, and I smiled at her. She sat back on the side of the bed, and I curled my arm around her hips and shut my eyes.

I heard the hum of familiar voices around me, but didn't listen to what they were saying. Instead, an instant replay at the pace of super-slow motion played against my closed eyelids.

Bellamy walking forward. Her long golden hair floating behind her like feathers. She turned to glance over her shoulder, smiling at me with a look of happiness in her eyes. Warmth suffused my chest. Love washed over me as I stared at her…

But then it changed.

Interruptive shattering blasted through the serene moment, and I watched in helpless agony as a metal bullet ripped through the air toward her.

I tried to yell, but no sound came out.

I hurled my body toward her, but my feet stayed glued to the floor.

I watched in supreme horror as the bullet tore into her flesh, a spurt of ruby-red blood jetting out of her as her body was violently thrown back with the force.

Bells collapsed right there on the carpet in front of me, her body falling motionless, her face turned toward me as a curtain of red bloomed over her body.

I yelled again. No sound. I glanced at her eyes, which had been sparkling and laughing just moments before. She was still looking at me. But the expression in her stare was no longer love. It was cold. Empty.

Lifeless.

I gasped aggressively, this time the force of it creating a sound. The body that had been sitting beside me lurched up, and cool hands grabbed at my cheeks.

"Liam?" Bellamy's voice floated overhead.

I blinked up, seeing her above me, concern on her face.

"Bells." I was breathless. I reached for her, and she came. "Should I get the nurse?" she whispered against my ear as I hugged her close.

"No," I protested. "Nah. I'm good." Cupping the back of her head, I reminded myself it was just a dream. Not reality.

The nurse bustled in a few moments later. I was still awake. Drowsy but awake. I fought for every ounce of consciousness I could have. I hated this feeling of being out of control.

That was good, right?

That meant I wasn't ready to reach for some pills.

Bellamy's lips pressed against my forehead. "We'll be in the waiting room. I love you."

"Love you," I replied.

The nurses shooed my family out of the room. My eyes clung to Bells until she was out of sight.

"Alex," I called out before my best friend could disappear, too.

Alex rotated and came back into the room, taking up space right beside my bed as they wheeled it toward the door.

"Stay with Bellamy."

"Of course." He assured me.

I grabbed his arm, forcing my drowsy eyes open so I could stare at him. "Don't let her out of your sight."

"You have my word," he answered intently.

I let go of his arm as they pushed the bed past and out into the hall. Staring up at the ceiling as we went, the sticky feeling of death clung to me.

And now we knew my deepest fear.

Losing Bellamy.

15

Bellamy

What was supposed to be an in-and-out procedure turned into an overnight at the hospital.

Perks of being a world-famous pro athlete?

Probably not.

However, I couldn't necessarily complain that the doctors and staff were being extra cautious with Liam because they wanted to give him the best possible chance at recovery.

So here we were, settling in for a night in the hospital.

"I could have gone home," Liam muttered, totally grumpy. The thermal shrinkage procedure had gone smoothly, but his mood was another story.

"Home is a plane ride away, not a short drive," I explained, even though the doctor already did. He was so annoyed when they were telling him he should stay. I didn't even think he listened. "And at least here you'll have your knee properly cared for and elevated instead of lying all night in an uncomfortable hotel bed. They already said they would discharge you tomorrow before we need to head to the airport."

"Hey, Bells?" he asked, his mood suddenly seeming less grumptastic and more conspiratorial.

"Yes?" I asked, dubious. Who knew what he was going to try and pull? Geez. He was probably plotting a hospital escape. He was so charming he might even convince me.

Stay strong, Bellamy. Don't cave to his manly wooing wiles.

"You ever done it in a hospital bed?" He lifted just one eyebrow and smiled.

A laugh burst from me, and I put a hand over my mouth to conceal some of the sound. After a moment, I pulled my hand away. "No, and tonight won't be any different." I scolded him. I had to admit… the thought did cross my mind. He was lying there all drowsy looking, with rumpled hair and nothing but a thin gown separating us.

"You have to lie still and keep your knee elevated. The nurses will be in with ice and to check on you."

"Maybe they'll join in." He wagged his brows, undeterred.

My mouth opened. Closed. Then a smiled formed on my lips. "You know… I just saw a pretty good-looking male nurse come on shift…" Liam's deep growl filled the room. My smile widened into a grin. "Not what you had in mind?"

"My knee might be busted, but not so busted that I can't get out of this bed and whoop some ass."

"But it was your idea." I reminded him innocently.

"No hospital sex," he declared, his eyes still molten silver. "I don't share."

I gave him a look. "Neither do I."

"Aww, sweetheart, I was just kidding. Come give me a kiss." He plastered a pitiful look on his face. "My knee hurts."

I made a rude sound but kissed him anyway. Liam was a lot of things, but interested in other women wasn't one of them. He was just being ornery. And slightly drugged up.

"You know I would never," he murmured when my lips left his.

I rubbed my palm over his beard. "I know."

He puckered his lips again, and I obliged. "I love you," he said against my mouth.

I pulled back after lingering against him for another moment. "Does it hurt?" I asked, sparing a look at his knee, which was elevated by some kind of sling hanging from the ceiling. It was wrapped, and there was some ice on it that the nurse would come remove in just a few more minutes. The doctor made several small incisions at the knee for the laser, so Liam had a few stitches.

"Nah. I'm still pretty numb. The pain meds they gave me work well."

They gave him a shot right before they started because he refused to take any pills. I knew he was only doing what he thought was best, and part of me was relieved. The other part of me didn't want him to be in pain.

"What about when that shot wears off?" I worried.

"They, ah, know the situation. The doc gave me a prescription for some anti-inflammatory you can get over the counter, just in a higher dose so I only have to swallow one instead of several at a time." He glanced at me, then down at his knee. "They aren't habit forming."

I went back to his side, gingerly balanced on the edge of the bed. "I'm not worried about that," I said.

"Maybe you should be." His voice was quiet.

I glanced at him sharply, but the door to his room opened and we were no longer alone.

Alex and his parents bustled in, carrying several bags and a tray of drinks. "Dinner is here," he announced.

I supposed dinner with Liam's family was a good distraction, though it wasn't lost on me I considered normal family time a distraction because the rest of my life was pretty much on fire. It was sort of hard to sit there and make small talk when someone had tried to murder me yesterday and we fled Chicago like criminals running from the law. I barely slept last night in the hotel room because every tiny noise had me alert and panicked.

We decided not to say anything about what happened in Chicago because Ren and Holly had enough on their plate. Besides, I didn't die. Technically, all was fine.

I picked at the takeout, mostly pushing it around in the box it came in, using the lid to basically conceal the fact I was doing more playing than actually eating. Liam didn't eat much either, but considering he just had surgery, I couldn't really blame him.

"Are you sure you don't want us to stay?" Holly worried, moving over to Liam's side. "It's only one night."

"There's no point in you guys getting a hotel room. I'm fine, and I know you'd rather sleep in your own bed tonight anyway," he told her. "I know I would."

"Tomorrow." I reminded him.

"Are you up for the drive, Alex?" Ren asked. "After driving in this morning?"

"I'm fresh as a daisy," Alex replied.

"I could do some driving for a while," Liam's dad offered.

Alex glanced at Liam slyly, then shook his head once. "I got this."

Ren frowned. "I have cancer. I'm not incapable."

Holly gasped. "Ren!"

"Dad, no one thinks that." Liam cut in.

Ren seemed doubtful.

Alex stepped in. "Nothing personal, Ren. You know my ride is new. Just enjoying being at the helm. You can take her for a spin if you want."

Ren relented. "I wouldn't want to get in the way of your fun," he told Alex. Then he glanced at Holly. "Maybe I'll sit in the back and hold hands with my girl."

Holly giggled.

Liam made a gagging sound. "I'm right here."

Alex chortled. "Mr. M's got game."

My heart squeezed a little because even though we were all joking and smiling, I couldn't help but think that sitting in the back, holding his wife's hand, was a good idea because moments like that were dwindling.

At the same moment, Liam and I glanced at each other. Something passed between us, and he held out his hand. I went to him. The feeling of his palm closing around mine was soothing, and I sat on the side of the bed.

Another thought occurred to me, and I smiled secretly.

Liam leaned up from the pillows he reclined against. "What's going on in that gorgeous head of yours?"

I glanced over, leaned in, and whispered. "I think we just had our first conversation with our eyes."

Liam cupped his hand around the back of my neck and pulled me down so he could kiss my forehead. "And so we did," he murmured.

"Now I'm the one gagging!" Alex so rudely interrupted.

I grinned.

"Your time is coming." Holly teased.

Alex shook his head. "Negative."

Liam yawned and adjusted on the bed like he was slightly uncomfortable. Both Holly and I flocked to his bedside to adjust pillows, make sure the sling was in the right place, and generally fuss over him.

"You should get some sleep," I told him, brushing back his hair. The past few days had been full of stress, travel, and now an overnight at the hospital.

"And we should get on the road so it's not too terribly late by the time we get back to BearPaw," Ren stated.

Liam rolled his head against the pillow and looked at his father. "You sure you're up for the drive back tonight? If you guys want, I can get you a hotel."

He was so sweet. I loved the loyalty and thought he gave his family, even when he was going through a lot.

"I'll be just fine," Ren replied patiently. He didn't seem too put off that Liam was considering his condition. Maybe he also realized his son just cared.

Holly leaned in to kiss Liam on the forehead. "I'm so glad everything went well. Do everything the doctors say, and we'll see you tomorrow when you both get home." When she finished talking, she turned and grabbed my hand. "Thanks for being here with him."

"Of course."

"Thanks for everything, bro." Liam held his fist out to Alex, and they bumped it out.

"Nothing you wouldn't do for me," Alex countered.

After everyone left, the nurse appeared to place a new ice pack on Liam's knee and check in on him. I think she had a crush on him. Hell, the entire floor of nurses all made up some reason or another to come in here and see him at least once. Liam attracted women like flowers attracted bees.

When she was gone, I pulled the large reclining chair toward the bed. It was heavy and boxy, so it didn't move much as I tugged.

"What the hell do you think you're doing?" Liam roared.

I stopped and turned. "What do you think *you're* doing?" I said back. He was sitting fully upright, his healthy leg slung over the side toward the floor as if he was going to somehow get up and yank his leg free of the sling!

Rushing over, I put both palms on his chest and pushed. "Lie down before you tear a stitch."

"I'm not going to tear a stitch," he argued.

"That's because you're going to lie down!"

"What the fuck did you expect me to do? You were trying to strongarm that chair! And with a shoulder still trying to heal." A few curse words dropped between us.

I stood back and planted my hands on my hips. "What did you just say to me?"

"Don't give me that look, woman. What the hell were you even doing?"

"I was trying to move the chair closer so I could sleep beside you. You big turd face! Clearly, that won't be necessary."

His lips twitched.

I narrowed my eyes. He'd better not laugh at me. This was not funny.

"Turd face?" he asked. Then the chuckle rolled right out of his chest.

I will not yell at him.

I will not yell at him while he is in the hospital.

With a huff, I turned away to grab the pitcher on the bedside table to escape into the bathroom to fill it up.

Liam's hand shot out and snatched my wrist. "Bells."

Why did he have to say my name like that? *Why?*

"You don't need to be moving that contraption. You're not sleeping in it."

I glanced at him.

He patted the mattress beside him.

I started to shake my head, but he gave my wrist a gentle squeeze. "I want you beside me. You're better than any medicine any doc could give me."

The pitcher went back on the nightstand.

"Come here." He cajoled.

With a sigh, I gave in. I was weak and powerless when it came to him. And I'm pretty sure I already mentioned how adorably rumpled and half asleep he looked.

I kicked off my sneakers and carefully crawled up on the bed. My body fit against him tightly. One of my legs draped over his, my arm over his middle.

"How's your knee?" I worried, glancing at it. I wasn't anywhere near it, but still.

"It's better now." He exhaled deeply. I could feel him relax into the mattress.

Lifting my face, I pressed a kiss against his scruffy jawline. "Go to sleep."

"Yeah." He agreed around a yawn. "I might do that."

I smiled into his chest.

It took him less than five minutes to fall sound asleep.

Then it was just me. Alone with my thoughts.

Liam

A strange sense came over me as I slept. A feeling so strong not even the meds I'd been given earlier could dull it.

I am not alone.

All sense of drowsiness vanished, and my eyes popped wide. Jolting upright, my back left the mattress as I balanced my weight on both palms. I scanned the room.

A shadow moved across the floor in front of the door. The dark shape stretched into the room, looming, lurking. But then it moved on, disappearing from sight as though it hadn't even been there at all.

More shadows moved past as hospital staff worked. My heart pounded, though, because they moved a lot differently than that first shadow.

Something was off.

My senses were screaming, my intuition on overdrive.

My arm jolted out to pull Bellamy closer into my side, the protective instincts in me hyper aware.

She wasn't there.

I forgot momentarily about the bad juju filling the room like a putrid odor and glanced at the empty place beside me so fast the muscles in my neck screamed.

I am alone.

Where the hell was Bellamy? She'd been in my arms before... and now she wasn't.

I glanced to the bathroom door. It was open. The lights inside were off.

"Bells?" I called out anyway.

No one answered.

A cold sweat broke out at my hairline. Pricks of warning made my breath pant. There was no use telling myself everything was okay. That we were safe here in this public hospital.

We weren't.

I had a feeling I wasn't alone. A feeling so strong it woke me out of a dead sleep.

But I was alone.

And I shouldn't be.

This time I yelled, "Bellamy!"

She answered.

With a scream.

Bellamy

You know what's more frustrating than not being able to sleep?

Lying next to a person who is sleeping without any issue at all.

Maybe I ought to ask one of Liam's admirers (aka his nurses) to get me some of whatever they gave him. A good night's sleep would be welcome about now.

Every time I shut my eyes, I was back in my old apartment with a bullet flying through the window on a mission to end my life. It wasn't exactly as soothing as counting sheep. Not that counting sheep ever worked. I ended up lying there wondering what I was going to name them and if their wool would make a nice sweater.

Blowing out a frustrated breath, I sat up. Clearly, this sleeping thing was a lost cause. I glanced over my shoulder at Liam and smiled. He looked peaceful, and I was glad.

The loud growl of my stomach disrupted the quiet of the room. Slapping my arm over my middle, I glanced down at it as if looking at it would somehow make it stop. It grumbled again, and I swallowed. Guess I should have done more than pretend to eat my dinner.

Right now the thought of food wasn't appealing, though. My mind and body were clearly at a disconnect. Perhaps it was why my body wouldn't let me rest.

The light from the hallway shone in the door, which was only pulled around halfway. I recalled the fancy coffee vending machine at the end of the hall and wondered if perhaps it also had some hot chocolate. Maybe something warm and comforting would make it easier to sleep.

And shut up my complaining stomach.

Slowly, I slid from the bed, taking pains not to jostle or wake Liam. After digging for some cash in my bag on the other side of the room, I slipped out the door and headed down the hall.

The hospital was much quieter at this time of night. There were no visitors walking around, and most of the patients were in their rooms asleep. The staff was still working, but it was a smaller crew than during the day.

Blinking against the too-bright overhead light, I passed the nurses station, which was empty, and headed toward the end of the hall. The vending machine was against the wall near the bank of elevators.

Perusing the options on the front, I noted it did indeed have hot chocolate. I pulled a couple dollars out of my pocket and smoothed them out on the leg of my jeans, hoping the machine would take it in one try.

Just as I was about to feed in the first dollar, a nurse walked by. "Oh, honey, that machine is out of order."

I pulled the money down as it continued to try and latch onto it. "It is?"

She nodded. "They were supposed to put a sign on it earlier, but clearly no one did. Guess I'll have to do it."

I frowned at the money in my hands, disappointed.

The nurse patted my shoulder. "There's another machine just like this one on the next floor down."

"Does it work?" I muttered.

"Sure does!" she sang, and off she went in her scrubs and Crocs.

I glanced back down the hall toward Liam's room, debating. My stomach grumbled again, and with it came a sense of nausea.

I hit the button for the elevator and then waited for it to ding open. The second it did, I stepped in, hit the button for the next floor down, then turned.

Something familiar moved toward the end of the hall. The nightmare-haunting tattoo drew my startled gaze.

A spider.

A black, long-legged spider. Right on the back of a bald man's neck.

"No!" I exclaimed and started forward.

The doors were closing. The gap showing the view of the man who wanted me dead became smaller.

Spidey pivoted when he heard me yell. His body stopped right outside Liam's door.

"No!" I yelled again. "Liam!"

In the narrowing space between the doors, I watched Spidey lift his hand, smile, and then wave.

Even though I was stunned, nearly in shock at the glimpse of the man who tried to shoot me then disappeared after the avalanche, my body knew what to do.

"Help!" I screamed and banged on the thick metal doors. I tried to pry them apart from the center, straining, feeling a twinge of warning in my shoulder and trying still.

The elevator practically laughed at my ineptitude and dropped to the lower floor. I sagged back, breathing hard when the doors opened. I rushed out into the hall, glancing wildly up and down the corridor, hoping to see a staff member or even security to have them call the police.

The hall was empty, this floor even quieter than the one Liam was on.

Liam!

I spun back around with a cry and rushed toward the elevator just as the doors closed completely. I banged on them with the side of my fist, then shoved off and lunged for the stairwell nearby. The door was heavy and made a squeaking sound when I shoved through. I was halfway up the steps when it banged shut behind me.

My vision tilted as I took the stairs two at a time. My stomach rolled, but I kept going and nearly collided with the door that led out into the hall where Liam was. I threw my body against it, totally expecting it to give way beneath my body, but it didn't.

I shuddered against the impact and bounced back. Without pause, I grabbed the door and pulled, opening it only enough for me to slip through.

"Liam!" I screamed his name so loud I probably woke the entire floor. My feet, which were only covered in socks, pounded over the sterile tile floor.

A nurse came out of the nurse's station, heading toward me with concern on her face. "Ms. Lane?"

"Liam!" I gasped. "He needs help!" As I ran, my sock-covered foot hit the polished floor at exactly the right angle, and I slid. Unable to catch myself, I landed in a heap on the floor.

The nurse reached my side, trying to help me up.

"No!" I shoved her hands. "Not me. Liam!"

"Bellamy!" Liam roared.

His voice sounded so strong, so alive… so ready to kick some ass that I stopped trying to scramble off the floor and actually sank onto it in a puddle of relief.

"Miss, what is going on—" the nurse was saying, but I ignored her.

Liam charged out of his room looking more like a linebacker than a snowboarder. The edges of the hospital gown flapped around behind him, sort of making it look like he was wearing a cape.

His gray eyes flared when they found me, and a broken sound ripped out of me. "Oh my God, are you okay?"

He stalked across the space between us and, without any effort at all, inserted himself between me and the nurse. His large, warm palms wrapped around my upper arms and lifted. Back on my feet, my knees were so shaky I knew I might end up back on the floor if he let go.

But I didn't think about that. Instead, I grabbed fistfuls of the front of his gown. "What did he do to you?" I pleaded. "Are you hurt?"

"Mr. Mattison, what is going on here?" the nurse asked. I noted there was much more movement at my peripheral vision, which meant I'd drawn a crowd... But I didn't look at them. I could only look at Liam.

"Give us a minute," Liam said flippantly to someone behind me.

"Bellamy."

"Are you okay?" I repeated as fat, salty tears spilled from my eyes and rolled down my face.

"Look at me." Liam encouraged softly. "I'm fine. All good. Everything is fine."

A sob was my only reply.

"Okay now, sweetheart," he said, gathering me against him. The center of my stomach turned over because being in his arms was just that good. "You're okay."

"I don't care about me!" I insisted. It sounded pretty pathetic because I said it between sobs.

Liam didn't laugh. Instead, he picked me up in his arms, cradling me against his chest.

"Your knee!" Someone cautioned him.

"I don't give a damn about my knee," he barked.

I sniffled, burrowed into him, and said, "Put me down, Liam."

"No."

"Sir, I really would advise against that kind of weight." The nurse continued, following him as he carried me back to the room.

"I'm not fat," I wailed. Clearly, I was having a brain hemorrhage of some kind.

Liam chuckled. "No, sweetheart, you aren't." But then his body went taut, and I felt him glance behind him. "You telling my girl she's fat?"

"This is ridiculous," the nurse replied, curt.

His smell surrounded me. Even in this hospital, Liam smelled like freshly fallen snow with a hint of pine. I inhaled deep and let the timbre of his voice wash over the worst of my frazzled ends. The hasty beating of my heart began to slow, and my brain finally caught on that the man I was so scared for was here and safe.

Liam carried me straight into the room and put me on the bed. The sling that should have been holding his knee was swaying slightly.

I gasped. "You're out of bed!"

Concern darkened his features. "You were screaming, Bells. I wasn't about to lie here."

I sat up, looking around the room, searching every corner. "He's here!"

"Who?"

"Spidey!" I scrambled off the bed. Liam tried to snatch me close, but I evaded and went rushing into the bathroom to flick on the light and check in the shower. "He's here, Liam! I saw him."

"I believe you," Liam replied, his voice calm and reasonable. How could he be calm and reasonable at a time like this?

"Could we have a moment?" Liam asked the nurse who was standing inside the door.

"Should I call the police?"

"Just a minute," he replied, barely holding on to his patience.

She left the room, and he shut the door, swinging to me. "Tell me what happened."

I leaned into the doorframe, gazing up and down his body as he stood in front of me. "You're really okay."

"I'm really okay," he echoed.

"I was so scared, Liam," I whispered, my voice wobbly.

"Hey now," he crooned, gathering me against him. I pressed close, rubbing my cheek against his chest. "I'm not going to let anything happen to you."

I pulled back forcefully. "I don't care about me. He was coming for you!"

Liam said nothing, just picked me up and put me on the bed. My feet dangled off the side, and that creeped-out feeling you get when you lie in bed and let one foot hang out of the covers drifted over me. I shivered, and Liam braced his palms on either side of my hips on the bed and leaned down.

"You should sit down." I worried.

"Just tell me," he snapped, his temper clearly thin.

"I couldn't sleep. So I went down the hall to get a hot chocolate out of the machine." I glanced up at him.

His eyes softened. "You like your hot chocolate."

"The machine was broken, but the nurse said there was another machine on the next floor down. I was only going to be a minute…"

Liam bent a little farther so he could catch my eyes with his. "You didn't do anything wrong, Bells."

"I left you alone."

"I'm a grown-ass man."

"You're *my* grown-ass man."

He laughed low. "Yes, I am, but that doesn't mean I'm not capable of taking care of myself while you get a cup of hot chocolate."

"When I got on the elevator, I looked back down the hall." I glanced up at him, swallowing. "He was here."

"Spidey?"

I nodded sagely, fear tingling my limbs. The sight of his tattoo flashed into my mind, and my teeth sank into my lower lip.

"Bellamy." Liam gripped my chin with one hand. "Look at me."

I did, his gray, thunderous eyes bringing me back to the present. "He was standing in the hallway in front of your room. He waved at me."

A low, aggressive sound rumbled out of Liam. "Then what?"

I scooted up on the bed a little more, trying to get comfortable. This bed was not at all. It was hard, and now it felt lumpy.

"I tried to get off the elevator, but the damn doors shut and I couldn't pry them open." I flexed my fingers, realizing my hands ached from the effort.

He made a sound, wrapping my hands in one of his. Both mine fit. In one of his. I stared down at the sight, unable to look away.

"So when the doors opened, I took the stairs and ran up here."

"And I heard you screaming."

Yanking my hands from beneath his, I grabbed his shoulders. "Did you see him? Did you scare him off?"

Liam pushed away from the bed and straightened. "He wasn't in here."

"What?" I exclaimed.

"When I woke up, the room was empty. I called out for you, but you didn't answer... Then I heard you scream."

"He was here, Liam! I saw him!" I jumped up from the bed and nearly slipped because this floor was freaking slippery when you were just wearing socks. I made a sound and fell back, throwing out my arm to steady myself on the bed.

Liam was there, grabbing my other arm, making certain I didn't fall. "You need to calm down, Bells. You're going to hurt yourself."

"How am I supposed to calm down?" I questioned. "He was here, and it wasn't me he was after this time!"

"Bells."

I glanced around, sharp. "Tell me you believe me."

"I believe you."

Just like that. He said it just like that without a hint of anything but seriousness in his tone. "Y-you do?"

"I will always believe you, no matter what. If you say he was here, then he damn well was."

How did I live without this kind of love for so long? How?

I started to turn completely, to go to him, but an odd sensation stopped me. "What…?" I whispered and turned back toward the bed.

It was dark in here, but there was definitely something there.

Definitely.

Reaching around me, I pushed at Liam. "Turn on the light."

"What?"

"The light, Liam! Turn it on!"

He flipped it on seconds later.

I gasped.

"Bellamy?"

With shaking hands and a heavily beating heart, I reached for the object I'd found on the bed. The reason it probably felt lumpy when I'd been sitting there. After slight hesitation, I scooped up the object and spun.

"He left us something." My voice was shaky.

Liam stared down at my hand cupped around the spine-tingling "gift." I didn't need it because Liam believed me, but if he didn't, I now had proof.

He reached out and grasped my hand, pulling it down from where I was holding it. "Let me see."

Extending my hand between us, I opened my fingers, exposing the black rubbery object filling my palm.

"What the fuck?" Liam wondered, staring down.

It was a spider. One of those real-looking toys with eight long black legs, an egg-shaped body, small head, and a red patch on its back.

A black widow.

One of the deadliest spiders out there.

Our eyes collided at the same moment. "He's playing with us," I whispered.

"Like a spider with a fly…" Liam murmured, his voice trailing away.

A spider is chaos to a fly.

18

Liam

Bells was turning me on.

There was nothing quite like watching your woman in her element, seeing flames of passion ignite in her eyes and an air of assurance mold around her body as she worked.

I was also mildly jealous.

Maybe more than mildly.

Pushing away from the island, I went into the kitchen where she was standing at the counter, working. She barely noticed me move up behind her. The girl was so involved with what she was doing with her hands.

Hands that were not on me.

Grasping her hips, I stepped into her, thrusting against her ass. "You're giving me a boner," I whispered against her ear.

She laughed and wiggled her fine ass against me, but didn't stop what she was doing.

With a growl, I picked her up and turned in a circle before planting her on the counter in front of me.

"Hey!" she exclaimed. "I'm cooking!"

"You laughed at my boner, sweetheart," I told her, serious.

She laughed again. "First of all, you called it a boner."

"Twice." I confirmed.

"Second, I think someone is jealous."

I made a rude sound. "I can't help it if you look all hot standing over here in the kitchen."

She groaned. "You are totally one of those types that like their women barefoot and pregnant... and in the kitchen."

A fizzle of desire spiked in me. My eyes must have betrayed me because she smiled knowingly. "So old school," she sang.

"I'll take you any way I can get you," I rumbled and pulled her into me.

My lips silenced her giggle and turned it to a sigh as my tongue stroked over her lips. I'd be a liar if I didn't admit that the thought of her pregnant with my baby didn't satisfy me on a purely instinctual level.

I didn't admit it, though. Not out loud anyway. I was too busy kissing her.

A moment later, Bells broke the kiss. "I'm finally cooking you dinner, and you're totally trying to distract me."

"You have flour on your nose," I said, brushing it off with my thumb.

"Leave that poor girl alone, Liam!" my mother said, coming into her kitchen like she owned the place.

She did, but I didn't appreciate the assertion.

"Mom..."

"Don't you mom me. The smells coming from this kitchen are divine, and I won't let even you get in the way of her finishing this family meal."

I glanced back at Bells, widening my eyes.

Bellamy nodded once. "She told you." Then she patted me on the chest and hopped off the counter beside me.

"The women in my life have let me down," I announced, woeful.

Mom laughed as she poured herself a glass of wine, and a large wooden spoon appeared before my face.

"Bells, now is not the time for spankings. My mother is in the room!"

Bellamy rolled her eyes. "Taste this."

I opened up so she could slip a taste of the sauce across my tongue. The second she was done, she pulled back and watched me carefully. As if she was nervous.

I might be a little nervous, too. I really hoped this stuff—

"Holy shit." I groaned and grabbed her wrist to pull the spoon back to my mouth to lick it dry.

"You like it?"

I didn't even pause even though the spoon was clean. "This is the best alfredo I've ever had."

"Really?"

"Well, I could have told you that just from the smell," Holly put in.

I dipped the spoon back toward the pot on the stove, but Bellamy smacked my hand away. "It's not done!"

"Tastes done to me."

"Get out of my kitchen!" Bellamy pointed to the door.

I raised an eyebrow defiantly. "It's my mother's kitchen."

"Out!" Mom backed her up.

I spun around and gave her a look. "I thought I was your favorite child."

She smiled and patted me on the cheek. "Oh, honey. You are my favorite son." I glanced over at Bells, but

Mom pulled my chin around. "But Bellamy is my favorite daughter. So out you go." She made a shooing sound.

"Come have a beer with your old man," Dad called from the bar. Clearly, he'd been listening.

I gave Bellamy one last longing look.

She smiled and waved. "It will be worth it."

Mom stayed behind, and from the bar, I could hear them tittering away, giggling as Bells created even more mouthwatering scents.

"Have you talked to your coach recently?" Dad asked, drawing me out of the jealous brooding I was doing about my mother and my girl.

"No." I turned toward him. Sometimes it was hard to look right at him, something that made me feel incredibly guilty.

It was hard.

Hard to look at a man who represented nothing but strength your entire life and now, beneath his skin, there was a disease literally trying to kill him.

"I told you, Dad. Snowboarding professionally is over for me. I'm ready to take on more here at the resort."

"Is that what the doctors have said? The physical therapist you've been seeing all week?"

I knew he was concerned. I knew he only cared. That's why I held on to the patience I had with both fists and fought the urge to snap at him to leave it alone.

The last thing in the world I wanted was any kind of recent memory where I disrespected my father—even a little bit, even out of frustration and pain—to look back on when all I had left of him were memories.

"It's too soon to tell," I replied. "It's only been a week and half since the thermal shrinkage. My knee is doing fine. I can put all my weight on it... but does that mean I can hit the half-pipe? I doubt it."

"Maybe in a few more weeks—"

"Dad," I said, much harsher than I intended. I relented immediately, pausing to take a sip of the draft I was drinking. "Pro boarding is not what I want anymore. I want to be here at BearPaw with you and Mom. With Bellamy. This is what I want."

He stared at me a moment, then relented. The firm weight of his hand settled on my shoulder. "More than anything, that's all I want, all any father wants for his son. To have the life he envisions. This resort," he mused, glancing toward the floor-to-ceiling windows nearby that looked out over the view of the place he built, "this was what I envisioned. It turned out better than even I imagined." Glancing back, he smiled and dropped his hand into his lap. "It was a lot of hard work and sacrifice. You're an only child because of it. But for me, in my life, that sacrifice was worth it because this is what I love. I don't want you to make sacrifices for something you don't love."

"Here I thought I was an only child because you got perfection on the first try," I quipped.

I couldn't help it. It was funny. And I needed to lighten the moment a little. The weight on my chest and the lump in my throat was making it really, really hard to sit there and breathe normally.

What was it like?

How scary, horrible, humbling was it to look out that window, see an entire world that you built with your own hands, and know that someday you wouldn't be here to watch it continue? To have spent your entire life building something you ultimately had to leave behind?

So much for trying to lighten things up.

Dad chuckled. "Well, that, too."

I tried to smile but failed. "Dad."

His reply was immediate and soft. "It's going to be okay, son."

I looked him in the eye, letting him see the sacred vow I was making. "I promise I will take care of this place. I might not love it quite as much as you do, but what I lack in that department, I make up for in how much I love and respect you."

I wasn't always much of a revealer—you know, the kind of man to reveal his innermost thoughts and feelings—but there were times when you had to tell people how much they impacted your life, how much you truly cared. Because if you didn't, one day all those unspoken emotions would turn into silent regret.

"I love you, too, son."

"I'm ready to do this. If you're up for it. I'm ready to come back to work."

He smiled. "I've been ready for this since you were born."

It felt good to be able to give my father that. Hell, he'd helped me achieve my dreams, and now I could carry his on.

I took a sip of the beer, glancing toward the kitchen where my girl was. "You know," I said, setting the glass down with a thud. "I have a couple ideas."

My father chuckled. "Don't even have an office yet and already trying to run the place."

"No one could ever fill your chair, Dad." I was sincere. "But I've been back a while, working at the resort, mingling with the employees."

The smile stretching across my father's face reached his eyes, which also shone with pride. "Let's hear it." He gestured for me to speak.

"I don't want to take up our entire night with business. We have tomorrow. But there are two things I'd like to run by you."

We finished our drinks as I told him, but before I could hear his response, Bells declared that dinner was ready. I abandoned all talk of business to hotfoot it to the table for the meal I'd been waiting for.

19

Bellamy

I'd never been so nervous to serve a meal.

Cooking was my passion, my education… Hell, up until my father shoved me inside a wall and I witnessed a murder, it was my life.

Being in the freaking amazing kitchen at Liam's parents' house was like a dream. Spreading out all the ingredients, getting out the professional-grade cookware, and just getting back to what I loved honestly felt like a gift. It was a chance to do something I thought I would never do again. At least at this capacity with this kind of kitchen.

Even though it had been nearly two years since I'd made a meal like this, it came naturally. Joyfully. The recipes I was making tonight I knew by heart. The scents took me back to a time in my life when I was wholly myself, before I had to give up everything I was.

A few times, tears sprang to my eyes as I was working because this felt so right and because it made me miss my mother even more than I already did. I loved cooking with her.

As I set the giant bowl of steaming creamy pasta alfredo in the center of the table, I felt a twinge of apprehension even though I'd already tasted it and knew it was good. *What if they don't like it? What if Liam thinks it's terrible?*

How embarrassing would that be?

Ren stepped up to the table beside me, touching my lower back. "I have to tell you, Bellamy. This is the most that kitchen has been used in years."

Holly laughed. "Yes, and when it had been used like this, it was the caterers."

"Thank you so much for letting me cook here. I loved every minute."

"Renshaw, did you know this girl even made the pasta? *From scratch!*" Holly told Liam's dad.

Ren lifted an eyebrow. "The sauce and the pasta? Impressive."

I felt my cheeks heat. In addition to the pasta alfredo, there was marinated grilled chicken, a mixed green salad with roasted vegetables, and a homemade balsamic vinaigrette. There were also rolls with a garlic butter I whipped up. And of course, a simple yet classic fudgy chocolate cake with homemade icing for dessert.

"Well, I'm ready to get at it," Ren said, reaching for his chair.

Liam popped between his father and me, leaned over the table, and stuck his fingers into the giant bowl of pasta. I gasped, and he pulled out a few noodles and shoved them in his mouth. White sauce clung to his upper lip as he chewed.

"Did you really just stick your fingers in the bowl of pasta?" I was incredulous.

He groaned. "Oh my God." He stuck his fingers in his mouth and sucked off the sauce, then licked his lip. "Heaven." He leaned back over the table toward the bowl.

I smacked his arm. "What is wrong with you?"

"It's only fair I got the first taste of your cooking." He wasn't even ashamed of himself!

"We have plates!" I exclaimed. "And forks."

"It's getting cold, Bells. Let me eat!" he grumped.

I shook my head. Holly pushed a glass of wine beneath my nose. "Here, dear. Have a drink. That's what I do when I eat with him."

"I feel the love, Mom," Liam said, grabbing a roll and shoving some of it in his mouth.

"Sit." She shooed.

The table was pretty quiet for a short while after that. We all passed around dishes, filled our plates, and began to eat. Well, I was too busy waiting with bated breath to know if they liked it or not.

Except Liam. He plowed through half a plate of pasta before he even looked up.

"If I didn't already love you," he said as he shoved more in his face, "I'd fall right now."

"I take it you like it," I mused.

"This is seriously the best pasta I've ever eaten," Liam declared, using his bread to get every last drop of sauce off his plate.

"It is delicious." Holly agreed.

"Really?" I asked.

Liam dropped his fork and turned to me. "I had no doubt you could cook, Bells… but you didn't tell me you were this good."

"Well, I'm just really good at this meal. It's my favorite to make."

Liam made a rude sound like he didn't believe me. I was going to kick him before the night was over.

"I have confidence that all the meals you make are just as good," Ren put in.

I smiled. "Thank you."

"What are you making us tomorrow?" Liam asked, shoveling some salad into his mouth.

I laughed.

He glanced at me, question in his eyes.

I paused. "You're serious?"

"You sealed your fate, sweetheart."

"Well, I'm sure your parents—" I started.

"Nonsense." Holly waved her hand. "We would love to have you for dinner as much as you want to be here."

Ren nodded. "Especially if you're cooking."

"And even if you aren't." Holly admonished. "I'll give you a key before you leave tonight. Just let yourself in anytime."

"Oh, that's not necessary," I hurried to say.

"It's decided," Liam's father announced like he was indeed a king and his say was final.

Liam caught my eye and winked. I felt myself blushing. Again.

Liam's fork clattered against his plate for the second time. His large, warm palm settled over my jean-clad leg, and his body leaned close. "I gotta tell you. I was nervous I'd be eating less-than-tasty morsels the rest of my life, but I'm saved. You did real good, sweetheart."

I wrinkled my nose. Was that a compliment?

A lopsided smile and an ornery look overcame Liam's features. He kissed me quick. "Love you."

The fact that they all enjoyed the dinner made my heart sing, and when Liam went back to eating but left his hand behind on my thigh, a warm sensation tingled across my skin.

"So what's it gonna be tomorrow?" Liam asked again.

"Tacos?" I asked.

"My favorite."

"I know."

"Fuck yeah!" Liam punctuated his excitement with his fork.

"Liam!" Holly admonished.

"Sorry, Mom." He went back to eating.

"Now, son…" Ren began. "Bellamy might be too tired tomorrow evening to cook for us. Especially after such an eventful day."

I looked up from my plate, wrinkling my nose. "I don't have anything planned for tomorrow…" I said, then gasped. "Did I forget your doctor appointment?" I said to Liam.

"That's not 'til the end of next week."

"Then…?"

We all turned to look at Ren.

"Bellamy, I think BearPaw Resort would be much improved if we could add your obvious culinary skills to our menu. I do believe there is a spot available at The Inn, and you are the perfect person to fill it."

I sat there almost uncomprehending for long moments. Eventually, his words sank in completely. "You're offering me a job?" I asked, awed. "At your highest-rated restaurant?"

"You'll still have to interview with Chef Paul, make sure you two get a long all right." Ren cautioned.

Liam scoffed and muttered, "If he wants to keep his job, he'll get along."

Excitement rose inside me. Sort of like light from a bulb I thought had burned out. Pushing my hands into my lap, I swallowed. They were shaking, and I didn't want anyone to see.

"Why would you do this?" I whispered, trying so hard not to get my hopes up. It was futile. Just the idea that I could have my dream job back… but not only that. I could have it here, at my dream location, and come home every single night to my dream guy.

It was overwhelming how much I wanted it all.

"Besides the fact that you are well qualified for the position and you just blew us all away with this mouthwatering meal?" Ren considered.

I nodded.

Liam's hand moved from my thigh to where my hands were shoved between my legs. It didn't matter how tightly my knees clamped together. His long fingers delved easily and grabbed them.

"BearPaw Resort is a family business, Bells. You're family."

For so long—actually, for my entire life—it was pretty much just me and my mom.

And then it was just me.

Here I was sitting in this gorgeous house with a tableful of people who just called me family. The emotion welled up inside me until the pressure on my chest was almost unbearable. Tears flooded my eyes, blurring my vision and embarrassing the hell out of me.

"Could you just excuse me for a moment?" The words rushed out, sounding wobbly and emo.

I fled from the room like it was on fire, feeling the stare of six eyes, rushing out of sight, down the hallway, and into the powder room on the right. The second the door was shut, I leaned all my weight on it and sank slowly down until my butt hit the floor.

The sob I couldn't hold in was muffled because I shoved the heel of my hand into my mouth. Unstoppable tears streamed down my cheeks as I tried to blink them away.

A knock on the door above my head caught my breath. "Bells," Liam said.

I swallowed and yanked the hand away from my face. "I just need a minute," I called back, trying to sound normal.

I must not have done a very good job because the handle on the door turned and he pushed. Digging my heels into the slick tile floor, I pushed my weight against the door to keep him from entering.

I wasn't heavy enough.

Liam pushed harder, and the door opened, towing me along the floor.

A frustrated sound erupted between my tears, and I glanced up. Liam poked his head in the opening he'd created, glancing around and then finally down to where I was.

His eyes softened the second he found me.

"Ah, sweetheart."

He pushed the door farther in to slip inside. Once it was closed, I scurried backward to sit against the wood again.

"You weren't invited in," I told him.

He ignored me and sat on the floor in front of me, spreading his legs so they were on either side of me.

"Mind telling me what's happening here?" He gestured with his finger to the room.

I wiped at my face, trying to conceal the tears he'd already seen.

Liam's voice was patient. "If you don't want the job, sweetheart, just say so."

"I want it," I said quickly. My voice was embarrassingly hoarse from the crying I was trying to conceal.

"Usually, when you want something, it doesn't send you fleeing into the bathroom to hide."

I groaned, dropping my chin to my chest. "I'm so embarrassed."

Liam made a low sound and scooted across the floor so we were closer together. I tried to look everywhere but at him when he lifted my chin with the back of his hand.

"Bellamy."

My eyes obeyed, answering his call.

"Your mom called me her daughter," I told him. "Out there in the kitchen. And then just now, your dad said I was family."

A puzzled look crossed Liam's face as if he wasn't sure why that was a big deal. Then he asked, "Too soon?"

A strangled sound erupted out of me. "I feel like I've been waiting my entire life for a family."

Understanding dawned in his eyes like a brand-new day. His hand moved from my chin to grasp the side of my face. I couldn't help but turn into his touch a little, inviting his fingers into my hair. "You've been alone a long time."

"Just a few years." *That have felt like forever.*

"And before that, all you had was your mother," he murmured, inching even closer. Liam's arm curled around me, pulling me off the door and into his body. I buried my face in the side of his neck and soaked up all the comfort he offered.

When I didn't say anything, just snuggled against him, Liam cleared his throat. "I'm still not sure how having a family is a bad thing. Or are these happy tears?"

I pulled back to look up at him. Gently, his knuckles dragged over the remaining wetness on my cheeks.

"Maybe I'm not meant to have a family. Maybe being here is just a recipe for even more pain."

"Because the mob is after you."

I nodded. "They took away my father. My mother. They're still coming for me... What's the point, Liam?"

He made a face. "The point?"

"The point of getting everything I ever wanted!" I burst out, suddenly emotional all over again. I sprang up out of his arms, stepped over his bent leg, and paced farther into the bathroom.

It was a very nice bathroom by the way.

"The last family I had was taken away. This one could be, too! I don't want to be the reason your family falls apart, Liam. I don't want to bring my bad luck into their lives!" I stabbed my finger in the direction of the kitchen and his parents.

He surged forward and grabbed me by the shoulders, giving me a gentle shake. Abruptly, he spun, pushing me up against the vanity, using his body to pin me there. We stood facing the large mirror. Staring at our reflection, I met his eyes.

"The point is you deserve to be happy." His voice was quiet, undemanding. "The point is there is no point to living if you aren't *alive*."

"It's selfish."

"To want to be loved and love in return?"

I tried to look down, but he caught my chin and held it firmly so I had to look at our reflection.

"No, sweetheart." He leaned forward and kissed the outer rim of my ear. "Didn't we decide we weren't going to do this? We weren't going to hide and cower. No more running, no more giving up what you want and who you are because of Perry Crone."

"I'm scared," I whispered.

Liam nudged me around, capturing my lips with his. The kiss was ice to a screaming burn, a dash of rich cream to a strong cup of coffee. A hiccup lifted my chest as he suckled my lips, but the motion of it only seemed to push me closer against him. Both arms encircled me, making me feel so small but so protected.

When he finally nudged away, my brain was heavy and foggy. My eyes felt like they were weighted down with sand.

"What if we lose everything?" I whispered, my greatest fear bubbling out.

"What if we don't?"

But what if we did? What then?

Liam sighed, cupped my face in his palms, and stared intently into my eyes. "Would it have been worth it?"

Of course. "Yes."

He smiled, and butterflies crowded my belly and under my ribcage. "Welcome to the family business, sweetheart."

I couldn't stop the smile from forming on my face. Even with traces of tears still there and fear still in my heart, I was happy.

Wasn't that the point of life? Finding happiness despite the obstacles?

"Can we go back to the table now?" Liam asked, stepping back. "I love you, boo, but this shit is interrupting my eating."

I laughed. "Heaven forbid!"

He held out his hand, and I took it. We walked through the house hand in hand, sitting in our seats, still clinging to one another.

I finished the dinner I cooked with my family.

It was a happy night.

Still, I couldn't help but pray deep down that this family I'd fallen so fast and so hard for wouldn't be ripped away.

Liam

"Yo!" Alex announced as he pushed into my father's office without knocking. I glanced up from the pile of papers on my father's desk. "You called. Here I am."

He was still dressed for skiing, with just the heavy jacket removed showing a long-sleeved thermal T-shirt in his favorite color, red. As he moved farther into the room, the fresh scent of outdoors and snow wafted toward me. I took a deep breath, and a sense of longing tugged at the deepest part of me.

I missed it out there. In the powder on the mountain with the wickedly cold air blasting my face and the sound of snow crunching and yielding under my board.

Alex seemed to sense the way I felt because he commented, "Everyone misses you out there."

"Feeling's mutual," I murmured, glancing back at the piles of paperwork.

God, the paperwork. It was endless. Keeping a resort this successful and large running smoothly required a small fucking forest of paperwork.

It sucked ass.

"Thank you so much for coming in," my dad said, standing up from behind his desk to extend his hand to Alex. After they shook, he gestured to the vacant chair beside me. Alex plopped down, sprawling back into it like the chair was blessed with his presence.

I grinned. I fucking missed him, too.

Being around all these suits and ties with their stuffy, near prim manners and no real sense of what BearPaw was all about was stifling.

"How's the knee?" Alex asked, glancing down at my sweatpants-covered lower half.

I smirked. The looks on all those suits' faces when I rolled into meetings with my sweatpants and hoodie was fucking priceless. The horror they didn't even bother to hide when my father announced I would be taking over soon was laughable.

Imagine! A bunch of number crunchers taking orders from a washed-up snowboarder who couldn't even dress nicely for the job!

I cackled gleefully before answering Alex. "It's still attached to my body."

"Got a brace on under those highly stylish pants?"

"The execs here are beside themselves," I said scandalously. Alex and I shared a gleeful chortle. "But yeah, knee's all strapped in beneath here."

It was one of the reasons I was wearing sweats. They were loose enough to cover the brace. Honestly, if it wasn't for that, I would have at least put on a nice pair of jeans.

'Course, now that I saw how scandalous it was to wear sweats, they might have to become part of my normal wardrobe rotation.

"Givin' 'em hell!" Alex reached out, and we bumped fists. "That's m'boy!"

I chuckled.

My father cleared his throat, and I glanced over. "Sorry, Dad. It's been a couple days since I've seen Alex."

"I haven't seen you smile like that since you started coming into work," Dad mused.

"I smile like this every day!" I rebutted. That was offensive to Bells.

Dad rolled his eyes. "At home with Bellamy, yes. At the office? No."

I made a sound. Now that he pointed it out... I guess he was right. "I've been focused on learning the ropes. No time to joke around."

"Hmm." Dad considered my words. "Here I thought it was because everyone on the executive floor is at least double your age."

"Well, there is that," I muttered.

"So what's up?" Alex asked.

"Besides the age of everyone on staff here?" I quipped.

Alex laughed.

"I've been considering something that Liam proposed to me last week." Dad began.

I sat up a little straighter.

"At first, I wasn't sure how it would work, but spending the week here with him and the other executives, I do see there is a very glaring gap."

A fissure of excitement kicked up inside me. A flame of passion even ignited. Yes, I'd always planned on taking over BearPaw. No, it wasn't really my passion.

But it could be.

With the right people.

With a team I could trust.

"I'm not really sure I know where I fit in," Alex replied, glancing at me with a question in his eyes.

I grinned, sat forward, and smacked him on the back.

"You want to clue me in?" he asked, amused.

"I'd like to offer you a position here at BearPaw, on the executive team."

A stunned expression froze Alex's face. After a moment, he recovered. "Um, what?"

I laughed low. "Hell yes!"

Alex turned to me. "You knew about this?"

"It was Liam's idea," Dad replied, drawing the attention of my best friend. "I think it would be a good idea to shake things up around here a bit, get a younger demographic in to help keep the resort fresh and prevent it from falling into a rut."

Alex turned to me. "They hate your sweatpants so much you already gotta hire on someone to watch your back?" He whistled low. "Damn, Liam. Put on a suit."

"They don't hate the sweatpants," I said, laughing.

"I beg your pardon," Dad interjected.

I laughed some more. "Fine. They hate them. But not me."

I glanced at Dad, and he nodded. "It's true. Liam is well liked, but his attire is not. Really, Liam, would it kill you to put on a suit?"

"It might," I said, grave.

Alex glanced at me, serious. "So why would you want to hire me, then?"

"You're my best friend. I trust you way more than anyone else in any of these offices."

Alex narrowed his eyes. "You want a yes man."

A rude sound ripped out of me. "If I wanted a yes man, I wouldn't hire you."

"As I said, a younger generation of executives might be good to mix along with the more experienced here. You and Liam both have worked among the employees, you frequent many of the resort restaurants, and you've mingled with guests."

"Alex likes his snow bunnies." I agreed.

"Yes, well, as a BearPaw exec, I would caution the amount of, ah, bunnies that you spend your free time with."

"You mean I'd have to say no to bunny tail?" Alex was forlorn.

I nodded sagely. "Just say no."

"This is a really generous and surprising offer…"

He was going to say no?

Oh, hell no.

"We both know you are way overqualified to be a ski instructor." I deadpanned.

"I like my job."

"You can still pick up some lessons," my father told him. "It would actually be good to keep your finger on the pulse of the resort."

"I'll be picking up lessons as soon as I can, too."

"How the hell you gonna do that running this place?" Alex asked.

"Because I'll have a team to help me, a team that hopefully includes my best friend."

Alex sat back and blew out a breath. "For real?"

I nodded.

His next words were directed at my father. "I'm not qualified."

"The skills you have will benefit this resort. Your army background would be useful with the security team. Your skiing experience here would be of use to the slopes management. And your fresh perspective would be refreshing on the board."

"The board!" he exclaimed.

I chuckled. "As an exec, you will have a seat on the board."

"And a pay raise," Dad added.

Alex blew out his breath again. "This is unreal."

"C'mon, man. You know I can't run this place without you. I'll go stir crazy."

"What if it don't work out?" he asked.

"It will."

Alex glanced away from me and turned toward the sprawling view out the windows. He was silent a while, and I actually started to think he was going to turn down the offer. Alex liked his freedom. He didn't like feeling boxed in, and hadn't I just basically said sometimes I felt suffocated?

Disappointment was a bitter pill to swallow.

Alex glanced at me. "Can I wear sweatpants, too?"

I burst out of my chair, laughing. "Hell yeah!"

Alex stood up, and we hugged it out. I squeezed him tight because I was so fucking happy he was going to be by my side for this. "Thank you," I said low.

He hugged me a little tighter in response.

"There is no reason for Alex to wear sweatpants," my father said, exasperated. "He doesn't wear a large brace on his knee."

"But, Dad…" we both whined at once.

My father's lips shook, but he managed not to smile. "I mean it, boys. This job offer is not so you can torture my entire staff. This is a place of business. I expect nothing but professionalism from both of you. Liam, you're out of the sweats as soon as the brace gets smaller."

"Yes, sir," we both answered, morose.

"This place is my legacy," he said, turning to look out his window.

He looked formidable standing there in his three-piece suit, poised, gazing out at the snow and mountains.

It hit me in the middle like it sometimes did when I least expected it. He was a sight I wouldn't be seeing forever. This man at the helm of the great place he'd built wouldn't be in charge much longer.

The joy I knew at bringing on Alex fell aside, and grief unlike anything I'd ever known welled up to swallow me whole. I wasn't sure how long I was going to be able to hold it back.

Alex and I moved simultaneously, going around opposite sides of the desk to take up a spot on each side of my dad. The three of us stood there gazing out at the winter wonderland.

"We won't let you down, Dad," I told him.

"We'll make you proud," Alex echoed.

"I know you will." He agreed, spreading his arms to place one on each of our shoulders. "You boys make me proud. Nothing honors me more than passing down BearPaw to the next generation of this family."

We stood there a while longer. No one said anything because the emotion in the room was palpable. After a bit, my father cleared his throat and lowered his arms. "I think I'll call it a day. Training Liam all week has been quite the exercise."

I frowned. "You feeling okay, Dad?"

He waved the concern away, but didn't meet my eyes. "Of course. Just a little tired."

"I'll drive you home." I began, but he shook his head.

A swift knock on the door was followed by my father's assistant letting herself in. "Mr. Mattison, here are the notes for tonight's meeting."

"Tonight's meeting," he repeated. "Ah, yes. I forgot."

My father never forgot a meeting.

I went around him and extended my arm for the notes. "I'm taking the meeting tonight."

His assistant seemed surprised. "You are?"

"If I need anything else to prepare, I'll buzz you."

"Of course," she replied, her surprise covered by professionalism. "I'll be at my desk."

"Thank you."

She offered me a small smile. "Of course, Mr. Mattison."

"Liam." I corrected. "Mr. Mattison is right here." I pointed at my father.

She nodded and excused herself.

My father seemed to wilt a little the second she was gone. How exhausting was it for him to pretend to be at top form so his employees didn't worry?

He wasn't just the head of this place. He was a pillar. A leader. Someone everyone looked to for strength and assurance.

That was my job now.

"I'm taking the meeting," I declared, heading over to the phone on his desk.

"That's my responsibility," he argued.

"There's no better training than on the job. This meeting is the perfect opportunity."

"Son, you haven't been briefed."

"I'll read the notes. I have a couple hours to prepare. If I need anything, I'll call your assistant."

"Call me." He relented. "Or your mother."

"Was just going to," I quipped, dialing.

Mom picked up her own extension. "Mom," I said.

"Liam, honey."

"I'm making Dad take off early. I'm gonna practice being him." I joked. "I think you should take off, too. Spend the evening with him."

"How is he?" she asked, her voice dropping.

I guess she heard what I didn't say.

When I didn't reply, she rephrased the question. "Is he very tired?"

"Yes, I think some takeout from The Inn would be perfect."

"I'll have them pull the car around," she said.

"Sounds good."

"Liam?" she called out before I could hang up.

"Yeah?"

"Thank you for calling."

I hung up because saying anything would tip off my father that Mom knew he was in a bad way.

"She's having the car pulled around."

"Are you sure you want to take this meeting?"

"I got this." I assured him. *I really hope I got this.*

He agreed. And that right there was proof he wasn't doing as great as he wanted everyone to believe.

It took everything in me not to walk him down to the car. I knew if I tried, it would hurt his pride. So I stayed in the office, and when he was gone, I turned to Alex and blew out a breath.

"I've been losing my fucking mind up in this wing without you."

He grinned. "We'll shake it up in here."

"I need you to do something for me."

"You mean putting on a suit on the daily and being your exec wingman isn't enough?"

"You can wear jeans." I assured him. "But you might have to get bunny tail somewhere else."

"Let it never be said I ain't loyal," Alex announced. "'Cause I love me some bunny tail."

I chuckled. His first paycheck would make up for it.

"So what's up?"

"Suddenly, I'm working late. So is Bells. I need you to pick her up and take her home. I don't want her wandering around the resort at night, alone."

"Sure thing."

"Thanks." I went back around the desk and set down the file the assistant had just given me. I had a very short amount of time to get up to speed on whatever the fuck this meeting was about.

Alex paused at the office door and turned back. "This place, it ain't just your father's legacy no more."

I looked up from the papers. "Yeah. I know." I agreed. "It's a family legacy now."

Our family.

21

Bellamy

I didn't want people to think I didn't deserve this job.

Because of that, I stayed late. *A lot.*

Right after the dinner when Ren offered me a position at The Inn, I had my official interview with the head chef. I'd been incredibly nervous, not only because this was another shot at my dream job, but because, generally speaking, head chefs were often temperamental and hard to please.

If this man didn't like me, then it didn't matter who recommended me for the job because even if I worked here, my career would be doomed.

Chef Jon D'alessio definitely ran a tight kitchen, and I could tell that some of the staff was intimidated by him the second I walked into the sprawling, amazeballs kitchen of The Inn.

I also noted that people were immediately intimidated by me. Seemed bizarre and unfounded really, until I realized how it looked. I was being escorted through the place by Renshaw *and* Liam Mattison.

Yeah. Hindsight on that decision.

Their presence definitely-probably helped me look like a favorable hire in the chef's eyes, but to everyone else? I looked like a spoiled, untalented kitchen brat who was only getting the job because I was boning the boss' son.

Regardless of how it appeared, Ren introduced me to Chef D'alessio and then left. Liam left, too, after he glared at my maybe boss and was dragged out by Ren.

Good Lord.

When I got the job as *chef de partie,* aka station chef, I liked to think it was because the executive chef thought I was a good fit for his kitchen.

Everyone whispered, though. Hell, even I kinda wondered.

Did I get the job because I deserved it or because of who I knew?

In the last couple weeks, as I learned the kitchen and tried to win over the skeptical staff, I told myself almost daily this was just reality. Lots of jobs and doors were opened for people because of who they knew.

It wasn't fair. But it was reality.

The difference was I knew I deserved to be here, and my God, I wanted to be. I was nearly bursting with passion every time I pulled up to the restaurant. My brain was overflowing with menu ideas, additions, changes, and specials. I kept a lid on it mostly, at least for now. I definitely didn't want it to seem as if I were waltzing in and trying to take over.

So, here I was staying late more often than I didn't because I wanted to prove I wasn't above hard work, and though I didn't start at the bottom of the kitchen ranks and work my way up, I was willing to be a team player.

Tonight, I was washing dishes. One of the dishwashers was sent home in the middle of his shift because he was throwing up in the bathroom, and that left the other dishwasher with a heavy load and no moment to breathe. When the kitchen was closed for the night and everyone was filing out, I stayed back and helped get the dishes down to something manageable. Then I told the poor exhausted girl to go home and I would finish.

Between you and me, she looked a little green around the gills herself. I was thinking she probably caught whatever her partner brought into work with him.

Lucky.

I could tell when she left that her opinion of me was a lot less hostile than it had been before. It was just the same for the prep station women two days ago and the sous chef before that. I was winning them all over, and it felt good to earn their respect.

All the extra work left me exhausted, though.

I wasn't about to complain. Not too long ago, there was a time in my life that I literally yearned for this.

I was alone in the kitchen. All the other staff had already gone. For a few minutes, I wandered around the spacious, pristine work area, shutting off lights over certain stations and making sure the pastry section was closed up right. Afterward, I went back to the massive dishwashing station and gazed at the piles of dishes still needing washed and run through the industrial-size machine.

Nearby was a radio, the old-school kind that didn't need to be synced to a Bluetooth device I didn't have. It didn't even play CDs. Just the radio. I smiled to myself as I turned it on and fiddled around trying to find a station. It was just like years ago when I first started out in kitchens. I washed dishes and listened to bad music.

A station came in playing some nineties music, so I cranked up the volume and got to work. I didn't know how long I hand washed giant pots and pushed racks of dishes through the machine, but by the time I was nearly finished, my fingers looked like prunes and my shirt was damp from all the splattered water.

When I shoved the last rack into the machine, I turned from the sinks with a heavy sigh. Maybe offering to do all this work alone wasn't my smartest idea. My arms felt like wobbly noodles and my feet ached from being on them all day.

I'd forgotten how much labor it took to work in a kitchen.

Rubbing the sore spots on my lower back, I grabbed a water out of the staff cooler and twisted off the cap. Glorious cool water rushed down my throat and coated my stomach. Feeling it fill my belly, I wondered about the last time I'd eaten and grimaced with the realization I'd missed dinner.

Cooking for other people left no time to feed yourself.

Abruptly, the creepy sensation of being watched along with an inkling of anxiety curled my toes, and I froze, paralyzed by familiarity.

I knew this feeling. I felt it that night in the grocery store in Chicago. Then again at my apartment later. I'd felt it enough times in the past couple years that I should be alarmed that I recognized it. I probably would be if I wasn't suddenly so afraid.

A faint click echoed through the kitchen, and everything shut down.

Darkness enveloped the room, robbing me of sight, and the radio cut off abruptly. Even the incredibly loud dishwasher shut down midcycle. The sound of water circling down the drain was eerie in the absence of all other noise.

Glug, glug, glug.

Body and limbs still immobile, I forcibly lowered the bottle from my lips and slowly straightened away from the cooler.

It's probably just a power surge. The breaker just needs flipped. It probably happens all the time. I told myself all those logical things.

I didn't believe any of them.

After everything I'd been through, it was basically an instinct to assume the absolute worst.

The pounding of my heart was irate, and the water in the bottle sloshed around from the trembling of my hands. I wrapped one arm around my middle and stood there in the pitch black, knowing I needed to do something, but my feet were unable to move.

A faint sound echoed through the kitchen. Or was it just my paranoia? Straining, I listened almost obsessively for any noise at all.

Are all the doors out there locked up?

Another thought had me blowing out a breath and sagging in relief. *I'm probably not the last one here!*

"Hello?" I called out. "I'm working late, too!"

No one answered.

"Hello?" I called out again, walking forward a few feet.

The silence ricocheting around the place did not help the anxiety gripping my windpipe like a madman intent to kill. I knew being afraid was useless. It wouldn't change the way any of this would play out. All fear would do was hinder me from thinking clearly.

But damn if I had a recipe for chasing away the feeling trying to control my mind and body.

Fighting it back, swallowing past the tightness in my throat and ignoring the way my chest squeezed, I glanced around the dark room, eyes adjusting so I could make out some shapes. I didn't know this kitchen as well as I would if I'd been working here for more than a couple weeks, but I knew it well enough.

The breaker box was in the back, the phone toward the front.

Before I could even decide which to make a run for, everything started up again, just as abruptly as it has shut down.

Lights flickered on overhead, the dishwasher started back up again, and bad music that seemed so much louder than before blared through the tiny, staticky speakers on the radio. Jolting in surprise, I pressed a hand to my chest as water managed to slosh from the bottle and splatter my hand.

Blinking against the sudden bright light, I set the water on a nearby stainless-steel countertop and used the hem of my T-shirt to wipe at the water on my hand.

A laugh bubbled up beneath my breath because clearly it had just been some sort of quick power shortage that had managed to scare the shit out of me.

"Get a grip," I muttered to myself.

That's when I saw it.

Right there in front of my face. Right there near my water bottle.

A spider.

Black, rubbery, and creepy as fuck. It was just like the one that had been left on Liam's hospital bed.

To my credit, I didn't scream. Instead, my teeth slammed down into my bottom lip so hard a tang of metallic teased my tongue. My stare whipped up, searching around the well-lit kitchen, expecting, fucking scared to death, that he would be standing there.

I saw no one.

But I knew he was here. Just seconds ago, he'd been creeping around in the dark so close by he could have slashed my throat without me even knowing it was coming.

Come to me said the spider to the fly...

I have no idea where that quote came from, but it bounced around in my brain, making my skin crawl and my knees quiver.

He was playing with me. I knew this. He'd done the same that night at the hospital.

Glancing back at the spider, I blew out a breath and tried to rationalize this entire situation.

He was probably already gone. Spidey got what he wanted—to send a message he was still lurking around, ready and able to kill me at any moment.

How the hell can we live like this?

Screw finishing the dishes. It was time for me to get the hell out of here.

My fingers visibly trembled when I reached out for the spider. I didn't want to touch it. I didn't even want to look at it.

I couldn't leave it here.

Just as the tips of my fingers brushed against the sticky rubber, the lights went out again.

This time I couldn't hold back the small scream that bubbled up. *He's still here!*

In the silence, my whispered name echoed.

Forgetting all about the stupid spider, I shoved away from the counter and rushed backward, toward the closest exit. My body slammed into something hard and hot, and I screamed.

Spidey chuckled as his beefy hands reached out and grabbed me. "You're so fun to play with; it almost makes me not want to kill you quite yet."

Acting purely on instinct, I raised my foot and slammed it down over his shin and foot. He made a sound and loosened his grip just enough for me to yank away. As I stumbled, I turned to run, but he shoved me and I fell back into the counter. The sound of the plastic water bottle falling over and water spilling out gave me an idea.

Blindly, I reached for it, the plastic crunching beneath my grip as I raised it and flung what was left of the water at Spidey.

He cursed, knocking the bottle away as I threw it at him. I dropped down on hands and knees and scrambled under the counter, out the other side. My shoes slipped in the water on the ground, but I propelled myself forward.

The sound of Spidey leaping right over the counter was not very encouraging as I rushed around the next station in front of me.

A large, gloved hand wrapped around my flopping ponytail and jerked me backward as though I were on a leash.

"No!" I screeched and grabbed the edge of the work station as an anchor. My eyes watered as he increased the pull on my hair, my entire scalp stinging, but I hung on to the counter. The cold metal was smooth beneath my fingers, offering nothing to sink my grip into at all.

I kicked at him, connecting only once, and it made him laugh.

The sound of my fingers streaking over the metal as he dragged me backward was worse than nails on a chalkboard, but I barely noticed.

When he managed to get an arm around my waist and pull me against his body, true panic fully set in.

"When I'm done with you, I'm going to that cabin of yours for your man," Spidey whispered roughly in my ear.

Eerie calm settled over me before the full threat was even out. Fear for my own life was indescribable… but fear for Liam's?

Oh, hell no.

It wouldn't happen. It was as simple as that. The idea that this man would lay a hand on the only man I'd ever loved was so reprehensible that my brain didn't even panic.

In a burst of rage, I shoved forward, even with his arm around my middle, and grabbed the handle to what I thought was a pan on the nearest counter. Gripping it soundly, I swung it around over my head and slammed it against Spidey's face.

He let go instantly, and I took off.

The sound of his laughter followed.

He's laughing. He actually enjoys this.

Maybe if I stopped fighting, his fun would run out.

But then my life would, too.

I had to stay alive because as long as I was alive, he would focus on killing me and not Liam.

"There's nowhere to run," he taunted from behind.

I slammed into the door leading out to the waitstaff area, but it didn't give way. I shoved into it again. It held. Next, I tried the handle, but it was clearly blocked.

I spun. Spidey's bald held seemed to shine like a lightbulb in the dark and his teeth flashed with his approach. He didn't hurry or run, which was scarier than anything else.

He'd trapped me in here. He knew I couldn't get away.

Still clutching the heavy cast iron pan, I gripped it like a baseball bat and swung when he was close. He evaded the hit with a chuckle. So, using my noodly-feeling arms, I chucked the heavy pan as hard as I could right at his face.

He dodged, but it still managed to hit him in the shoulder and knock him off balance. I rushed by, running back into the kitchen, deep into the room holding me prisoner. My shoes squeaked as I rushed around one of the corners, and it made me stop moving instantly.

I couldn't run. But I could hide. At least until I figured a way out of here. Being noisy was not the way to hide.

"Bellamy," he sang.

I dropped down to the floor and ever so quietly pulled off my shoes and set them on the floor. Staying low, I crawled along the bank of cabinets against the far wall.

Spidey made a sound on the other side of the kitchen, and I felt a tiny sliver of hope.

Quickly, I scurried past the coolers and into the back room where the bread was made. It was a basic square with only one entrance/exit, but it was the only idea I had. As I crawled over the tile, my hand slipped into the drainage vent built into the tiles. My finger went right through one of the small circles, and pain made me fall back onto the tiles. Cradling it against my stomach, the pain ebbed in my hand. As I felt it gingerly, the warm stickiness of blood smeared around.

With no other choice, I pushed aside the pain and crawled soundlessly around the large center island to a cabinet on the end. I stared up at the ceiling in silent prayer as I pulled open the cabinet door.

Please be quiet. Please be quiet.

I got it open just enough to slip inside without any sound to give me away. Before crawling in, I spied the knife block sitting atop the counter, so I snatched a large knife and took it with me.

I barely fit inside the cabinet. There was an oversized mixer stored there, and it poked the side of my hip angrily.

The sound of my breathing was loud and ragged. I tried desperately to get it under control as I also tried to keep my body from shaking so much it gave me away.

Spidey called out my name again, and I squeezed my eyes closed, gripping the handle of the knife like a lifeline.

A cold sweat broke out over my forehead and dizziness washed over me. Memories of that day two years ago assaulted me. The way my father shoved me between the drywall in that dingy apartment room. How I sat there, breathless and scared as hell, listening to the sounds of my father being beaten.

I despised being trapped. Feeling helpless and terrified.

I heard Spidey in the doorway. My breath caught, my lungs squeezing. He moved so quietly I had to strain to hear him, but I could. He was less careful now that I knew he was coming for me.

He wanted to scare me. To smoke me out.

One of the cabinet doors on the island opened. The sound of metal dragging on metal made me wince.

Sweat dripped between my shoulder blades.

He was opening each door… Eventually, he would get to me on the end. Leaning my head against the metal wall, I took a breath and formulated a plan. The second he opened the door, I would burst out, plunge the knife down in his shoe, and then run like hell. I could go out the window in the employee lounge even if I had to bust it open with something.

A little of the terror inside me eased just enough for me to catch a full breath. I could do this. I had a plan.

The cabinet door beside the one I was hiding in started to open.

Loud banging from out in the kitchen brought my head up.

"Bellamy!" a muffled voice yelled.

A low curse close by gave me pause.

"Bellamy!" a clearer voice yelled this time. "Girl, where you at?"

Alex! Alex was here!

Oh shit. Alex is here!

"No!" I roared and burst out of the cabinet a hell of a lot less gracefully than I went in. I fell out on hands and knees, the knife clattering against the tile. My sliced finger screamed as I gripped the knife and leapt up, brandishing the weapon toward where I knew Spidey was standing.

He was gone.

The lights came on for the second time, and everything came back to life.

Everything but me.

A dark figure came around the corner, and I jerked back and raised the knife. The wildness inside me was scary, but I used it.

"Whoa, whoa!" Alex skidded to a stop at the other end of the island. He lifted both hands and held them out, palms up. "Is that any way to greet your ride home?"

I searched around behind him and realized Spidey had gone. Alex must have scared him away.

The knife clattered at my feet, and I sagged backward with a cry. I would have hit the floor, but Alex rushed forward and caught me.

"Are you okay?" I worried as he supported me. I grasped the front of his shirt and searched his face.

"I'm fine." Alex assured me, stark concern taking over his features. He pressed a hand over mine where I gripped his shirt. "Tell me what happened, girl who got away."

My face fell and tears came so easily.

Alex pulled his hand away from mine and glanced down at the blood smeared over his fingers.

Everything about him changed. "What the fuck is this?" His voice was cold and toneless. "You're bleeding!"

I scrambled back, still holding his shirt for balance. "We have to go. We have to get out of here in case he comes back!" I said, frantic. "He didn't come back before, but tonight he did."

"Who?" Alex bellowed.

I shoved away and started to run for the door. My sock-covered feet slipped, and I went flying.

Alex cursed loudly. His arms went around my waist and lifted. The next thing I knew, I was cradled against his chest.

"We have to go." I urged, tears spilling over my cheeks. "I don't want him to hurt you, too."

"Ah, baby girl, the only person that's going to get hurt tonight is whoever the fuck did this to you." Alex walked out of the back room as he spoke, holding me as if I weighed nothing at all.

My stomach clenched and nausea followed.

"Why was the door in here barricaded? Why were all the lights off?" Alex pressed.

My eyes found the fat, black spider still sitting on the counter.

I lifted a weak hand and pointed to it.

Alex's body went rigid.

"He was here," I told him and then went slack in his arms.

Liam

The second I unlocked the cabin door, I knew something was wrong. Nothing appeared off, including the giant slobbering dog wagging his tail at me the second I appeared.

But the way everything felt?

Major alarms in my head.

"Where's Bellamy?" I demanded, gruffly pinning Alex with a stare.

"In the bedroom," he said, his voice equally as gruff.

I paused by where he was sitting at the island, his back still to me. "What happened?"

Alex moved only a few inches, sliding over enough to reveal what he was sitting in front of, glaring.

The blood in my veins turned to ice.

"Why didn't you call me?" I yelled. "Jesus, fuck…" I started as I rushed toward the hall.

"She begged me not to," Alex replied, not even fazed by my cussing tirade.

I stopped and turned, angry. "I thought you were my best friend."

"I am, and you fucking know it. But she is, too, now." He gave me a look. "I kinda see why you can't ever tell her no."

"She cry?" I worried.

He nodded.

"Bellamy!" I roared.

Alex caught me as I started back down the hallway, his hand clapping down on my shoulder. "Slow your roll," he demanded. "She's had a rough night. Don't go back there yelling and ordering her around."

I glanced down at his hand on my shoulder and then around at him. His icy eyes levelled on mine.

"You telling me how to handle *my* girl?"

"I'm telling you to calm the fuck down."

I spun back around, knocking his hand off my shoulder. My pointer finger drove into his chest. "You didn't call me."

"I had it handled."

Red tinged the outer parts of my vision. I stepped up to my best friend, our toes hitting. "You don't ever handle my girl."

"I will if you aren't there to do it."

I reared back as though he'd punched me, my fists clenching at my sides. "What the fuck did you just say to me?"

"Liam?" Bellamy's small voice from the doorway at the end of the hall cut my anger like a hot knife through butter.

I spun instantly, forgetting about my bonehead of a friend.

My chest caved in seeing her there. She was maybe half my size (or less), standing there with wet hair, bare feet, dark circles beneath her eyes, and frighteningly pale skin. Her body was drowning in one of my BearPaw T-shirts and nothing else.

"Sweetheart," I practically crooned. "What happened?"

Her lower lip wobbled.

Without looking away from her, I reached back and shoved Alex toward the living room. "Don't leave," I ordered.

"What a nice invitation to stay," he muttered, but I tuned him out.

My legs made short work of the distance between us, and the second she was within distance, I picked her up, her legs winding around my waist. I felt the quiver in her thighs and noted how weak they felt. Even though the image of the spider sitting on the kitchen counter haunted me, even though I wanted nothing more than a full report of whatever the fuck happened, I didn't demand anything.

Instead, I held her a little tighter when her face pushed into my neck and carried her into our dim bedroom, lit only with the bathroom light.

Wet strands of her long hair fell over my arms and dampened the front of my shirt. I sat on the end of the bed, keeping her tightly in my lap. I felt her feet fall against the mattress behind us. Her body relaxed against mine, so I supported all her weight.

Behind us, Charlie jumped on the bed and lay down, taking up more space than us. My palm rubbed up and down her back as I kissed the side of her head.

"Bells," I spoke gently. "What happened tonight?"

"He was at The Inn tonight," she said, still collapsed against me.

The muscles in my jaw ticked. "Spidey?"

I felt her nod against me.

"Like that night at the hospital? He showed up and left the spider, then disappeared?"

Bellamy pushed up. Her hands fell between us, and she gazed down toward them. I followed her gaze, immediately stiffening when I saw the crudely wrapped bandage around her finger, blood staining it.

I cursed and lifted her hand. "What the fuck is this?"

I heard Bells swallow. It sounded as if her throat were the Sahara Desert and her spit a giant rock. She pulled her bandaged hand from mine and glanced up.

"He didn't just leave this time."

I felt like a lit fuse that someone just doused in gasoline. I stood up brusquely, jolting both of us. "Tell me now," I demanded, unable to keep composed.

Bellamy slid down my body and squirmed a bit, right out of my arms. I watched her race across the room and rush into the bathroom. Seconds later, the sound of her retching filled the silence.

I went instantly, opening the door she weakly tried to push closed on her way through. Heaviness settled on my shoulders seeing her on her knees in front of the toilet, her small frame spasming with every heave.

Reaching down, I gathered her hair and held it back, noting how wet the T-shirt was from the long strands. Bells paused long enough to lift her head slightly. Her voice was raw when she spoke. "I don't want you in here."

"Too bad," I said and squatted down behind her until she finished.

Even after she stopped vomiting, her body remained poised over the porcelain until she was sure she was done. Once she was, she sank back onto her butt, almost curling into herself.

I wanted so badly to pull her against me, to tuck her against my chest and make all this go away. I didn't like feeling helpless...

It was a feeling I'd become well acquainted with as of late.

Forcing myself off the floor, I grabbed a cup of water and handed it to her. Bells took it without looking at me, rinsed her mouth out, and spit in the toilet. I took the empty cup back and tossed it, then grabbed one of those fluffy hair things—a scrunchie I think she called it—and tied her hair back in a style that definitely wasn't going to win any awards.

When that was done, I retreated from the bathroom. Each step that took me farther away from her actually caused pain to lance through my chest. Moving fast, I grabbed another one of my shirts and carried it back to her.

"Arms up," I said. She obliged, and I quickly swapped the wet shirt out for the dry one. "You done?" I asked gently, reaching toward the toilet lid.

She nodded. I closed it, flushed, and picked her up off the floor. Before heading back to the bedroom, I grabbed the first aid kit, which was still open and mussed on the counter.

Charlie moved down to the foot of the bed when I approached, and I moved to lay Bells on the mattress. When her arms tightened around my neck, I slid between the covers, propped myself against the headboard, and let her settle against me between my legs.

"Do you need to go to the ER?" I asked.

"No."

I figured as much. I might be miffed at Alex, but if she needed the ER, he would have taken her there immediately.

Glancing down, I lifted her poorly bandaged hand. "He do this to you?" I couldn't help the coldness in my tone.

I felt shake her head. "I did it. Trying to get away."

My teeth slammed together forcefully enough it made my jaw ache. He'd been chasing her. While I'd been sitting at some boring-as-shit dinner meeting in a stupid tie. I should have been there tonight. Not Alex. Me.

Why hadn't I been there?

Because you were doing something for your father.

I didn't know how to feel, so instead of thinking about it, I went about taking off the crooked, half-done bandage on her finger to replace it the right way.

"My hands were shaking when I did that," she admitted. "I'm sorry."

"Don't apologize," I murmured and kissed the top of her head.

We didn't talk as I cleaned up the cut, which probably could have used a stitch or two. I got it to stop bleeding, though, put a couple butterfly bandages on it, and then wrapped the entire finger in gauze and medical tape.

What? I'm a thorough guy.

Once that was done, I tucked her hand against my chest and pulled a blanket around her legs.

"I need to know what happened." I reminded her.

"He told me once I was dead, he was coming here to take care of you," she wailed, her voice breaking partway through the sentence. Charlie lifted off the bed and looked at her, tilting his head.

Bellamy started openly sobbing, and the darkness inside me rose up to match the anger. My tongue slipped along my teeth, and my arms wound around Bellamy so tight I thought she might complain.

"Tighter," she said.

I obliged.

Eventually, her crying turned into sniffles, the sniffles gave way to hiccups, and then she lifted my tie and used it as a tissue.

There was a brief pause, and then she glanced at it. "Why are you wearing a tie?"

"Sweatpants piss off the execs," I muttered.

After a few quiet minutes, Bellamy's voice filled the bedroom. "I thought he was just playing a game like that night at the hospital. But he wasn't. He came back and tried to kill me. I hid, b-but he almost found me. Alex showed up and scared him off."

"You're safe now." I promised, stroking the side of her head.

"Until he comes back," she echoed, almost as if she was warning herself.

Chills raced up my spine.

"Get some sleep, sweetheart. We can talk more in the morning."

"I don't feel so good."

"I know," I murmured. "I got you now. Everything's okay."

I held her for a long time, staring over her head at the wall, just thinking. I felt pulled in many directions. Between the business, my father, my girl… hell, even snowboarding.

I might say I was done with my career, but the truth was I still yearned for a board, the crunch of snow, and a pristine halfpipe.

Every single thing I loved was being threatened. I could lose it all in the blink of an eye.

How the fuck was I supposed to hold it all together while being stretched in so many directions? A rubber band could only bounce back so many times before it snapped.

Before *I* snapped.

A while later, the sound of the kitchen door opening and closing and booted footfalls against the floor drew me from my stormy thoughts. Charlie gave a low woof and leapt off the bed to go see what was up.

I knew it was probably only Alex because Charlie stayed quiet once he was out there. Bellamy was sound asleep against me, her breathing calm and even. I didn't want to move. I liked my position far too much, but answers couldn't wait 'til morning.

Slowly, I slid out from beneath her, tucked two pillows at her sides, and made sure the blankets were securely tucked around her. I glanced toward the door, and as if on cue, Charlie bounded back in and hopped on the bed, taking up position right in front of Bells.

"Good boy," I whispered, scratching behind his ear.

Alex was standing in front of the fridge, his body bathed in the harsh light from inside. He grabbed a beer from one of the shelves and tossed it in my direction, all without even looking to see if I was actually there.

Dude had like fifty eyes. He never missed a thing.

I snatched the bottle out of the air, opened the top, and took a long pull. Alex grabbed another for himself and did the same. The kitchen plunged into darkness when the fridge door closed, leaving only the light from the hallway behind me.

"I told you not to leave." I bitched.

"Oh, my bad. Did you suddenly become the boss of me?"

I gave him a salty look and then went to the living room and flipped on the fireplace. It was fucking freezing.

"Where'd you go?" I asked, staring at the red flickering flames.

"The Inn. Someone had to clean up the place."

I spun from the mantle, crossed to where he stood, and offered my fist. He looked between me and my knuckles, then touched his against mine.

"I'm grateful," I told him.

"I know."

"You still shoulda called me."

"She wanted to make sure the house was clear before you got here."

My beer slammed down on the top of the mantle. "And you fucking let her make that call?"

"She was so upset she could barely walk, man. I wasn't gonna argue. I knew no one was here, and I swept the place when we got here."

I felt my eyes flash and my tongue get ready to fling out some harsh words.

Alex's eyes landed on mine. "He would've had to go through me to get to her, and you fucking know it."

I relented. I did know it. Alex was a tough son of a bitch, and I knew Bells was safe with him.

"Don't put my safety above hers again."

He made a sound. "That's not what this was. I knew by the time we got here you'd be wrapping it up anyway. We were only here long enough for her to rush into the bathroom and puke up her guts, then take a shower."

"She was sick before I got here?" I murmured.

"Stress and adrenaline will do it to you, man. Every time."

"What happened?"

"He was there when I got there. Had the door barricaded shut, the lights off. This fucker is some twisted shit, Liam. When I made it into the kitchen and walked into the back room, Bellamy climbed out of a cabinet, with no shoes, brandishing a knife."

"She said she was hiding," I murmured, recalling the little bit she'd told me. How much more shit was this girl gonna have to live through?

Alex nodded. "Guess he shut off the lights a couple times on her. One time, he left the spider before showing up to take her out."

I let out some curse words while Alex dropped onto the couch. "They tried to kill her in Chicago, then showed up in Denver at the hospital."

"Dude," Alex intoned. It was a lot of implication in one simple word.

Huh. Maybe Bells was right. Alex and I had our own language.

I nodded. Something had to be done about this. "What did you get back at The Inn?" When Alex said clean up, he also meant casing the place for any kind of clues the asshole left behind.

He shook his head, regretful. "Not a damn thing. This guy is good at what he does."

"We have to be better."

"So we will be."

Snatching my beer off the mantle, I dropped down in the chair near the sofa. "Tell me everything Bells told you." Hopefully, it was a hell of a lot more than what I'd managed to get out of her.

We talked for a while.

Until Bells started to scream.

23

Bellamy

Darkness enveloped me like a protective blanket, but I didn't feel secure.

If anything, I felt as though the darkness wouldn't protect me, but the evil that lurked within it.

I didn't have to contain the shudders wracking my body again and again. The enclosed space did that for me. The drywall was hard and solid, the space between it so tight it actually hurt to be squeezed inside.

I had no idea what was going on out there, but the sounds couldn't be ignored. Moaning, hitting, and the slap of skin on skin was crystal clear. My fingertips pressed against the drywall as if I would be able to claw my way through if needed.

"Please, no," a familiar voice begged, and everything inside me seized. Bile rose up the back of my throat, and the panic I was holding back flooded through my entire body.

The loud sound of a gunshot reverberated through the room. It seemed extra loud in this enclosed space. I shoved the heel of my hand into my mouth to muffle my sobs. Another shot rang out, and the gurgling noises that filled the silence between shots ceased.

Daddy.

"Next!" demanded a man on the other side of the wall.

I sucked in a breath as terror consumed me. Pressing close against the wall, I strained to hear what was happening. Shouldn't they be leaving? Wasn't that how this went?

There was a loud thump and the sound of a slamming door. "Tell us where she is!"

"Fuck you."

I'd know that voice anywhere.

"Liam," I whispered, shocked.

Flesh hitting flesh was the only reply to his words. It seemed to go on forever, and tears rolled down my cheeks as I strained to hear anything at all.

"Tell us where your girlfriend is, and we'll think about letting you live," the man demanded again.

"Never," he spat, his voice weaker this time.

They took him to get to me! And here I was hiding, cowering while the men in my life were being murdered.

Not Liam. Not him.

"Hold him," the man instructed. A few grunts followed, and I knew they were hitting him again.

"Liam!" I screamed and beat on the wall, trying so hard to get through. "Don't hurt him!"

"Shut up!" someone yelled, but I was beyond listening. I was fighting the stupid space to get out, panicked I wouldn't make it in time.

"She's here."

"No!" Liam yelled.

The sudden explosion of the gun made me shriek. It plowed through the wall just above me. I ducked, cowering as low as I could in the crammed space. Light shone through the newly ripped hole, a beam in the dark.

I'd been wrong before.

The darkness had been concealing me. It was the light that would reveal my presence.

Silently, I lifted my chin, glancing up to that beam of light that others might have equated to hope. In horror, I watched as a black object crawled through, unfolding its body and stretching out its legs.

The black widow seemed to zero in on where I was and silently began crawling down the wall. Biting back a scream, I returned to the struggle of getting out of this space. Why was it so hard? Why did I feel trapped?

Momentarily, a shadow moved over the hole, blanking out the light beam and drawing my attention. The second I looked at that roughly blown hole, an eye appeared.

It bored into mine with chilling intent.

"Gotcha!"

I screamed, but the sound was drowned out by Spidey reaching into the hole that was suddenly so much bigger and ripping a huge chunk of the wall right down.

"Bellamy!" Liam surged to his feet but was shoved back onto the floor as a boot kicked right into his ribs.

I screamed again and practically fell out of the crudely ripped wall. He was covered in blood and bruises, one of his eyes swollen shut.

"Liam," I whispered, stumbling over and falling onto my knees beside him. "I'm so sorry, so sorry."

Rough hands grabbed my hair and forced me to my knees.

Liam struggled to get up. "Don't touch her!" he yelled.

The other man with Spidey punched him and laughed.

"We've gone to a lot of trouble to find you," Spidey said, practically ripping the hair out of my head. I glanced away and saw the body of my father lying on the other side of a dirty mattress.

The blood spilling from him was still fresh, and the scent of death clung thickly to the air.

I began to fight, managing to hit Spidey in the balls. He groaned and bent at the waist but didn't loosen the hold he had on my hair.

"You're going to pay for that," he said, the words chilling. "And it seems the best way to hurt you is to hurt him." He pointed to Liam. "Hold him."

I began to scream and kick as the man forced Liam to his knees. Liam was weak and bloody, but he tried to fight, to no avail.

I cried as I fought, and Spidey only laughed.

"This is all on you," he taunted, levelling a black pistol right at Liam.

"No!" I begged, my knees going weak. "No."

Liam and I locked eyes. He mouthed the words *I love you.*

And then Spidey killed him.

Liam

The reaction was immediate. I leapt up out of the chair I was in, knocking over the bottle of beer balancing on the arm, and lunged down the hallway while the animal inside me roared.

The bedroom door slammed against the wall when I shoved it wide and raced inside.

I didn't bother scanning the room first. If anyone was in here, I'd tear them apart after I got confirmation that Bellamy was okay.

Charlie barked, standing over Bells as I rushed forward, reaching for her.

She was having a nightmare. Something I was innately shocked she hadn't had until now. After everything she'd been through, I couldn't believe it wasn't a nightly occurrence.

Tonight must have pushed her over the edge.

"Sweetheart," I said loud enough to hopefully cut through the screaming she was still doing. The second I reached for her, Charlie did something to me he'd never done before.

A deep rumble ripped out of him, and he snapped at my arm. On instinct, I pulled back to stare at my dog as though he'd grown three more heads.

"Charlie," I intoned and reached for Bells again.

The dog showed his teeth.

He was protecting Bellamy. If I wasn't so anxious to pull her close and assure her she was safe, I might have been proud of my dog.

But this was getting in my way.

I leaned down and met the dog's eyes, not backing up an inch. "*No*," I said. It sounded more like a growl than anything.

The dog relented and lowered his head.

"Charlie, c'mon," Alex said, taking him by the collar to lead him off the bed.

He went but refused to go any farther than his position beside us.

Bellamy was tossing fitfully in her sleep, her face screwed up in pain and fear. I slipped my arms under her and pulled her upper body against mine, holding her close.

"Bellamy," I said clearly. "Wake up. You're having a nightmare."

Her body stilled and then stiffened. Pulling her head away from my shoulder, she squinted up at me. "Liam?"

"Right here." I soothed her.

Both her arms went around me, her face pressing into my shirt.

"We'll talk tomorrow," Alex said from the foot of the bed.

I started to nod, but Bellamy pulled back. "Alex?"

"Yeah?"

"Stay."

Alex ducked his head, making a sound as he rubbed the back of his neck with his hand. "Liam's my boy…" He began. "But, ah, we ain't that close."

Bellamy made a sound, looking at me, then toward the doorway. "I meant on the couch."

Alex straightened and made a sound like he was relieved. "For a minute there, I thought you was suggesting some kinda brother husbands or some shit like they play on TV."

Bellamy giggled. A real giggle. My stomach clenched, and I found myself wondering when the last time was I heard that sound.

Fuck. I was fucking this up. I wasn't taking care of her the way I should.

"What's a brother husband?" she asked, still clutching the back of my neck.

"I'm just thankful you don't know," Alex replied solemnly.

"Get the fuck out of my bedroom, man," I said, amused.

"Wait!" Bellamy exclaimed and then patted me on the back of the shoulder. I glanced down at her. "I need off the bed."

I suppressed a smile. "Allow me."

Once I put her on her feet, Bellamy tangled her fingers in mine and tugged me across the room toward the closet with her. Alex watched from the doorway, and Charlie trotted along behind her like a loyal servant.

Pretty sure he wasn't my dog anymore. He was hers.

Not letting go of my hand, Bellamy pointed up to the pile of folded blankets and extra pillow on the shelf in the closet. I lifted them down, and she tugged me along back to Alex.

"Here," she said, gesturing to them. "Safety in numbers, right?"

Wait a minute. Was she asking Alex to stay because she felt safe around him?

"Do you think he can protect you better than me?" I burst out, surly and confrontational.

What. The. Fuck?

Bellamy jolted and looked at me, her eyes wide. Her half-dry hair was rumpled, and the scrunchie I'd tied in it earlier was lost somewhere in the bed.

"Of course not!" She gasped. Yanking her hand out of mine, she planted her fists on her hips. "I don't want Alex out this late and going home by himself! Spidey probably saw him tonight." Her lower lip wobbled.

I wished she would quit with that shit. It made me feel like a frozen piece of glass about to crack.

With a soft sound, I pulled her into me, cradling the back of her head with my palm.

She sniffled and glanced at my best friend. "What if he goes after you next?"

Alex's shoulders moved beneath his shirt, a surprised look flitting over his face. "You're worried about me?"

"Duh!"

"I guess I could stay," he replied gruffly.

Could it be? Was the impervious bunny chaser actually getting a little soft toward a woman?

I felt my eyes narrow.

"But don't be getting no ideas," Alex told Bellamy. "Just because you have this guy wrapped"—he pointed at me—"doesn't mean I'll just do whatever you tell me."

Bells went forward and hugged him.

He looked at me over her head, the whites of his eyes growing. I grinned.

With one arm, he awkwardly hugged her back and cleared his throat.

"I didn't say it before, but thank you for tonight." Bellamy pulled away. "You might have saved my life tonight."

"*Shiiit,*" Alex drawled. "I saw you with that knife. You had that shit handled."

Bellamy smiled, but it fell quickly. "I was going to stab him in the foot and run for a window."

My hand balled into a fist at my side.

Alex didn't seem nearly as affected by that plan as I was. He angled his body toward her and spoke with confidence. "Hey. You had a plan. That's the number one step of surviving. Thinking. Planning. Fighting."

I didn't want that for her. I didn't want her to have to fight every single day just to live.

That's what your dad is doing, too. My subconscious reminded me.

"I'm tired of fighting," Bellamy whispered, bringing me back.

"Even the best warriors get tired sometimes," Alex whispered.

"Okay," I said, shooting forward and wrapping an arm around my girl. "This bonding time is cute and all, but it's over." I needed her. Just her. Alone.

Alex guffawed. "Jelly."

"I am not," I declared through gritted teeth.

Alex turned and sauntered down the hall. "You better kiss your boy, Bellamy. He's jealous as hell."

"Don't be here when I get up in the morning!" I yelled.

"I'm making breakfast for all of us!" Bellamy yelled right after.

I swung around and glared at her accusingly.

"Shut the door, Liam," she murmured. "I want to be alone with you."

I guess I was wrapped, just as Alex said.

Know why?

'Cause I did what she asked and reached for her.

25

Bellamy

In Liam's arms was the easiest place to be.

It didn't require work or thought. There was never a second of hesitation when it came to his touch or asking for it. The way I felt for him went beyond want. Beyond need even. He was as essential to me as the sun to a flower, nectar to a bee, the winter's air on a snowy night.

Pressing my nose into his shirt, I inhaled deeply, taking in the fresh scent of snow and pine. If home had a scent, it would be him.

Sure, there'd been a couple jokes a few minutes ago. Alex seemed to be the king of diffusing a tense situation, but it didn't erase the nightmare or the feelings of helplessness it stirred in me.

I hated feeling helpless. Being scared. I was growing so very weary of it. Now more than ever, I wanted to be strong.

Reluctantly, I pulled back from Liam just enough to gaze up into his face. I loved his face. The unruly scruff on his jaw, the way his eyes reflected his moods, and how his hair never behaved. "I trust you more than anyone else. Hell, even more than myself. If I ever had to choose, it wouldn't even be a choice. It's you, Liam. Only you."

His eyes shone against the backdrop of darkness in our bedroom, silver stars lighting up the night. He didn't say anything, but his body shifted even closer to mine, settling against me in all the right places. His large hand came up, palming the side of my head. How small I felt with him like this, how utterly protected.

I swallowed, still consuming every detail of his face. That dream felt too real, his death too devastating. "I couldn't get back here fast enough tonight. I was so afraid you beat us here and that you'd be caught off guard… that I would lose you all over again."

He made a sound I didn't hear, but I felt it. All the way down to my core. My feet tilted against the floor, going sideways a little as my toes curled under.

The gruffness in his tone, the deep timbre of his words, made me feel like a guitar, and he was striking all the right chords. "Oh, baby. You will never, ever lose me."

My fingers encircled his wrist right beside where he palmed my head. I sank forward slowly, resting my forehead against his shoulder. "I didn't mean to upset you by asking Alex to stay."

"Ah, sweetheart, you didn't upset me."

"I had a bad dream."

His free hand rubbed up my back. "I know."

"Make it go away, Liam."

With our bodies still pressed close, Liam guided me toward the bed with an unhurried pace that made my blood bubble with impatience. The need inside me rose swiftly, catching my limbs on fire and tingling my fingers and toes. It felt as if there was always so much death chasing us, and the only way to escape it was by coming alive beneath his touch.

My legs hit the side of the bed. Liam steadied me, keeping me close. The softness of his lips brushed over mine once, then twice. He lifted his mouth just long enough for me to make a sound so he'd come back. The roughness of his facial hair was a direct contrast to the silkiness of his tongue. The kiss was languid and heavy, chasing away all thought and replacing it with hazy reality that had the power to make a girl drunk.

My lips were wet and slick when he untangled our tongues and drew away. Encircling my waist, Liam lifted me off my feet and set me on the bed, using his body as a guide to push me back until I was sitting in the center of the mattress.

Fingertips dragged down my bare leg when he withdrew, returning to his feet and reaching for the loosened tie around his neck. It was rare to see him dressed so formally, and while I noted how imposing he was in a tie, I couldn't even put forth the small effort it would take to admire him this way because the fact that he was undressing totally stole the show.

The silky tie slid from his body, falling somewhere I couldn't see. His eyes caught mine and flashed when his fingers reached for the buttons of his dress shirt and moved down until the fabric fell open to reveal the solid contours of his body.

Teeth sinking into my lower lip, I leaned forward, reaching out to skim a hand over the exposed skin. He leaned just out of reach and smiled.

Liam abandoned the shirt and reached for his belt, soon having his pants completely open. The solid length pressing against the tight fabric of his boxer briefs was a dead giveaway that his little game wasn't just turning me on.

The belt made a soft jingling sound when he peeled the fabric over his muscular legs.

"Liam," I beckoned, enjoying the show but craving his skin on mine.

He smirked and rubbed himself through the fabric of his boxers. The way his ab muscles rippled as he touched himself had me lifting up to my knees. Grasping the hem of the T-shirt I wore, I slowly pulled it up, exposing inch after inch of my thighs.

Liam's eyes flickered, and the hand over his cock rubbed a little harder.

I peeled the shirt up, bunching it so it was just beneath my breasts, revealing my waist and the lacy undies I had on.

With a sound, he reached for me, but I pulled back and gave him the same smile he'd given me.

"Is that the way it is?" he murmured.

"You show me yours, I'll show you mine." I confirmed.

In one swift movement, his shirt fell to the floor behind him. My stomach fluttered a little just looking at him, just knowing he was mine.

Liam gestured to himself and then lifted a brow.

I took off the shirt and tossed it at him, the fabric hitting him right in the face, obstructing his view. He yanked it down and chucked it over his shoulder.

We froze there like that, both barely wearing anything, chests rising and falling, deeply engaged in a contest of who could last the longest just looking, no touching.

The electricity in the air hummed, vibrating my body and causing a fever to burn my skin. Without losing eye contact, Liam shucked the boxers, revealing his thick cock, which caused the air to turn static.

He moved first. The mattress dipped under his knees, and I reached for him to steady myself. We ended up both on our knees, chest to chest, with his hot palms griping my hips.

As we kissed, Liam's hands traveled up so his thumbs could draw lazy circles around my erect nipples, making them pucker so forcefully that pain/pleasure shot all the way down into the center of my panties.

His movements were so swift and graceful I didn't even know he moved until I felt the cool sheets at my back and his warm skin covering mine. I moaned softly, arching into him and rubbing my body against his.

Liam's lips latched onto the inside of my neck to suck and lick until my hips started to grind against him. He straddled my hips and rose up, grabbed my hand, and pressed a barely-there kiss to the finger I'd sliced open.

My heart skipped, and I wrapped a fist around his arousal. Both his hands settled over my breasts, and we stroked and touched one another until I started tugging at his hips. Liam settled between my legs, rocking against me as his tongue fucked my mouth.

I moaned, whispered his name, and spread my legs just a little bit wider.

Liam kissed down my body, slipped the panties off, and dragged two fingers up my drenched center. He said something under his breath, but I couldn't understand. Then he swirled his fingers in the silky heat again.

I shuddered, and he came over me, reaching out for the nightstand.

"Liam, no."

He paused and looked down.

"You want me to stop?" he asked, already moving off me.

I grabbed him, the loss of contact making me ache. "The fact that you would stop right now, knowing you want this as bad…" I murmured.

He kissed my forehead. "I'd do anything for you."

"Would you make love to me without a condom?"

His eyes flared with wild hunger. It was almost predatory.

I shivered and pressed closer.

"You've been through a lot, baby. I'm not sure you know what you want."

"I want everything," I whispered.

Liam entered my body without hesitation. The feel of his throbbing, thick hardness made me cry out. He covered my mouth with his and began moving with a pace that literally made it impossible to breathe.

Sensation after sensation rolled through me, making my body go boneless against the bed. My chest started to squeeze, but I didn't notice until Liam paused deep inside me.

"Breathe, sweetheart."

I gulped in air, and my lungs relaxed.

A low moan vibrated his throat, and his arm muscles contracted as he lowered so we were chest to chest. "You feel incredible," he whispered in my ear.

I turned my face and kissed his cheek and then the underside of his jaw as he rose up to hammer into me all over again.

The orgasm hit me hard and fast. I clutched at his shoulders, pulling myself up against him as he shuddered and shoved deep.

"Bells…" His voice was strained, warning me he couldn't hold back.

I wrapped my legs around his ass and held him deep, rocking against his dick. Liam shoved his face into the pillow beside my head, muffling his shout.

His body quivered and spasmed. His hips involuntarily thrust into me with each aftershock. I cradled his cock inside me until he groaned and rolled off me onto the mattress.

"I just love you," I told him.

"Ahh, sweetheart, I just love you, too."

We slipped under the covers, and I pressed as close to him as I could get. Charlie leapt back on the bed and took up the rest of the available space.

And for a little while, everything was perfect.

26

Liam

"I want to learn how to shoot."

Bellamy's announcement made the perfect bite of pumpkin bread in my mouth turn into tasteless sawdust.

"Excuse me?" I said, pausing mid-chew. A crumb fell out of my lips onto the island where Alex and I were stuffing our faces.

"Shoot what?" Alex asked dubiously. Clearly, he wasn't as alarmed by her sudden announcement because he was still able to chew. Loudly. "Pictures with a camera?"

Bellamy turned from the stove where she was scrambling up some eggs. For a minute, I forgot she was spouting off insane comments because she looked hot as hell standing there with a spatula in her hand and an apron tied around her. Her hair was so long it brushed against the tie at her waist.

"A gun." She elaborated, then turned back to the eggs.

My best friend and I looked at each other, back to her, and then back at each other. "Did you hear that, too, or am I hallucinating?" Alex wondered.

"You're being ridiculous," Bellamy called over her shoulder.

I threw the chunk of bread in my hand onto the plate she made me use and stalked around to where she stood. "You just announced you want to shoot a gun like you ask for a refill of coffee."

Bells made a sound and thrust her cup out at me. "Actually, I could use some more."

"Is this the twilight zone?" Alex asked from behind us.

"Now, baby." I reasoned, filling up her coffee. "You have to realize how out of character this sounds. You hate guns."

Bellamy flipped off the cooktop and piled all the perfectly scrambled eggs into a large bowl, sprinkling some cheese over them before putting the bowl on the island.

I caught her wrist when she was done and gently tugged her around.

"I hate feeling helpless more."

Her blunt statement felt like that time I landed wrong on a halfpipe and broke a couple ribs.

Like shit.

So shitty, in fact, I could only stand there and hear the words echo inside my head for what felt like endless moments.

Alex, of course, had a comeback ready. "I saw you with that knife last night, girl. You ain't the definition of helpless."

She looked at Alex, her voice matter-of-fact. "If you hadn't gotten there when you did, I'd probably be dead right now."

"Don't say that!" I burst out, angry.

Bells glanced back at me, her blue eyes wide. I felt my nostrils flare, and I took a breath, trying to calm down. She was *not* going to die.

I took her by the shoulders, giving them a little shake. "Don't even think that ever again."

"Liam…" She lifted her palm toward my face.

I pulled away. "You don't feel safe."

"How can I? How can any of us? The mob wants me dead, Liam. Perry Crone himself has ordered a hit on me. He's not going to stop until—"

I glanced up sharply, daring her to say the D-word just one more time.

She pressed her lips together, saying nothing at all.

"You didn't even want guns in this house. Guns scare you, and now you want me to teach you how to shoot one?"

"It's a good idea," Alex inserted. I looked at him as if he were fucking insane, but he merely shrugged. "Learning to use something she's so afraid of would be taking her power back."

Bellamy nodded enthusiastically. "I can't just sit here and wait for the next time they come. I won't cower behind you like some heroine in a superhero movie. I want to *do* something."

"No," I stated, flat.

"No?" Bellamy raised her eyebrow. Then she glanced at Alex. "No?"

Alex made a sound beneath his breath and shoved a huge forkful of eggs in his mouth as if that would make him unavailable for the shitstorm brewing.

"No," I repeated, not an ounce of give in my voice.

Bellamy stepped up to me, the red apron shifting as she moved. She barely came to my shoulder. She had to tip her chin back so she could glare into my eyes. The spatula still had egg on the end, but she poked it into my bare chest regardless. "You do not get to tell me what to do."

Alex made a sound of agreement. "Dude thinks he's the boss of err'body."

I looked up sharply, and he shoved more eggs in his mouth. *Bastard better not eat all of them.*

"I don't think it's a good idea," I said, gently taking the spatula and tossing it into the sink. I was pretty sure there was egg stuck to my chest, but I wasn't about to glance down to check. We were in the midst of a staring battle.

Backing down would mean defeat.

"Well, if *you* don't think it's a good idea..." Bells said, and I smirked.

Victory would be mine.

"Alex will teach me." She finished swiftly, spinning away from me and walking toward Alex.

I felt my eyes widen as she sauntered her damn fine ass away. "What the fuck?" I roared. "If anyone is teaching you to use a deadly weapon, it's going to be me."

"Thanks for breakfast." Alex started to rise from his stool. "But I need to be going."

"Sit down!" Bells and I yelled at the same time.

"Aww, man," Alex whined, returning to his seat.

Charlie trotted over to his side and laid his big head on Alex's leg. Alex gave him some bacon.

Bellamy whirled to face me. She did that adorable thing where she slammed her fists on her hips and looked at me with blue fire in her eyes. One day I was going to have to tell her she turned me on when she got mad.

"Liam Daniel Mattison," she announced.

Ah, shit. All three names.

Alex grimaced.

"You just had the balls to tell me no, so I found someone who thinks it's a good idea to teach me."

"I'm Switzerland!" Alex chimed in. "Neutral."

We ignored him.

"I thought you liked my balls," I deadpanned.

Hey, the sarcasm worked for my bro. It would work for me, too. Right?

Bellamy blinked. "That was illegal use of balls."

"No such thing," Alex and I said at the same time.

Bellamy threw her hands up in the air. "This is ridiculous. I wasn't asking for your permission to learn how to protect myself. You said no, and I said I'm doing it anyway." Turning back to Alex, she said, "You taught Liam how to shoot, right?"

"Uh, yeah."

"So you're going to teach me, too."

I narrowed my eyes on my best friend, practically firing laser beams out of the slits in warning.

Alex heaved a giant, relenting sigh. "Fine."

I started to growl, and Alex looked up. "What the fuck you want me to say? If I say no, she'll find someone else to teach her, and he won't know his head from his ass. Then what? I ain't having your girl running around BearPaw with a gun some asshead taught her how to use."

Asshead?

"Is that the same as an ass taxi?" Bellamy deadpanned.

Alex and I burst out laughing.

The second we were done, Alex met my stare. "If you ain't gonna do it, then I will."

"So you're forcing my hand." I surmised, pissed.

Bellamy came forward, slipping her hands around my waist. I didn't look down at her. I couldn't. I'd melt.

I didn't want to melt.

"No one is forcing you, Liam. How many more times will Crone's men come after me before I fight back?"

"You shouldn't have to fight at all." No one should have to fight for their life. And Christ, it was my job to protect her.

I was doing a bang-up job of that, wasn't I? So good that now she wanted to tote a gun around.

A sudden urge slapped me so hard it actually shocked me. It was brief, like a bolt of lightning, but it left behind a sizzling scar. For the first time in a long time, I actually felt the urge for a bottle. A few pills. Not even the whole bottle. Just a couple, just something to numb the worst of my demons so I could be here for everyone.

"In my nightmare last night, he killed you." Her voice was small and quiet.

My eyes flew down to her, and the brief pull of addiction was wiped out by something greater.

Her.

All I could see was her bowed head, but if the look in her eyes matched the tone of her voice, I was about to be slayed.

"He killed you right in front of me, and I stood there and watched."

Unable to stay so frigid with her so close, I reached for her, curling my hands around her waist. "Bells…"

Her face lifted, and yes, what I saw in the depths of her jewel-toned eyes slayed me. "I won't be helpless, Liam."

Locking my arms around her, Bells folded right against my chest. Rubbing my chin lightly over the top of her head, I spoke. "All right, sweetheart. You want to learn to shoot, then I'll teach you."

"Alex, too."

I glanced at my bro. He shrugged. "My afternoon's free."

Today? Damn. I was hoping for a couple days to get used to this idea. I was hoping maybe she'd change her mind.

Deep down, though, I knew this was the best. I was even fucking proud of her. To literally pick up something she feared so much, something with the absolute power to kill, and take its power away…

That was something.

"Alex, too." I agreed, pulling her a little tighter into my chest.

"Can I go home now?" he asked, sipping on some coffee. "I mean, I love you guys, but I need to take a shower."

Bellamy laughed against my shirt, the sound muffled but distinct.

"Go," I told him.

He stood but hesitated and looked at my girl. "Uh, Bells?"

My eyes narrowed a little at the use of the nickname.

Bellamy pulled away from me long enough to hug him. "We'll pick you up later," she said and returned to her place in my arms.

On his way out the door, Alex muttered something about having a secondhand girlfriend. I couldn't help it. I laughed.

Secondhand girlfriend = all of the work but none of the benefits.

He was so wrapped I'd be jealous if it wasn't funny as hell.

Once the door was shut, he gave me the finger through the window. I laughed harder.

Bellamy looked up to see why I was laughing, but the sound died away.

"Hey," I murmured, picking her up and sitting her on the kitchen counter. "I'm sorry I wasn't there last night. I should have been, not Alex."

"It's okay."

But it wasn't. Bellamy might not think so, but she was biased and scared.

I needed to do better. Starting now.

Bellamy

Learning to shoot wasn't as terrifying as I thought it would be. The range where Liam and Alex went wasn't some seedy hole in the wall that made it seem like the people who went there were all in training to be murderers.

Although, wasn't that the reason I was there?

Okay, so maybe that was a little bit of a stretch, but I went there to learn to defend myself, and as surprising as it might be, my personal philosophy for this current situation was shoot to kill.

I refrained from sharing that little wealth of thought with Liam because he was already on edge. The entire time we were there, he was extremely focused, almost to the point of being cold.

What saved the situation from feeling so clinical was the way he felt against me. Every time he slid up behind me, fitting his body against mine to show me how to hold the gun or how to aim, I felt his deep intake of breath and the electricity between us crackled.

Liam didn't acknowledge it, though. He remained fixated on making sure I understood the mechanics of a weapon and the proper way to use one. Then he gave me a ten-minute lecture on how I should aim to wound to give myself enough time to flee.

You know, in the knee, the foot, or something that would make any attacker unable to give chase.

Hence the reason I kept my little shoot-to-kill mantra to myself. I was so weary of running. Of looking over my shoulder every single day. I just wanted this over, and if I had the chance to make that happen, I was going to take it.

Alex seemed to be of same mind because when he spent a little time with me at the targets, his instructions were more on par with aiming for a kill shot.

By the time we got back from the range, it was almost dinnertime, and I felt frazzled and a little stressed out. I'd been nauseous half the day, and I knew it was likely because I needed to eat something. We were due at Liam's parents for dinner. I had steaks already marinating and baked potatoes ready for the oven.

The thought of food was unappealing, so I opted to put it off a little bit longer. Backtracking to the door, I leaned out. The wintry air was heavy with the scent of snow, and the sky was dense and gray. There was a forecasted blizzard heading toward BearPaw Mountain, and I couldn't help but feel perhaps this was the calm before the storm.

"I'm going to take a shower," I called across the deck to where Liam was standing in the yard with Charlie. "Want to join?"

He glanced around, a red ball clutched in his hand. Before speaking, he threw it, and the dog barked, taking off after it through the cold. "Like you even have to ask." He smiled fast, the white of his teeth matching the pristine snow on the ground.

There he was. The more relaxed, snow-loving man I knew so well.

Charlie nearly collided with him as he bounded back with the ball, snow flying up around his legs and spraying Liam, who laughed and bent to get the toy.

He missed the snow. The mountain. Being outside.

His entire life had been turned upside down since I'd showed up here that night. Most of it was my fault, some of it just cruel fate.

The urge to protect him had always been there of course. But seeing him out in the snow now made it stronger somehow. Liam was so good. A man with demons but a man who put everyone he loved ahead of himself.

He was hell bent on protecting me. Who would protect him?

I would.

He was the reason I went to that range today. He was the reason I shoved the fear of guns deep. I realized it wasn't myself I felt frantic to protect; it was Liam. The way Spidey continued to taunt me with Liam's safety and the nightmare I had was the final straw.

His booted feet made a thunderous sound as he rushed up the deck stairs with Charlie beside him. I smiled as he approached, shaking his head to fling off the freshly fallen snowflakes from the dark-blond strands.

"Why aren't you naked yet?" he demanded playfully.

"You want me to get naked right here? Right now?" I reached for the zipper on the coat.

He caught my hand and growled like a bear. "Woman, keep them goods to yourself 'til we get in the house. That's for my eyes only."

I giggled and went inside ahead of him.

"Go ahead, sweetheart. I'll be there in a few. I'm just going to put some stuff up."

He meant the guns.

"Okay," I called out as I went down the hall. I'd just have to ask him to show me where they were later. I liked this more relaxed Liam. I hadn't seen him enough today, so I wasn't going to ask now.

In the bedroom, I stripped off all my clothes, then went into the bathroom to turn on the shower so the water could heat. After putting my hair in a knot on top of my head, Liam still hadn't joined me. The mirror was steaming up, and I wondered what could be taking so long.

Wrapping a white, fluffy towel around me as I went, I stepped into the hallway. At the other end, the closet was open, the door blocking where I figured he was standing on the other side.

"Liam?" I called out, securing the end of the towel around me.

Stillness smacked into me first, causing my bare feet to stutter against the floor.

The damp strands of his hair poked around the edge of the door, followed quickly by his face. Gone was the relaxed Liam I'd just left in the snow. Back was the man enveloped by cold.

"Liam?"

His hand shot out and grasped the edge of the door. He shoved it closed just enough to reveal what was lying at his feet.

"What the fuck is this?" His voice was harsh, and he stabbed a finger down at the duffle.

"M-my emergency bag…" I stuttered, queasiness washing over me.

"It's packed," he clipped out. "Why the fuck is your emergency bag packed and in the closet, ready to go?"

"I put it there."

He stared down at it, anger swirling around him. The muscles in the side of his jaw clenched.

"Why would you do that, Bellamy?" His silvery, stormy eyes flashed up to mine. "Are you planning to run away?"

28

Liam

First the gun and now this?

Bellamy was standing at the end of the hallway, wrapped in nothing but a towel and all her hair pulled up, revealing every feature.

Including the alarm in her eyes.

I stabbed a finger at the bag again. "Are you planning to leave me?"

"No!" She gasped. "I just..." She fretted, her stare dropping to the floor.

Anger burst inside me, and I slammed the closet door shut, then kicked the bag against the wood. Charlie slinked off behind me into the living room.

"Just what?" I demanded.

Bellamy lifted her chin. "I learned a long time ago that sometimes you need an escape plan."

I let out a lot of curse words. Yeah, yeah, I cussed too much.

I don't know what stung worse—the fact that she thought about leaving or the fact that she was still scared enough to pack for it.

"You said you weren't going to run." I held on to what very little patience I had.

She tugged the towel up a little farther on her body, grasping it tightly against her chest. "I'm not."

"But you packed this bag, the same bag you used to run last time."

I was being a gigantic dick right now, but fuck, it was too much. First she wanted to learn to use a gun, and now I realized she had an escape plan in our fucking hall closet that didn't include me!

"They threatened you!" she burst out, her own anger rising up.

"So?"

Her eyes widened, and a stubborn glint came into them. "So if I wasn't around, then they wouldn't care about you."

I laughed. It was not a nice sound. "They're coming for me no matter where you are."

Her face paled, and I felt the first prick of guilt.

"If anything happens to you…" The amount of pain in her voice was something I recognized well.

"You leaving here would kill me, Bells. I'd be the living dead. Is that what you want?"

Her face fell, and she buried it in both of her hands.

I'd gone too far, and it was too late to take it back. Rushing down the hall, I grabbed her, pulling her into my body. She stiffened, and I felt the move like a knife, but I didn't let go. I deserved that. That and more.

A floodgate opened up inside her, and she began to sob into her hands, pressing against my chest. I cradled her head, rocking her back and forth a little while I held her tight.

"I'm sorry, sweetheart," I murmured. They were stupid words, seeming far less meaningful than the barbs I'd tossed out earlier.

Why was that? Why were harsh words so much sharper than those of apology and regret?

"Shh," I whispered. "Fuck, I'm sorry. I shouldn't have said any of that shit. I was already on edge from last night and the damn gun range. I opened the closet and saw that bag... It was like a damn arrow to my chest."

Her face was damp when she looked up. "The last thing I want to do is leave. I put that bag there weeks ago... out of habit."

"Out of survival mode." I finished, gently wiping the tears off her face.

She nodded. "It's why I wanted to learn to shoot. If I'm going to stay, I have to be able to fight." She leaned her forehead on my shoulder, whispering to herself. "Being able to fight is so important, now more than ever."

I paused, tilting my head. "Why now more than ever?"

She shook her head softly, almost as if she were trying to clear it. "I just feel this kind of urgency, you know? Like everything is spiraling."

I pressed a lingering kiss to her forehead, and she sniffled. My heart turned over. I shouldn't have yelled at her. I hated that bag and everything it represented, but I shouldn't have yelled.

Saying I'm sorry just wasn't good enough.

I wrapped my hand around one of hers, tugging gently so she would follow along into the bedroom. The shower was running in the bathroom, a total waste of water, but some things were just more important.

She was clutching the towel to her breast when I swiped another tear off her cheek and went into the closet. When I came back out, she frowned, lines pulling close on her forehead.

"What are you doing?"

I dropped the duffle on the bed and unzipped it. "Packing. If you have an escape plan, then I'm going to have one, too."

"Liam—"

I stopped in the midst of pulling a few random shirts out of a drawer. "It'll sit right next to yours in the closet, and if there ever comes a time when you have to run, we'll run together."

I shoved some stuff in the bag, very aware of her watching me, and grabbed a few more things. Without a word, she turned and left the room. Before I could go after her, she reappeared, toting along her duffle. It landed with a thud on the bed beside my half-empty one.

"I'm unpacking," she announced and literally dumped everything out of the bag and tossed it on the floor. Then she kicked it beneath the bed.

I took her shoulders, staring into her eyes. "I shouldn't have yelled at you, sweetheart. I'm sorry. So fucking sorry. I should have thought about it from your point of view. You were only doing what came natural."

"You've been a grouchy grouch all day." She sniffed and looked away.

"Well, you pack emergency getaway bags, and I act like a grouchy grouch. We all have our ways of dealing with stress."

A giggle escaped her lips.

I tried not to smile because I shouldn't smile while I was trying to grovel. It was damn hard, though, because she was standing in front of me practically naked, giggling.

"You can put that bag back in the closet, and I'll put mine beside it. I won't mention it again."

"You would run away with me?"

"There is *nothing* I wouldn't do for you."

She whispered, "Same."

Tucking a loose strand of hair behind her ear, I pulled the edge of the towel so she would tumble into my chest. "Think there's any hot water left in there?"

Her eyes softened with the deep timbre of my voice. "Does it matter?"

I half smiled, pulled the towel off her completely, and lifted her in my arms. Her eyes widened when she settled against the raging hard-on beneath my jeans.

Bells reached between us and undid my pants as I carried her into the bathroom. Just outside the door, I paused long enough to shove them down and step out.

Inside the shower was steamy and humid. Water splashed against my back and splattered my hair. Bellamy made a sound and grabbed my shoulder. "You're still wearing a shirt!"

"I want you."

Her eyelids drooped as I pushed her back against the wet tile wall.

My lips latched onto her neck, sucking all the way down to the collarbone where I latched on again and sucked deeper. Bellamy moaned and pushed her fingers through my hair. The wet strands curled around her hands.

I retreated just enough so her body could slide down the slick wall so just the tip of my dick penetrated her entrance. Pulling my hair, she yanked my head up for a kiss.

My tongue entered her mouth at the same time my dick slid deep. I slapped my hand against the cold tile wall, bracing myself, and began to thrust inside her.

"I love you," I grunted between thrusts.

She pulled my hair again, forcing me to look into her eyes. "I won't leave you, Liam. I won't."

The worst of the storm inside me abated, and I lost myself right there in her arms. I thrust deep again and again. Her body was so slick and warm, so perfectly matched with mine. Too soon, I was breathing heavy and the steady sound of water falling around us was joined by my shouts of release.

Her fingertips dragged up and down my back, playing against my skin and in the water until I came down from the high I always got with her. Once I was coherent, I pulled back, kissing her gently on the lips.

Then I smiled a devilish smile and lifted her off the wall. Her baby blues widened with surprise when I laid her across the bottom of the shower floor and dropped to my knees between her legs.

She lifted her head, gazing at me with a question in her eyes.

I smiled wolfishly, already anticipating her coming across my tongue. Without a word, I lifted her legs and draped them over my shoulders. One stroke of my finger made her shudder and lie back, boneless.

The water cascaded over her body, making her look like some kind of goddess in the rain. Her erect nipples beckoned for attention, so I pinched and played with them before settling back down at her center.

The water stayed hot the entire time I lapped up her juices, or maybe that was just us generating heat of our own.

Regardless, when I was done and holding her close beneath the spray and pure bliss cocooned us, I knew I had to do whatever I could to not let anything get in the way of this. Of us.

It was time I stepped it up.

Bellamy

I knew something was up when Alex sauntered into the kitchen.

People turned to stare at him, abandoning their tasks as he walked through the lines and past stations of people chopping and sautéing as if he didn't notice the attention he was drawing at all.

Maybe he was used to it. Or maybe he hadn't expected it. It had only been a few weeks since he was promoted from ski guide to basically everyone's boss. That little change in the business hierarchy set multiple tongues a wagging. I'd heard very low murmurs of staff members wondering if Alex was qualified for the job he was promoted to or if it was perhaps only because of Liam.

Alex and I were sort of kindred in that, I supposed. Everyone around here was either intimidated or thought me undeserving of working at The Inn. I knew all too well what it was like to walk into a room and have people stop talking or whisper conspiratorially behind my back.

I also knew the jealousy some of the, shall we say, less-confident employees clung to.

"Yo, girl who got away!" he called out before even reaching the station I was working at.

I cringed because the curiosity in the air reached a new level. "I have a name, you know," I told him, prim.

He lifted an eyebrow. "Bellamy."

"More like Belladonna," one of the women working nearby said under her breath. The girl working beside her stifled a laugh.

I sighed.

Alex frowned, then turned his attention to the ladies who I definitely hadn't won over in the last few weeks. It didn't matter how many nights I stayed late or how many tasks I helped out with that weren't even my job. The fact was you couldn't make everyone like you, and in my case, you definitely couldn't make jealous, catty women be nice.

When I just ignored them, Alex made a sound and started toward them. My hand shot out and grabbed his arm. "No," I said, quiet.

He glanced back at me with a defiant look on his features.

"Please," I said, weary.

The last thing I had energy for was a bunch of kitchen bitches. Next to Spidey, they looked like an episode of *Barney*.

It wasn't even worth my time. Or Alex's.

He relented, reaching across and grabbing up some crudité I was cutting up for a large platter. The crisp carrot made a sharp crunching sound when he bit into it, chased by sounds of his indelicate chomping.

Did no one teach him or Liam any manners?

"How bad is it?" I said, leaning a hip against the counter.

"How bad is what?" He shoved the rest of the carrot into his mouth, then reached for a few cherry tomatoes.

"The reason you're here."

He tossed a tomato into the air and caught it with his mouth.

A few ladies walking by giggled, and he spun, offering up a wide grin. "How are you ladies today?"

"We're fine, Mr.—"

"Alex." He cut them off.

They actually blushed, and when they saw me watching them, they scurried away.

"Wow, you are super good with people," Alex quipped, turning back to me.

I levelled him with a stare. "You're really going to make me stand here and worry, especially considering the last time you picked me up instead of Liam"—I stopped and glanced around, leaning in to speak low—"there was an incident?"

"Everything is all good. Liam just had somewhere he had to be." He spread his arms wide. "So here I am."

I pursed my lips. "What aren't you saying?"

"I'm offended." He admonished, reaching for more crudité. I slapped his hand away. He pulled back and cradled the slapped hand against his chest. "Savage."

I rolled my eyes. "Liam didn't call to tell me you were coming instead."

Alex shrugged, averting his gaze. "It was a last-minute thing."

Liam always called. Always. Even when he didn't have to. The fact that he didn't sent alarms ringing in my head.

"You're scaring me," I whispered.

Alex caught my shoulders, leaning down to stare steadily into my eyes. "Liam is fine."

"Then where is he?"

He scrubbed a hand over his face. "You about finished here?" He gestured to the veggies. "We can talk on the way to your place."

"This isn't even my job," I muttered. "I'm beginning to think it doesn't matter how helpful I am in here. People won't like me anyway."

Alex's voice deepened but grew louder as his body stiffened. "People are giving you a hard time?"

I felt a few stares like daggers in the back of my head. Tattling to the boss definitely wouldn't help either.

"No." I lied. Signaling to the girl I was helping out, I let her know I was done and had to go.

After a brief check-in with Chef D'alessio, I grabbed my stuff and walked out of The Inn toward Alex's Hummer, which was parked right at the entrance like a giant roadblock.

We didn't even have our seatbelts on when I turned to Alex. "Talk."

30

Liam

I wasn't scared of what I was about to do.

Apprehensive? Yeah. Walking into any potentially dangerous situation was enough to make any sane man a little nervous, but it wasn't anything with the power to stop me.

Nothing was going to stop me from doing this.

In my eyes, this was something that had to be done. I didn't know if it would help, but at this point, it sure as hell couldn't make the situation any worse.

That's the thing… When the situation a man was in was life and death, he'd already hit the bottom of the problem barrel.

Bottom of the problem barrel = losing my pro-athlete career, watching my father battle terminal cancer, and waiting for the people trying to kill my girl to succeed.

I was spiraling out of control. Everything and everyone around me was volatile. I couldn't—*wouldn't*—just sit back and wait for literally everything to slip through my fingers. I was taking some of the control back. I would use everything in me to fight what I could.

As a pro snowboarder, I learned early and quickly that the only way to thrive in the frigid world of snow was adaptability. Being able to adapt to any kind of condition was key to being successful.

So adapt is what I would do.

Pulling the rental into a spot in the large, barren asphalt parking lot, I shut down the engine and leaned back against the seat.

Ahead, there was a huge concrete building with barbed wire, chain-link fences, and watch towers surrounding everything. The massive floodlights took up a lot of airspace. Everything was sparse and downright depressing.

My phone began vibrating against the cupholder to my right. Without taking my eyes off the building, I picked it up to glance at the screen.

I knew this call was coming. I'd been expecting it. I'd just seen Bells this morning, but I already missed her. And I felt guilty as hell for lying to her.

But I had to do this.

I just hoped after I explained, she would understand.

"Hey, sweetheart," I said into the line.

The call wasn't an easy one, and I kept it short. I knew if I didn't, she would wear me down, and telling her what I was doing wasn't something I wanted to do over the phone. Besides, I'd rather tell her after the fact, when I was home in front of her, rather than have her stress and worry the entire time I was gone.

Hearing her voice and feeling her anxiety was a reminder I didn't need that I had people at home waiting for me. People I wanted to give my time to, but instead, I had to be here.

Swiftly, anger and resentment rose in me. It mingled with the darkness I'd spent a lot of effort battling back. Closing my eyes, I stopped fighting.

Embracing it wasn't nearly as hard as fighting against it. In fact, I quite enjoyed the rush of power that filled my limbs, bringing with it a newfound confidence I knew would be visible when you looked in my eyes.

I might not be as dangerous as the men locked up inside the maximum-security prison I was parked in front of, but I wasn't powerless.

Despite the storm raging inside me, there was also a stillness. An absolute calm that, frankly, I found more unnerving that the anger. I grabbed on to it, though, gripping it like a fine-edged sword.

After retrieving the paperwork I'd already filled out, I made my way across the parking lot to the entrance of the New York State Correctional Facility Getting inside a place like this wasn't a fast, simple process.

The fact I already had clearance and was on the list made it a little easier, but it still took a while to get through security, get a visitor badge, etc. The longer it took, the more time I spent standing inside this cage, the angrier I became and the more deadly calm I grew.

Eventually, I was led into a room with the same windowless concrete walls the rest of the place had. The room was divided in two sections with a large concrete half wall separating one side from the other. A clear partition I knew was highly durable met the half wall and continued up to the ceiling.

The wall itself was separated into four sections, creating four "private" areas for people to visit. Someone was already seated closest to the door, waiting for whoever they were visiting to come out.

A uniformed officer pointed for me to go to the far end. The metal legs of the chair scraped against the polished concrete floor when I pulled it out and lowered into it. The lighting in here was harsh, the overhead fixtures hummed slightly, and even though the walls were concrete, the sounds of buzzing doors and people moving around in rooms nearby filtered in.

Leaning my arms on the counter in front of me, I waited, staring at the empty seat on the other side of the glass. A few moments later, a door opened at the edge of the room and an officer stepped in, held the door open, and gestured for someone to come through.

I kept my eyes trained on the empty metal chair in front of me. I wasn't about to give this man the satisfaction of flying my stare to his face as though I were desperate or even scared.

No.

Not today.

Instead, I sat back slowly, keeping my movements controlled while keeping my eyes on the chair.

A body dressed in an orange jumpsuit stepped around that chair. His hands were cuffed in front of him, his fingers clasped together as if he didn't even notice the handcuffs. I clutched a little tighter to that deadly calm inside me, reminding myself the best reaction to give someone like this was no reaction at all.

It was hard. Oh, was it hard to not rip his arms off and beat him with them.

As I watched the body lower into the chair, my eyes lifted just slightly to the patch sewn onto the jumpsuit on his left breast.

CRONE.

Casually, calmly, I raised my stare and met the eyes of the man who ordered the hit on my girl.

31

Bellamy

"I cannot believe he did this!" I declared for the umpteenth time as I marched through the door at home. I slapped my bag down on the island and spun toward Alex. "Why would he do this?"

"I told you," Alex answered. "There was a last-minute opening, and Liam didn't want to disrupt your work schedule."

"You keep saying that," I murmured, bending down to pet an excited Charlie. "Hey, boy," I crooned, rubbing his oversized ears. "Your Uncle Alex is a liar, liar pants on fire."

"Don't be filling his head with that nonsense."

I stood, flinging out my hands. "Why? You're trying to fill my head with it."

"Why you so stubborn, woman?"

"Why are you lying, Alex?"

"God, I knew generals in the army who weren't this persistent."

I didn't bother responding. Instead, I just glared at him.

He sighed rather dramatically. "Liam's doctor called. They had a sudden opening for this afternoon at the hospital and wanted to know if he could move his appointment up a few days. There was a flight leaving right away, so Liam hopped on. He'll be back later tonight or tomorrow morning at the latest."

"Why wouldn't he call me?"

"He was in a rush to get the airport."

Liam was a lot of things, but it didn't sit right that he wouldn't tell me about this.

"He knew I wanted to be at his appointment."

"You were at work. And you work tomorrow, too. He didn't want to disrupt your schedule."

"He's more important than my work schedule. I would have left without pause."

Alex made a scoffing sound. "Yeah, and from the sound of it, you probably would have been flogged by wagging tongues for weeks."

"Nothing new about that," I muttered.

"Liam know that the people in that kitchen are less than receptive to you?"

"It's not everyone." I rebuked. "And it's getting better."

Alex's eyes narrowed, and just a smidge of that hard edge he sometimes seemed to emanate crept into his voice. "You telling me it's been worse than that?"

I made a frustrated sound and spun, going to the fridge for the pitcher of lemonade I'd made. Charlie danced around nearby, his tail beating into the island, threatening to knock my bag off onto the floor. I moved it aside and set the pitcher down.

The dog got even more excited and clumsy when I pulled out his treat bag. He leapt forward, knocking me back into the island.

"Charlie," Alex warned.

I glared at him. "He can't help it he's big." After withdrawing a snack, I handed it to him, and he flopped down right there on the floor at my feet to eat it.

"You know how it is," I told Alex, getting down some glasses. "I saw the way everyone looked at you when you strolled into the kitchen today."

"How did they look at me?"

"Like they were intimidated."

He made a rude sound. "They should be. And if they know what's good for them, they'll act right toward you, or Liam will clean house."

I threw my hands up. "That's what I'm talking about! People only think I got the job because of Liam, because him and his daddy said so. I've been working for weeks to prove myself."

"Haven't they ever eaten your food?"

"Of course."

"Then what the fuck else do they need, a hand-engraved letter from the Queen of England?"

I ignored him. He was ridiculous. "And to top it all off, now I have you coming into work like we're BFFs and you're the boss, too!"

"We aren't BFFs," Alex remarked.

I couldn't help it. The offhand comment kinda stung. I thought we'd gotten close over the months I'd been here. I'd come to trust Alex almost as much as I trusted Liam.

Aside from the fact he was totally lying to me right now about Liam's whereabouts.

"We're family."

My eyes flew up to him. "What?"

"You don't have just Liam in your corner. You have me, too. Family takes care of family."

My eyes started to mist over, so I got busy pouring the drinks and then putting the pitcher away.

Alex took a long chug out of his glass and set it down with a thunk. "I'm thinking maybe I need to be making more appearances in the kitchen. People need to recognize."

"That will just make things worse."

"People love me," he said, totally clueless. His face lit up like a lightbulb went on over his head. "This why you've been working late all these nights?" Anger crossed his features. "You've been doing other's people's work?"

"It's not like that."

His rude sound filled the kitchen. "Then how is it?"

"It's called earning my place."

He laughed. "The only place ass kissing earns you is that of a whipping boy."

I started to shake my head.

"You don't earn respect, Bells. You demand it."

He didn't get it. I guess we didn't have as much in common as I thought. Of course, people were more accepting of him and his promotion. He grew up here. People knew of the bond Liam and Alex had. And yes, maybe they were intimidated, but as Alex so eloquently pointed out, he liked it.

I didn't blame him for it. Actually, I admired it. Maybe I should learn to be a little more like him. I definitely did feel like life's whipping boy as of late.

"Did you learn that in the army?" I asked.

A dark shutter came down over his piercing blue eyes. It made me so curious as to what those years of his life had been like. I knew there was a story there. Liam said as much. But he also seemed to want Alex to be the one to tell me about it.

"Among other things." From the tone of his voice, I knew right now wasn't going to be the time Alex and I had that talk.

I let it go. I respected his privacy and the right to his own demons.

"About Liam…"

He groaned. "My God, girl. Now I remember why I don't have a bunny. Too much damn work."

"That wasn't very nice."

He chuckled. The sound was very warm and such a contrast to his icy eyes. "Aww, bring it in." He opened his arms wide.

I sniffed.

The chuckle turned into a laugh, and he came forward, grabbing me up for a hug, lifting my feet off the ground. I shrieked, and Charlie barked.

"I love ya, girl who got away. I was just playing."

I was entirely too emotional lately. Going from sass to tears at the drop of a dime. One second, I was ready to fight. The next, Alex saying he loved me turned me into a mushy mess.

I pulled back and looked at him. The crystal of his stare seemed to see through me. "You are a piece of work, but I really do love ya. Like a sister, of course."

Aww, hell. I started to cry.

Alex put me down and stepped back, holding up his hands as if he didn't know what to do. "I was trying to be nice!"

"You were." I sniffled.

"Then why are you crying?"

"'Cause I love you, too," I wailed.

"Women," he muttered.

I laughed and swiped at my eyes. "I was just by myself for a long time," I tried to explain.

Realization dawned, and his face softened. "Ah, I gotchya." He nodded. "You aren't alone anymore."

I sipped at the lemonade, trying to compose myself. Geez, I was acting ridiculous. I was also worried about Liam, something that was not helping anything.

"I'm going to call him," I announced, feeling lighter just thinking about hearing his voice.

Alex nodded. "Good idea. You can grill him for a while."

I held out my hand. Alex looked between me and it.

"I need your phone."

"Where's your cell?"

"I haven't had time to get one."

"Still?" he drawled, pulling it out of his jeans to hand it over. "Well, we have a free evening, so guess what we're doing tonight?"

"So Liam asked you to babysit me until he got back?"

"I hate to break it to you, girl who got away, but you don't have the best track record of being alone."

"Yeah, yeah," I muttered and called up Liam's number on the screen. "I'm going to take a shower before we go. Want to pick up a pizza while we're out?"

"Now you're talking."

I started down the hallway with the cell, the line ringing in my ear.

"Hey! Where you going with my phone?"

"I need some privacy!"

"Leave that in the bedroom when you're showering! I can't be having my phone in the bathroom with you while you're naked!"

I cackled at the horror in his voice and then shut the bedroom door behind me.

My stomach twisted uncomfortably when the line rang again. *Where are you, Liam? Why did you take off without telling me?*

Just when I thought it would go to voicemail, his voice filled my ear.

"Hey, sweetheart."

And just like that, the clenching of my belly eased and a feeling of calm washed over me. "Liam." I sighed.

"Everything okay?" The concern in his voice snapped me back to the reason I was calling.

"Actually, no, everything is not okay."

Tension burst through the line. Liam's voice grew louder in my ear. "What's wrong?" He insisted. "Is Alex with you?"

"Yes, Alex is with me, and that's what's wrong. *You* should be here, not him. I want to know why you got on a plane without telling me and why Alex is trying to feed me some bullshit story about an early doctor appointment."

Silence answered me.

"Liam!" I insisted, clutching the phone.

His voice was quiet when he finally replied. "Do you trust me?"

"Of course I do. So don't take advantage of it."

"I'm doing what I have to do right now. For you. For *us*."

I didn't like the sound of that. "You aren't at the doctor."

"I'll explain everything when I get home."

"When will that be?"

"I'm not sure yet. Tomorrow at the latest."

I walked into the bathroom and stared at myself in the large mirror. "Why won't you tell me what's going on?"

"I will. When I get home."

"Liam…"

"I have to go, sweetheart."

"Liam!" I called out, afraid he would disconnect the call.

"I'm here."

I relaxed against the counter and stared at my feet. "You're safe, aren't you?"

"I'm safe, and I'm coming home to you as soon as I can."

My teeth sank into my bottom lip. "Okay."

"I love you, Bells."

"I love you, too."

He ended the call first. I stood there gripping the phone in my hand, wondering what he was doing that he didn't want to tell me about.

32

Liam

Our stares met and held. Neither of us flinched. Neither of us blinked. His hands remained folded in his lap as though perhaps he were sitting at church, preparing to listen to a sermon.

He didn't fidget. His nostrils and eyes didn't flare when our eyes met. If it weren't for his control, I wouldn't have been impressed by this modern mobster at all.

He was smaller than he appeared on TV. Probably about five feet eight, one hundred sixty pounds. His hair was thick and dark but was peppered with gray, especially at his temples and around his ears. His face was completely clean shaven, and his eyebrows were bushy.

He looked Italian. I think I'd read somewhere he was. Not that it mattered. He could be a blue Martian for all the fucks I gave. All I cared about right now was results.

I didn't bother to lean toward the holes in the glass separating us. I stayed where I was, my eyes not leaving his when I spoke. "I'm—"

His voice cut me off. He had a definite New York accent. "I know who you are."

I didn't react. Frankly, I would have been more shocked if he didn't know who I was.

"Then I'm sure you know why I'm here."

"What I don't know is how." Ah, so he might know who I was and what I was here for, but he didn't know everything. Like how someone like me got in without being approved by him to be on his visitor list.

"Pays to know people."

He seemed amused. A ghost of a smile lifted is face. "You mean the FBI? I'm sure they didn't approve this visit out of the goodness of their heart. What's in it for them?"

"I'm not here to talk about the FBI with you," I replied, mild. My heart beat heavily in my chest. This guy was the scum of the earth, and we were sitting here conversing as if he wasn't.

"You came to offer me money?"

I half smiled. The notion of me trying to pay this monster off was ridiculous. "Will money make you go away?"

"You know it won't." His eyes were dark and flat. I wondered if it was because of his lack of conscience or because he was just very good at shuttering all his thoughts.

"I didn't come here with money," I answered, quiet.

"What, then?"

"I came to ask you a question."

He spread his hand out in a sweeping gesture, offering me the floor.

"What's it going to take?" I said, keeping my tone even and free of the intense anger and hatred flooding me. "What's it going to take to get you to call off your assassins?"

"My assassins?" He scoffed. "What makes you think they're mine?"

I glanced up at the guard standing behind him near the door. My upper lip curled, and I leaned forward. "Let's not lie to each other. We both know you're the one trying to punish her for those cuffs around your wrists."

"Do we?" he asked but smiled. A knowing sort of smile with a glimmer in his eyes. He wouldn't make the admission out loud, not where he could be heard. But Crone didn't have to. The look on his face, almost gleeful and sinister, said it all.

A moment later, his face cleared. He glanced calmly over his shoulder at the guard. Seconds later, the guard disappeared through the door, leaving him alone.

When the guard was gone, I glanced at the empty spot where they had been and then back to him, my eyes flickering with knowledge.

"Let's not lie to one another," he said.

"What do you want?" I deadpanned. Now that he wasn't being listened to, he could spell it out.

"I want her dead."

In my lap, my fists clenched. How I'd love just five minutes alone with him. No glass divider. No handcuffs. No police.

I could do a lot of damage in five minutes.

Cool it.

"Again, I ask… What's it going to take to call a truce?"

He chuckled. "You think I'd call a truce?"

I took a moment to pointedly gaze around the cage we sat in. "Why not? It's not like you have anything else to lose."

"That does not mean I would allow someone else to win."

My shoulders stiffened, the muscles in my neck bunching. "You blew her world apart. More than once. You murdered her father. Separated her from her entire life. She didn't win."

"So you suggest I just take that as sufficient payment for the betrayal, let her live in that charming log cabin of yours with you and your dog, high up on that ski mountain, free to live out the rest of her days in bliss, while I'm in here like a caged animal?"

I gave no reaction. Of course he would know all about our life together, our house. Hearing it, though? Hearing him say it, painting it into a picture, was unnerving.

The thought that someone could be watching her right now and I wasn't there to protect her made my toes curl in my boots and the urge to get up and run out of here overwhelming.

I kept my ass in the chair.

"You aren't here because she tattled on you. You're here because of the decades of criminal behavior you've engaged in."

My words fell on deaf ears.

"She took something from me. I take something for her."

"There has to be something you will trade for her freedom."

"I don't trade. I don't make exceptions. A man in my position lives the laws he made, and everyone beneath him does, too."

I knew coming here was a long shot. It still stung like I was standing in forty-below weather without any clothes. If I didn't know it before, being here, looking into the eyes of this asshole, I knew it. Bells and I were being backed into a corner.

I didn't like it.

"What if I absorb her debt?"

That got a reaction. His bushy brows rose and a glimmer of surprise sparked in his eyes. It made the tiniest spark of hope flicker inside me. "Her debt is her life."

"I know."

"You would die for her?"

A thousand times over. "Yes."

"Making her live, knowing she was the reason you died… That's almost—*almost*—equal to the fact I have to rot in here."

My stomach clenched. This entire situation was so fucked up. And to think, just a year ago, I thought the worst thing that could ever happen in my life was the day I took that fall and ruined my career.

Oh, how wrong I was.

My vision dimmed as I stared at the gangster in front of me. Everything around me seemed to fade as I thought about the gravity of what I just said. Of what it would mean to my family and to my friends.

Even though it mattered, even though they all mattered so damn much, it wasn't enough. I would do anything for Bells. Including giving my life.

Besides, I had a better chance of surviving repeated assassination attempts. She'd totally kick my ass for saying such a thing, but it was the fucking truth.

I'd rather have these assholes come after me than her.

Just to make this clear, though—this deal did not mean I was giving up. Quite the contrary. I would fight like hell. I just had to know she was safe.

I said nothing else. I just sat there while a blizzard raged inside me, leaving me cold yet determined. I sat straight, kept my face blank, and waited for whatever it was he would say.

Crone's head tilted to the side, his eyes shining with something that appeared slightly like surprised admiration. I didn't let it fool me, though. A man like him probably took pleasure in crushing something he admired. In his twisted mob mind, it probably made him think he was somehow better.

"I can respect a man who is willing to come all the way here without anything to barter with except his own life."

"But?"

"It changes nothing."

Cold, bony fingers clutched my heart and squeezed. "One girl means that much to you?"

"It's not the girl that matters. It's what she symbolizes."

I sat there for a few long, silent minutes, reining in the anger threatening to explode. It wouldn't do any good. To rage. To give a reaction. It's what he wanted. I knew that.

But fuck. It was hard.

I wanted nothing more than to punch this glass until it shattered so I could lunge through and wrap my angry hand around his throat. The sound of him choking and gurgling as the example I made out of him would be sweet.

After allowing myself to live in that thought, I pushed it back and sat forward. My elbows hit the concrete counter, and I leaned close to the holes drilled into the glass.

"Remember this moment," I intoned, my voice quiet and chilling. I let that chill, the power of the arctic wind inside me, rise to the surface of my silvery eyes. "Remember the chance I gave you to walk away from her." I tapped on the glass in front of him. "Because if you keep coming for her, then I'll have no choice but to come for you."

His eyes flickered. Something that admittedly surprised me. I didn't show it, though.

Instead, I stood, the metal legs of my chair making an ear-cringing sound as they were forced back to accommodate my body. I towered for just the briefest moment at the glass, gazing down on the physically weaker man before dismissing him completely.

The door buzzed before I even got to it. The guard held it open, anticipating my arrival.

"Thanks, man," I said low as I went through, not even slowing my pace an ounce.

The second that heavy door latched behind me, I halted, turning back. The guard was there, waiting for me to look.

"First time that man has ever sat still and watched someone walk away from him," he told me, approval in his tone.

"Maybe being inside is making him soft." I deliberated.

"Or maybe he's never met someone as hard as him."

I dropped the cloak of black armor I'd wrapped around myself and smiled. "Me? Nah. I'm just a snow jock with a bum knee."

The guard made a sound, glancing up and down the corridor as if to note we were still alone. The whites of his eyes were a stark contrast against the midnight color of his skin. "A snow jock who smacked his head, broke his jaw, and dislocated his shoulder during a qualifying match but still managed to finish competing and secure a spot on the Olympic team."

"Good times," I mused, thinking back to that day. Sheer will kept me on the board. Just like sheer will was going to keep Bells alive.

The guard cleared his throat and stepped away from his post at the door. When he was a few steps closer, his voice lowered. "I don't know why you're here to see a man like that." His eyes rolled back to the room I'd just left. "But I do know that if it was enough to bring you here, then it's not good."

"Every man's gotta look a threat in the eye," I replied.

"It's a good thing you got snow in your veins." He began. "Because dealing with a man like that, you have to be cold."

I nodded and started to walk away.

"Hey," the guard called.

I turned.

"It was an honor. You represented our country well during your times in the Olympics." He held out his hand.

I slid mine into it and shook. "Thank you."

He nodded. Then in a low voice, he added, "You ever need anything, just ask. Name's Reggie."

My eyes met his for a meaningful second, and I knew if I ever needed it, I had an ally. "I respect the work you do here. Can't be easy sitting inside this concrete cage day after day."

He moved back to his post. "It's a job."

"You know the Olympics are finally coming to the U.S.," I said. I tried to ignore the pang of regret it gave me. Those should have been *my* games. *My* gold.

He grinned. "'Bout damn time. Already looking forward to next year."

"What's your favorite winter game?"

"Snowboarding, of course."

I chuckled, even though I had to force the sound past the rock in my throat. "Of course. I'll see if I can get ahold of some tickets for you. Will be a nice change of scenery from this concrete jungle."

His eyes rounded. "No shit?"

I laughed. "No shit."

"Damn. That would be something."

I started to walk away again. The walls of this asylum were closing in on me.

"Any chance you might return to defend your title? On your home turf?" His voice rang out behind me.

My steps faltered, and I closed my eyes briefly. "Don't think the knee will hold up," I said, keeping my tone passive.

"If anyone could make a comeback, it would be you."

I laughed and continued on. I didn't have it in me to stand there and fake it anymore. I was suddenly beyond exhausted. My limbs were limp, my feet heavy.

I wanted to go home. I wanted to see Bellamy.

A comeback, he'd said.

It wasn't a comeback I needed. Not for everything going on in my life right now.

It was a miracle.

33

Bellamy

I went and got a phone. Then we picked up a pizza. The entire time we were doing these things, I was wholly preoccupied with Liam and what he was up to.

Where is he?

Alex told me not to worry. Liam told me not to worry.

I worried regardless.

You know what all the worrying and pizza got me?

A stomachache.

After just a slice and a half, I found myself in the bathroom in front of the toilet, bringing it all back up. Just FYI: it doesn't taste as good the second time around.

TMI?

Too bad. If I have to suffer, so do you.

I shut both the bedroom and bathroom doors and turned on the faucet to try and disguise the noise. I didn't want Alex to know I was puking. He'd just tell Liam and make him worry more.

Liam worried way too much lately. He carried the weight of everyone on his shoulders. I knew whatever he was doing right now had to do with it, but for the life of me, I couldn't figure out his plan.

I was worried about him. I was worried about everyone, and clearly it was starting to take a toll on my health.

After rinsing out my mouth and splashing water over my face, I patted it dry while studying myself in the mirror. I was tired and queasy, my skin too pale.

How much more of this could any of us take?

I wondered not for the first time if staying here had been the right choice or if it just dragged too many good people into the mess of my life.

It's too late now. They're all involved.

Swallowing past the lump in my throat, I dropped the towel onto the sink, noting that it knocked something onto the floor. I bent to pick up the small, white paper bag, staring at it clutched in my fingers.

Oh.

Glancing inside, I pulled out the receipt, scanning it for the date.

The second I saw it, I shoved the bag on the counter and snatched up my new phone. It took a minute to find the calendar, but once I did, I stared at it dumbfounded, just as I had the white bag.

I'd gotten those birth control pills weeks ago. They'd been sitting on the counter, waiting for me to start them the Sunday after my next period.

A period that never came.

Numbly, I put down the phone, glancing between it and the bag.

It couldn't be.

You damn well know it could.

Maybe it wasn't the extreme stress and anxiety I'd been under that had me running for the bathroom and vomiting what felt like almost every night.

Maybe it was something else.

34

Liam

It was *very* early in the morning when I unlocked the door and stepped inside my place. Charlie, with a low woof, was the first into the kitchen.

I dropped all my shit on the counter and petted the dog while looking through the kitchen and into the living room. Bellamy was curled up on the chair near the fireplace, a blanket draped over her. My heart tumbled beneath my ribs seeing her there, looking so innocent and vulnerable. It made me angry all over again that the face-to-face with Crone pretty much got me nowhere.

She deserved so much better.

My eyes stayed fastened on her as I moved quietly into the room, stopping just a few feet away to stare at her.

"Yo," a voice whispered from the couch. I glanced over at Alex sitting up on the couch, rubbing the sleep from his eyes. "How'd it go?"

I shook my head regretfully. "Pretty much like we predicted."

Alex grunted. "You had to go."

"Yeah, I did," I murmured, glancing back at Bells. I'd do it again, too, if I thought I might get anywhere.

There weren't many people I could genuinely say I hated in this life, but Perry Crone? That asshole had a special throne in hell just waiting for him.

"How was she?" I gestured to her with my chin.

"How do you think?"

"Fuck," I muttered. I put her through all that and still came home with nothing to show for it.

She stirred on the chair, the blanket sliding down, hanging partway onto the floor. "Liam?"

"I'm home." I confirmed.

Her eyes widened, still looking drowsy. She pushed out of the chair so fast her legs tangled in the blanket, which sent her spiraling to the floor. I moved quickly, scooping her up and holding her against me.

Bellamy tilted her chin and smiled up at me. "I've been waiting for you to get here."

Everything around us was so fucked up. But damn, when she smiled at me like that, all felt right with the world.

I leaned down and kissed the tip of her nose. Sweeping her up off her feet, I cradled her body against mine. "We're going to bed," I called over my shoulder.

Bellamy's arms wound tight around my neck, her soft breath tickling against my skin. The bedroom was cool and quiet, the only sound the wind outside.

"It started snowing about an hour ago," I murmured, setting her down in our bed.

"The blizzard," she whispered.

I nodded. By tomorrow, everything would be buried under a world of white.

"I don't want to talk tonight." Her words surprised me.

I began pulling off my clothes. "You don't?"

She shook her head. "Will you just hold me?"

The second I slipped between the sheets, I pulled her close. We both sighed in contentment. I didn't think I'd be able to sleep, but I was wrong.

***

The snow was still fiercely coming down the next morning, the wind gusting with ferocity, and the visibility out the window was practically zero. Leaving Bellamy cocooned in bed, I slipped into a hot shower, wanting to wash off the travel and the prison. I'd wanted to do it the second I got home, but Bells's request and the way she felt all warm and soft in my arms superseded that by like a million.

I lingered under the spray because it felt good against my tight muscles and because I wasn't looking forward to the conversation I knew I was going to be having this morning.

Eventually, I coaxed myself out of the steamy bathroom, clad in nothing but a pair of loose sweatpants, still rubbing a towel over my head.

Bellamy was sitting up in the center of the bed, blankets piled around her, with a dog who easily outweighed her at her side. He beat his tail against the mattress as I approached, which made him seem like far less of a traitor.

"I didn't mean to wake you." I spoke quietly.

"You weren't at the doctor, Liam."

I let the towel fall out of my hand onto the floor. "I wasn't at the doctor."

"Where were you?"

"You aren't going to like it." I warned.

I was stalling. I was a procrastinating procrastinator.

Bellamy rolled her eyes, enhancing the adorable just-woke-up look she had going on. "Well, when you didn't walk in with a diamond, I figured it probably wasn't good news."

I paused. "You want a diamond?"

A frustrated sound escaped her lips. "What I want is to know where you were and why you lied to me."

"I didn't lie," I insisted. "I always intended to tell you. I just wanted to wait until I was home."

"Semantics," she injected.

I blew out a breath and went for it. "I went to see Perry Crone."

Her entire face and eyes went blank, sort of like a computer screen that died right in the middle of a big project. Slowly, I watched her reboot. A little realization came into her blue eyes, and she blinked.

"What did you just say?" she whispered.

"I wanted to look him in the eye. I had to see if—"

"You went to the *prison* in *New York* to visit the man who is trying to *kill* me?"

"Y—"

"The most notorious mobster in the modern era…"

"I—"

"How the hell did you even get access to him?" she burst out.

I remained silent. Clearly, she wasn't really ready for my explanation.

"Well!" she demanded as I stood there and said nothing.

"Can I talk yet?"

"Don't you take that tone with me, *Mr. Mattison*!" She shook her finger in the air. Charlie licked it with his giant tongue, and she wiped it on my pillow. "I cannot believe you!"

"That I went to see Crone or that I asked if I could speak?"

Her eyes narrowed.

I sighed. "The FBI got me in to see him. A special favor, I guess, because you know, they've almost gotten you killed more times than I care to count."

"Do you have any idea what you've done?" she exclaimed, rising out of the nest of blankets like an angry snake ready to strike. "My God, Liam! You've made even more of a target of yourself!"

She crawled over the dog and nearly fell out of the bed. She would have had I not caught her. She didn't linger in my arms. Instead, she yanked herself away and stalked across the room. "Why would you do this?" she stressed. "Don't you understand how powerful he is?"

"I don't give a damn how powerful he is!" I yelled.

She spun around, wide-eyed.

"I'm not going to let that son of a bitch sit in some cell, feeling all superior, thinking I'm just going to sit back and let him do whatever the fuck he wants to my girl!"

Her shoulders slumped. "What did you say to him?"

"I asked him what it would take to get him to call off the hit."

"What did he say?"

I shook my head, still hating him for being exactly who I knew he was.

"He wouldn't do it, would he?" Bellamy scoffed. "Of course he wouldn't. He doesn't have to. And now you've put yourself on his radar."

"I don't give a flying fuck about me!" I roared.

"Well, I do!" Bellamy roared back.

She swayed a little on her feet, blindly reaching out to steady herself on the dresser. I rushed forward, not even hesitating to grab her by the waist.

"Hey..." My voice was instantly calm and concerned. "What happened?"

"Nothing," she said, looking pale. "I'm just... I can't believe you went there."

"You deserve better than this, Bells. I'm tired of watching you look over your shoulder, swallowing panic every time someone knocks on the door, and staring at the phone longingly because you want to talk your mother."

"Liam." She reached for my face, but I pulled back.

"Life is too fucking short as it is. You have a goddamn escape bag in the closet, and you've been learning to use a gun!" I paused to take a breath, trying my best not to yell at her because this wasn't her fault.

"What else?" She urged.

"My father is dying," I burst out. "He gets weaker every day. He's at the office less and less because it's just too fucking much for him. I will *not* lose him and you, too. I won't fucking do it, Bellamy."

She started forward. I hitched a breath and took a step back.

"So yeah, I went to the prison, and I looked into Crone's eyes. I told him exactly what the fuck would happen if he didn't step away from you, and you know what?"

"What?" she whispered, almost as if she were afraid to ask.

"I meant it. I meant every threat that came out of my mouth."

Bellamy put a hand up to her throat. The color returning to her cheeks leeched out again. "You threatened him?"

"No," I intoned darkly. "I made him a promise."

"I really wish you wouldn't have done this."

"It's exactly why I waited to tell you until now, so you couldn't try to stop me."

"This is how it's going to be, then?"

My brow furrowed. "What?"

"You just do whatever the hell you want, and I wonder every time you aren't in sight what you're doing and what kind of danger you're putting yourself in?"

My chest ached because I knew this was hurting her, but what choice did I have? "I will do whatever I have to do to protect you."

"You're scared."

I drew up short. I really wasn't expecting her to say that.

"I'm scared, too. Everything is chaos right now." She put a hand to her stomach, holding it there for a moment before dropping it to her side. Bellamy came forward, reaching for my face. This time I let her grasp it, allowing her soft palms to brush against the scruff on my jaw. "You just want some control."

I nodded, mesmerized by the blue of her eyes, the tone of her voice, and the feel of her skin on mine.

"Promise me, Liam."

"Promise you what?"

"Promise me you will never go back there. That you will never see Perry Crone again."

I started to shake my head, but her fingers tightened on my face, holding me so I had to look nowhere but her eyes.

"I need you home. Your family needs you safe."

Something about the way she said that struck me.

"Bellamy…"

"Promise."

The desperation in her eyes forced my hand.

"I promise."

She released my face and fell into my arms. I couldn't help but notice the slight tremble in her limbs. Had I really scared her that badly by going to that prison?

Or was there something else?

35

Bellamy

I buckled way too fast. I let him off the hook for doing something so dangerous and utterly insane. Hell, I couldn't even really get on him for lying.

Because right now I was doing the same.

Liam

Word was out. People knew of my father's diagnosis, and they knew his time was limited. I guess really it was only a matter of time before people found out. After all, I was being groomed to take his place, and before, I'd barely been in the executive offices, having spent all my time out on the slopes.

God, I fucking miss the slopes.

The second I started showing up in meetings and frequenting the offices, tongues started wagging. And with him being present less and less, he felt it best he make an announcement.

I hated it and wished we didn't have to tell anyone anything. I wanted to protect him from the prying eyes, the pity looks, and the tears half the staff was raining all over the place.

Everyone at BearPaw was family, though. Some days I loved that, and some days I completely hated it. My father wasn't just *my* father. He was the father of this entire place. He created it. He nurtured it and made it what it was today. The staff loved him; everyone did. I supposed they all had a right to know.

Still. He might be everyone's father, but he would only ever be *my dad*.

While everyone else cried and was all *woe is me*, I was buckling down. Learning everything I could, taking meetings, and reading a billion financials and documents that honestly bored the living shit out of me.

It wouldn't always be like this, though. Once I filled the tank with all the knowledge I needed, it would become a muscle memory, and I could spend more time running this place and less chained behind a report.

At least I hoped so.

It was like learning how to board. I had to get the basics down before I could get to the fun. With my brain going right back to snowboarding, I pushed out from behind the desk and turned to the window.

My neck and shoulder muscles were sore and tight. I rotated my head and pulled my arms back for a stretch while staring out at the snow.

The sky was heavy with the promise of more. The two feet we'd already gotten lay thickly over everything, pristine and untouched because most outdoor activities were suspended due to the gale-force winds.

I itched beneath the jeans and dress shirt I was wearing. My skin felt suffocated and tight. All that untouched powder beyond these windows beckoned to me like the most dangerous siren to ever rise from the sea. What I wouldn't give to go out there right now, wind and knee be damned, and cut through it all. My board leaving distinct indents that might as well be my initials.

I used to own that mountain.

And now?

Here I was standing behind some glass, looking at it like an animal cut off from the wild.

Glancing down at my leg, I wondered how my knee would fare. Physical therapy was going well, even though it was hard to find time to fit it in. Last time I was injured, I did more for recovery than I was currently.

I had more time back then. Less responsibilities.

A father who wasn't dying.

I was sorely tempted to burst out of this office, raid the locker I still kept in the instructor quarters, and break out on that mountain. No one could stop me.

I could take that mountain back.

God, what I wouldn't give to feel the work of my muscles, the bitter bite of winter across my cheeks. Hear the sounds of crunching snow and the whistle of the wind as I barreled down the mountain.

The glass of the window was shockingly cold when my hand pressed against it. I glanced over, not even realizing I'd moved. So close to it all yet so fucking far away.

Going out there right now would be a dipshit move, and I was no dipshit. My knee needed more time, and I had work to do in here.

Regardless, I stood there at the huge windows and watched drifts of snow blow, the air turning white with powder, and imagined the way it would feel spraying against my bare cheeks.

My phone went off behind me, forcing me out of my happy place. A gruff sound ripped from me, but I spun to snatch up the device. I wouldn't just let it ring, not on the off chance it was Bells, my parents, or Alex.

Everyone else, though, I wished I could order straight to hell.

I made the mistake of not looking at the caller ID. I guess I was still kinda lost in the snow. "Yeah," I bit into the line.

"I have to say I'm shocked. I was beginning to think you were avoiding me."

My eyes closed briefly, and that feeling of homesickness I felt at the window intensified.

"I've been busy," I replied, resigned to this call. I had been avoiding it like the plague.

"That surprises me. Used to be nothing else was as important as your career."

"Things change," I murmured.

"I've been hearing whispers you reinjured the knee."

"Snooping is not your best quality, Joiner."

Tom Joiner was my trainer/coach. He'd been with me my entire career as a pro snowboarder.

"You saying it's not true?"

A rude noise filled the line. "I stretched my ACL a few weeks back."

"That why you haven't been returning my calls?"

"Partly." *Totally.*

"How bad is it?"

"Not as bad as before. I didn't need surgery, and I already had a treatment to tighten back up. I've been doing PT. It can bear full weight already."

"Then I repeat: why haven't you been returning my calls?"

I sighed loudly. "I'm not up to competing. I'm nowhere close to Olympics ready."

"Not yet. It's my job to make you ready. I can't do that if you're avoiding my calls."

"My personal life is a mess right now, Tom," I admitted, turning back to the window. "Even if my knee could somehow withstand the training, I don't have that kind of time right now."

"If I remember correctly, boarding was always therapeutic for you."

"There are people that need me right now."

"We can work out a schedule. I'll come to you."

My chest squeezed. *"No."*

He paused and cleared his throat. "I've been holding off all your sponsors, all the potential new ones reaching out because they want to be part of your comeback."

"There is no comeback," I told him. "Not for me."

"Talk to me, Mattison. Tell me what's going on. It's my job to make this work."

With my thumb and forefinger, I pressed into my closed eyes. "I think it might be time for you to find a new job."

"We've been together a lot of years. I know you. You don't want to end your career because you have to. You've always wanted to go out on your own terms."

I shut my eyes. Didn't he know what he was doing? Baiting a fish that had already been caught. He didn't have to tell me who I was, but the truth was it didn't fucking matter.

"I said I can't."

Yeah, I could tell him about Dad. I could tell him about my new role here at the resort. I could even tell him I was in a committed relationship. Did any of it really matter, though? The answer was still the same.

"I can probably hold off the sponsors another week or so. But not much more than that. There's a window to these things; you know that. Take a few more days. Really think about this, Liam. I can't promise that when the Olympics come back around in a few years, this opportunity will come with them."

I knew that. I knew exactly what I was closing the door on right now. I glanced at my reflection in the window, then back out to the slopes. I thought about Bells and my father, about all the people depending on me.

"I don't need a few more days." My voice took on a hard edge. "My days as a pro boarder are over." I paused, swallowing. Those words burned. "Please give my regrets to Chevy. They've always been damn good to me."

Before Tom could make me feel any worse, I ended the call.

The urge to pitch it across the room in a fit of frustration was pretty fucking strong. Instead, I spun away from the view and tossed it onto the desk covered in papers I only half understood.

Movement in the mostly closed doorway brought my eyes up.

The large wooden door pushed wide, revealing my father. I thought he'd gone home. Guess I thought wrong. And from the look on his face, he'd totally just eavesdropped on that call.

"I think we need to talk."

Bellamy

I snuck out of work without telling anyone.

Actually, I told Chef D'alessio. I lied and told him I wasn't feeling well and didn't want to be around the food our guests would eat.

He sent me out of his kitchen instantly.

I definitely wasn't feeling well, but what I had wasn't contagious.

Liar-itis? Freaked-out-as-hell disease? Or maybe it was a combination of both.

Actually. No. I was pretty sure what I had was a baby. Liam's baby growing inside me.

The instant I thought it, butterflies swarmed my tummy, my heartbeat rose, and a warm sensation that felt a lot like joy tingled through my limbs.

Then I remembered.

This was the worst timing ever for a surprise pregnancy. Liam was already freaked out enough by everything. Adding an innocent baby to the mix would push him over the edge.

Correction: adding *his* innocent baby who was growing inside a target for the mob.

Can you see the conundrum here?

If he was willing to go to such extremes as visiting Crone personally on my behalf, what would he do with an innocent baby at stake?

Ever since I realized how long ago I should have started those pills, ever since I looked at my calendar, I'd been unable to shake it—the absolute certainty that I was pregnant with Liam's child.

I wanted to be happy. But how could I be, knowing everything I was bringing this child into?

We shouldn't have been so careless. Because of me, another innocent person might suffer. And this one would be the worst yet.

I'd been so angry and frightened when Liam told me where he'd gone. But how could I give him hell when I had this big secret hanging over my head? How could I fight with him about trying to keep me (and consequently, his child) safe?

Maybe it wasn't true. Perhaps the feelings of certainty I had were just my fear. I'd done the right thing by saying nothing because there might be nothing to say.

Which was exactly why I had to find out.

So I ducked out of work without telling anyone. It was the only time Liam and Alex weren't watching me. The only time I didn't have a freaking babysitter scrutinizing my every move.

The blizzard blanketed everything with two feet of snow. The newscasters said it was only intermission, though, that Mother Nature, or maybe it was Jack Frost, was only resting to dump another two feet on us starting tonight. I might have scoffed at the idea of another two feet, but the winds were still wild, creating dangerous conditions, promising more was to come.

Other places would have been under emergency, but not BearPaw. This place was equipped to handle the snow. That meant full electricity and indoor activities were a go. The roads were closed, though, which presented a problem.

Getting into the hospital for a blood test wasn't an option.

I couldn't wait. I couldn't go another single day without knowing if I was carrying Liam's baby.

I woke in the middle of the night and remembered the doctor's office here at the resort. It had been opened a few years back for the comfort and peace of mind of all visitors. With so many outdoor activities available, the odds of injury went up. Not to mention the roads were closed frequently due to snow. Ren thought it good business to have a small office available, and thank goodness for that.

I walked to the main building. By the time I got there, my toes were numb and I couldn't feel most of my face. It didn't matter, though. I wouldn't be deterred. I slinked along the hallways like a frozen ninja, terrified that an employee would see me and go running to Liam with news of me being in the building.

The small doctor's office was empty when I walked in, and I breathed a sigh of relief.

The nurse at the front desk glanced up then back down at whatever she was doing. "Hi, what can I do for you today?" she asked.

As I walked closer, I undid the scarf around me and pulled the blue hat off my head. "I'd like to see the doctor, please."

"Bellamy!" she said, recognition dawning.

I forced a sweet smile and reminded myself it was nice to have people know me. It was much better than having to be invisible.

But damn, being invisible right about now sounded pretty enticing.

"Hello, nice to see you today." I had no idea who she was. But everyone knew me. I was the one who took Liam off the market, you know.

eye roll

"Is everything okay? Are you sick? Should I call Liam?" She fretted, picking up the black phone on the desk.

"No!" I said, practically leaping over the counter.

The nurse's eyes widened.

I leaned back and straightened my coat. "Liam is very busy. He's in meetings, you know." The nurse nodded. "This isn't serious at all. I'll just tell him about it when he gets home tonight."

She hung up the phone. "What's it like to live with him?"

Oh my gosh, she said that as if she daydreamed about it all the time.

I seriously considered screaming, *I'm pregnant with his baby, you ho, so forget it!*" but I refrained.

"He snores," was what I said instead.

She giggled. "Really?"

Geez, that was supposed to make him more unattractive, not the opposite.

"Is the doctor available?"

The nurse straightened and cleared her throat. "Sure. Sign in, please."

I hesitated but then signed the log. I didn't really have a choice. When I was done, I cleared my throat.

"You can have a seat," she pointed at the waiting room chairs.

"Would it be possible to wait in a room? I just…" I leaned close. "People gossip around here. Not everyone is as cool as you."

The nurse smiled. "Oh, don't I totally know it."

She ushered me to a private room, and before she shut the door, she told me how lucky I was to be with

Liam. I smiled and thanked her, even though I wanted to kick her.

Once I was alone, I peeled off my coat and dropped it on the chair with my hat and scarf. I was pacing the room when a middle-aged doctor with a bald head knocked, then entered.

"Miss Lane," he said, using the name I was legally given by the FBI.

I missed my old name. My real one. I took comfort in the fact at least everyone here knew me as Bellamy and not Bella.

"The nurse wasn't able to tell me what you are here for today."

I nodded. "I didn't tell her."

"Would you like to tell me?" he said, halfway smiling.

I gestured between us. "Doctor-patient confidentiality applies here, right?"

He frowned. "Well, yes, unless there is something illegal going on."

"Oh no!" I hurried to assure him. "It's nothing like that at all. I just want to keep this private. People around here like to talk."

He glanced at me again. "Bellamy, you said… Isn't Liam Mattison—"

"Yes." I cut him off. "I'm his girlfriend."

"Ah," the doc mused. "I understand. Yes, everything you say to me stays in this room."

"I'm pregnant," I burst out.

"I see," the doctor said, keeping his expression neutral.

"Actually, I don't know if I am or not. But I'm late. *Way* late, and I'm never late. And I've been throwing up a lot… usually at night, though. Is night sickness a thing?"

"I take it this is a surprise?"

I nodded vigorously. Then I paused. "Well, I mean, it wasn't planned, but I guess it's not really a surprise." I blushed.

"How about we run a test so you can know for sure?"

"You can do that here?"

"Sure can."

"Thank God," I mumbled.

"What was that?"

"I said great. I'd like to do it now, please."

After I filled out some forms and answered about a thousand personal questions, he handed me a cup and told me to pee in it. When I was done, I slipped back into the exam room where he was still waiting. I couldn't think of any instance that handing a cup of pee over to a man in a lab coat would ever be *not* awkward.

I climbed up on the table, the stupid white paper on it crinkling so loudly I cringed. I watched the doctor, with his back to me, dip some little thing into the cup.

A few moments later, he turned toward me. "It seems that you are in fact pregnant."

I sucked in a breath. "You're sure?"

"Well, these tests are very accurate. I can also do a blood test if you'd like?"

"Yes," I said without doubt.

He chuckled. "Okay, but I won't have those results back for a couple hours."

I bobbed my head.

He drew the blood himself, seeming to understand that I didn't want that busybody nurse who was obsessed with my boyfriend anywhere near any of this. When he was done, he handed me a script for some prenatal vitamins and promised to call me later in the afternoon. He also gave me the name of a good baby doctor down in Caribou so I could make an appointment.

I don't think I took a breath until he left the room and I was alone. Still sitting on the table, I glanced down at the prescription for vitamins.

Oh my God.

I was pregnant.

38

Liam

"There's nothing to talk about, Dad."

"I beg to differ."

"I thought you went home to rest."

"I went to your mother's office, not home."

I nodded and went around the desk to the chairs in front of it. I didn't sit behind the desk when my dad was there. For me, this was still his office. I picked up some papers and sat down. "Well, since you're here, I have a few questions about this—"

"Business can wait."

"I don't want to talk about it."

"That was Tom on the phone?" He continued as though I hadn't even spoken.

I was a grown-ass man, but my parents sure had a way of reminding me I was their kid. I blew out a loud, forceful breath and tossed the papers back on the surface. My dad took a seat behind the desk and looked at me.

He was thinner than before. His appetite was on the decline. According to Mom, the only time he ate enough to satisfy her was when Bells was cooking, which was often, but clearly not enough.

"Why don't you and Mom take the rest of the day? Go have a late lunch."

"Liam."

I resigned myself to the conversation. "Yes, Dad. It was Tom."

"From the sounds of it, he seems to think you can compete next year in the Olympics."

"He doesn't want to lose his biggest money maker."

"Come on now, Liam. You know Tom Joiner isn't about that. Besides, you've made him more than enough in the past nine years."

"It doesn't matter." I got right to it. "I told him no."

"Because of me."

I shook my head. "Because I have a life here. One I'm not willing to abandon. Not like I did eight years ago."

"You didn't abandon anything. You went after a dream."

"And I made it come true. Now it's time for a new dream."

My father regarded me quietly for long moments. I squirmed under his watchful eye. "Is this really your dream?"

"What?" I played dumb.

"Taking over *my* dream. Being contained in this office. Not competing in the Olympics."

"Jesus, would everyone just quit it with the Olympics!" I burst out, jumping out of the chair to pace. "How many times do I have to say I'm done before everyone believes me?"

"When you actually mean it."

I muttered beneath my breath, then turned toward him. "I'm a grown man, Dad. I'm capable of making my own decisions and owning them."

"I know how quickly life passes," he intoned thoughtfully, quietly. "I don't want you to get toward the end of the road, look back, and have regret."

My chest tightened. "I could never regret doing right by my family."

"No. You couldn't." His chair rotated to the window. "But you could regret missed opportunity."

"We can't have it all, Dad."

He spun back around. "Says who? I certainly do."

"And how's that working out for you?" I quipped, bitter.

Instantly, I felt like a dickwad. Like the biggest asshole to ever exist.

"Dad…" I started toward the desk, remorse heavy in my voice.

He held up his hand and smiled. "I understand your bitterness. I have some of my own."

"I'm sorry." I atoned. "I—" Beginning to make an excuse for my words, I shut it down. There was no excuse. Not a good enough one anyway.

"In truth, though, it's worked out very well for me."

I collapsed into a chair as he spoke.

"I've been a lucky man. To live my dream of creating this place, not just some resort, but a place that people come back to again and again. A place that continues to grow and prosper. A home. And I did it all with the love of my life at my side. If that wasn't enough blessings, I was given you. I'm so proud of you, Liam. I hope you know that. You chased your dreams like I did mine. I might even allow that I am lucky in death."

I shook my head, overwhelmed with emotion but also with grief. "I don't know how you can say that."

"I know my time is marked. It gives me a chance to say good-bye. To make sure you and your mother know just how much I love you."

I glanced over at the bar cart and the giant bottle of Jack Daniels sitting atop it. My vision went a little blurry with the tears forcing their way into my eyes as I thought about that drink.

I blinked them back as vehemently as I could.

I didn't know if I would be remarkable enough to ever think dying was a chance to tie up loose ends, so to speak. I didn't know if I would ever be able to see past the anger and all the years I was going to miss because I was robbed of time.

I couldn't say any of that. My voice barely worked. All I could manage was, "I love you, too, Dad."

My chest ached so much it reached into my belly and ached there, too. The kind of ache that made you feel like you might die a little inside and there would be a hollow spot left behind, one that would whistle when any kind of strong feelings traveled through.

"I admit I feel much more at ease with… the future because I have you to pass down my legacy. But I can't leave this life knowing that my legacy is stopping you from creating your own."

"I'm already an Olympic medalist. I think my legacy is already carved in gold."

Dad smiled. "What a day that was." His eyes turned wistful. "I wish I could be here to see you do it again."

The ache deepened, and though the pain was dull, it was incomparable to anything else. After making sure my voice wouldn't give out, I responded, "You won't miss it, Dad, because that chapter in my life is over."

"I hope it's not."

I fell back against the chair, heavy with grief. "Why are you doing this? Why can't you just let me be a good son?"

He pushed away from the desk, coming around to stand beside where I sat. His hand landed on my shoulder and gave it a squeeze. "Because you are so much more."

His words seemed to echo around the silent room even after he'd gone.

39

Bellamy

I went back home, getting a ride from one of the valets so I didn't have to walk. He swore he'd keep the ride he gave me a secret, and I swore the next time Liam's truck needed driven somewhere, he'd be the one to do it.

Charlie was excited to have someone home early and bounced around the cabin like a giant bouncy ball, knocking over several things and slobbering all over my clothes.

Since I had a few hours to impatiently wait around for the results of the blood test, I figured a good way to spend a few minutes of that was by taking him outside. He definitely needed to run around, especially before the snow started again.

The dog practically took a running leap off the deck when I stepped outside with him. I laughed and threw the ball. It hit the piles of snow and practically sank. I worried he might not be able to find it, but he surprised me and bounded back a few moments later with it in his mouth.

I threw it again, and off he went. Lifting my face toward the sky, I glanced up at the grey, heavy clouds and took a deep breath. The scent of snow was thick in the air, and it reminded me of Liam.

Putting my hand over my middle, I wondered what I was going to tell him.

What would he say?

What if he wasn't happy? Was I happy?

A baby would change everything.

How in the world was I going to keep him safe?

Charlie barked. It echoed with the wind whipping through the ends of my hair. I glanced around, expecting to see him with the ball in his mouth, but he wasn't there.

"Charlie!" I called out.

He barked again. This time he didn't stop. He barked repeatedly, and something about the tone of it sent warning shivers down my spine. Gripping the wooden railing, I stepped off the deck onto the narrow pathway Liam had shoveled early this morning.

It sounded like Charlie was around the side of the house. He never went around that way. He always stayed in the back where the yard was open and there was room to run.

"Charlie!" I called again, my voice catching on the wind. "Here, boy!"

He continued to bark, the sound more and more hair raising with every step I took.

Maybe I shouldn't have come home alone. Maybe I should have called Liam or even Alex. Hell, I could have gone back to work.

I'd only wanted a few hours of quiet solitude to work through some of my thoughts and to figure out what I was going to say to Liam. If there was anything to say at all.

The shock of realizing I was likely pregnant, with the added bonus of waiting for the blood test, forced all other thought from my head. Even thoughts of Spidey and the fact that I was vulnerable here. Alone.

I remembered the guns inside. I might be alone, but I wasn't vulnerable. Not anymore.

The dog made a whimpering sound, and alarm spiked through me. I rushed forward, my feet sinking into the heavy, immense snow as I turned the corner of the cabin. "Charlie!"

He was toward the front of the home, staring out into the trees, tail low, ears back. I scanned the yard, studying the area where he seemed focused, especially around the trees. The entire time, adrenaline pooled into me, slamming my heart repeatedly against my chest and making my hands shake.

I didn't see anyone.

But the dog clearly did.

"Charlie!" I yelled.

He glanced back, then came bounding toward me, putting his nose against my hand. I stood there huffing, my breath coming in great white puffs and swirling around me like ghosts.

Ghosts of my past coming to haunt my present.

"C'mon," I said, tucking my fingers beneath his collar and heading toward the house. I managed to walk briskly to the bottom of the deck stairs, but once there, I raced up them like there was some demon hot on my heels.

Charlie burst inside first, and I slammed the door and locked it immediately. Next, I yanked the curtains over the window and fell against it wheezing. My God, fear had a way of stealing your breath and making your knees weak. It was as if I'd just run six miles, when really I'd done nothing at all. Charlie stood in the kitchen watching me, wagging his tail, waiting for a treat.

"What did you see out there, boy?" I asked him.

He tilted his head and puffed up his ears, listening, but of course he didn't have a response.

Forcing aside the worst of the jitters, I grabbed a snack out of a tin on the counter and handed it to him. Then I washed my hands at the sink and peeled off my coat and boots.

I felt colder than when I'd trekked through the snow to the main building to get to the doctor. I put on some milk to heat for a cup of cocoa and went to turn on the fireplace.

Back in the kitchen, I pulled my phone from my bag and debated calling Liam. I was scared, and it made me feel incredibly stupid. I was at home, for crying out loud. What kind of person is scared in their own home? Besides, I needed time to think. To process.

Going through the motions, I made a rich, steaming cup of hot cocoa and plopped some whipped cream on top. Shoving my phone into my back pocket and wrapping my hands around the warm mug, I went out to the living room to sit by the fire. Lifting the mug toward my lips, I inhaled the milk-chocolatey scent, expecting to be comforted and calmed.

Instead, I started to gag, the scent too rich and not comforting at all. I set it down on the brick surround, some of the contents sloshing out and making a mess. Ignoring it, I took off down the hall, burst into the bathroom, and dropped to my knees in front of the toilet.

I brought up what little was in my stomach and then heaved some more, which caused an aching back and burning throat. When I was finally done, I fell back onto my haunches and wiped my mouth with a tissue.

It was more than obvious I didn't need the extra assurance of the blood test. I was pregnant, and I couldn't keep telling myself it wasn't for sure.

I wanted to be happy, but there was just so. Much. Fear.

At this point, I didn't even think I would recognize life without it.

Oh my God, what am I bringing this baby into?

I wished for probably the millionth time that I could call my mother. I was beyond lucky to have Liam and Alex, even Liam's parents, but really, there was no one quite like a girl's mom. Especially mine.

Tears dripped down my cheeks, the wetness like a giant wake-up call.

Stop it. You will not sit on the bathroom floor, pity party of one, because life is hard. This is not the kind of woman you are, and it's definitely not the kind of mother you're going to be.

Pushing off the floor, I brushed my teeth, combed out my hair, and then smoothed some moisturizer over my face. Since I was still dressed in my work clothes, I went into the bedroom and replaced them with a pair of black leggings and one of Liam's red plaid flannel shirts. It was too big, but I wore a tank top beneath it and buttoned it up so it stayed around me. After I was dressed, I cleaned up the cocoa I'd spilled by the fireplace and dumped the rest down the sink. Just looking at it made me queasy.

The second I turned off the faucet, I reached for a towel, but an odd sound stopped me in my tracks. A low growl, almost like a snarl, filled the space. The hair on the back of my neck rose at the same time I spun.

Charlie was standing in the doorway of the kitchen, facing out toward the living room and hall. The hair on his neck was standing straight up, and the sounds vibrating out of him were more aggressive than anything I'd ever heard from him before. He wouldn't act this way over nothing. Something was wrong…

My heart leapt into my throat. The bottom fell out of my belly.

I didn't bother to call out to the dog. He knew where I was, and he was protecting me.

I reached around for my phone, patted my back pocket, and then nearly had a heart attack right there on the floor. My phone was still back in the bedroom.

Instantly, I glanced to the landline mounted to the wall on the other side of the fridge.

Still holding the towel and mug, I crept forward, trying to be quiet. Charlie didn't let up on his menacing growl, and his hackles remained raised.

When I reached the dog and the wall with the phone, his growl became even more aggressive. Swallowing down my insane fear, I leaned around the wall and looked where Charlie was focused.

There was a man. Motionless and filling out the doorway of our bedroom. A black ski mask covered his face, black leather gloves on his hands.

Most of him was concealed, but not the look in his eyes.

In his eyes, I saw a promise to kill.

40

Liam

I took a shot of the Jack Daniels.

Actually, I tossed back two.

Once the warmth spread down to my belly and loosened the worse of the ache, I returned to the desk, back to the view, and immersed myself in documents.

I tried not to think of the conversation between my father and me. But trying not think of that would be like trying to only see in black and white.

When the phone on my desk rang, I snatched it up, grateful for the distraction.

"Liam, I have the front desk on the line. He is insisting to speak with you."

"Put 'em through," I said. In that moment, I probably would have taken a call from Ronald McDonald.

"Mr. Mattison?"

"Liam." I corrected automatically.

"Liam. This is Kenny from the check-in desk?"

"What can I do for you, Kenny?"

"Um, sir, we have your dog."

I sat up. "What?"

"The big St. Bernard. Answers to Charlie?"

"What's he doing downstairs? Did Bellamy bring him over?"

"He's alone, from what we can tell. He came in the front doors. He was wet from the snow."

The unmistakable sound of Charlie barking came over the line.

"He seems agitated, sir. He won't stop barking."

My pulse spiked. Any relaxation I'd found from those shots was instantly gone. Charlie had been at home. Safe inside with the doors locked and the alarm on. He shouldn't have been able to get outside.

I stood up.

"Put him in the employee lounge, okay? I'll be down to get him in a minute."

"Sure thing."

I hung up the phone and hit another number. The second Alex picked up, I spoke. "You been at my house?"

"No."

I hung up with no explanation, a sense of urgency exploding inside me.

I dialed another number.

"Chef D'alessio," the chef answered after a few rings.

"It's Liam Mattison. I need to speak to Bellamy."

"Bellamy?" he questioned, and that urgency turned to full-blown alarm. "She went home a few hours ago. Said she wasn't feeling well."

I slammed the phone down and ran for the door. With a curse, I doubled back and picked up my cell, dialing hers.

It rang. And rang. Rang some more. When the generic voicemail came on, sweat dripped down my back. "Call me," I demanded, then hung up.

Shoving the cell into my jeans, I ran for the door. It banged against the wall when I wrenched it wide. My secretary nearly fell out of her chair when I charged into the hall.

"Liam?"

"Call the police," I yelled. "Send them to my house."

And then I started to run.

41

Bellamy

I didn't scream. Maybe I was beyond screaming. It never helped anyway. Jerking back around the wall, out of sight from the intruder, I picked up the landline and dialed 9-1-1.

Charlie started going crazy, and I looked up in time to see the big dog lunge at the man who was suddenly right there, rushing around the corner.

This time I did scream.

The dog attacked, knocking the man onto his back. He shouted in pain, and I knew Charlie hit his mark. Seconds later, the dog was shoved away. He skittered across the kitchen floor, hitting the side of the island.

The phone was still in my hand. I still needed to press the final button to actually send the call through. Just as I was about to, the intruder produced a gun and took aim right at Charlie.

"No!" I yelled and threw the cordless right at him and leapt in front of my dog.

A shot exploded in the house, so loud my ears rang. Still trying to protect Charlie, I glanced up, realizing the shot had gone wide because the phone hit the gun.

The pistol was lying near the intruder, and I briefly thought to lunge for it, but the chance I would make it first was slim. And it would leave Charlie unprotected. The man's ski mask was ripped, and red dripped out of the tear and over his lips.

Blood coated the back of his hand as it extended for the gun.

Seeing him recover snapped me back into action. I grabbed the dog by his collar and dragged his heavy body toward the back door. I fumbled with the lock with one hand as Charlie began barking and growling again. I felt sick with fear. If I didn't get him out of here, that man was going to shoot him.

The door flew open as another shot fired, and the sound of wood splintering made me shriek and duck, but I didn't stop. I shoved and pushed a very reluctant and aggressive Charlie outside. "Get out of here!" I yelled at him. "Run!"

A heavy hand clamped around my hair. The leather of the gloves seemed to tangle it instantly as he dragged me back into the house.

Charlie started to lunge, but I kicked the door shut, forcing him to stay away.

As the man dragged me backward through the kitchen, I started to fight. The excessive length of my hair gave me freedom of movement, so I spun, ignoring the way it tugged on my scalp, and kicked out.

I hit his knee, and he stumbled, so I took advantage and slammed my arm down over his, dislodging his hold on my hair.

I ran for the hallway. The sound of my phone going off filled the bedroom, but my phone wasn't what I was after. Wrenching open the closet door, I glanced up to the emergency bag I had packed… and then I looked beside it. To the case with the gun inside.

Frantic, I went for it, but the man grabbed me from behind. His arms were like vises, clamping down around me, lifting me off my feet. I kicked and yelled, and in a fit of desperation, I slammed my head backward, headbutting him.

The force of the hit caused him to let go and stumble away. I dove at the gun case and yanked it down. Several other items fell with it, littering the floor around me as I hit my knees and threw open the top.

The cold, unmistakable butt of a pistol slammed against my temple. I fell to the side but quickly pushed back up and reached for my gun.

He kicked the case just out of reach. It skittered beneath a large scarf that had fallen.

I went for it, but he appeared in front of me, pushing the gun right between my eyes. I froze. The memory of my father being shot and the way the blood splattered haunted me. I had a moment of clarity. *So this is how he felt.*

"Any last words?" the man intoned, and I jerked up.

I didn't know that voice. "Who are you?" That wasn't Spidey underneath that mask. This was someone new.

"Your own personal grim reaper." He had a New York accent.

Since I was low to the ground, I had the perfect vantage point. I swung out with everything I had and punched him right in the nuts.

A choked sound gurgled overhead, and I scrambled away, crawling until I could jump to my feet. He was standing in front of where my gun was, so instead, I ran for the door.

He fired again, and the shot went past me and shattered the window. Snow and cold air rushed in. It was snowing again, the kind of snow that seemed to attack the ground.

Glass crunched under my feet, slicing through my socks and piercing my skin. I didn't cry out, but kept going, yanking open the door as more snow drifted inside, spreading over the threshold and covering the floor.

He caught me before I could rush out into the blizzard. This time when the gun hit me in the side of the head, everything around me went dark.

***

I came to on my back, the hard floor pushing into my shoulder blades creating sharp jabs of pain. Blinking awake, consciousness surged over me, and I gasped, the force of it bringing me up.

"Not so fast." The man grunted and shoved me back with his meaty hand.

I fell back, the ache in my head real. His heavy weight settled over me when his body straddled my hips. My stomach churned, and my limbs felt weak. I couldn't shove him off, but when he forced his face down near mine, I grabbed the ripped mask and tore it off his head.

His hair was gray and buzzed close to his scalp. A large scar cut through his right eyebrow and down to the corner of his eye. His face was smeared with blood, the gash still bleeding, and it gave me some satisfaction.

"Take a good look, sweetheart," he rasped. "This is the last face you're ever gonna see."

I twisted, trying to get out from beneath him. He pushed his body down against mine even more. Breath stalled in my lungs when he reached out and caressed my chest with a knife I hadn't even noticed he had.

I turned my face away, looking behind him to where I knew my gun lay. If I could just get there, if I could get it in my hand, everything would be okay.

A strong gale of wind made the door slam against the wall, and frigid air came with it. The sound of more wind beating against the side of the house filled the place with an ominous feeling.

"Did Crone send you?" I asked, trying to figure out my next move.

"It's nothing personal, doll. I'd come after anyone whose death was worth two million."

So that's what my death was worth?

What about my life?

"Please." I gasped. "I'm pregnant."

He laughed. "Nice try, sweetheart. I'm a man of no conscience."

I grabbed his wrists and started to fight. The knife he held fell out of his hands when he moved to subdue me. I twisted, grabbed it, and felt a moment of triumph.

A moment that was entirely too brief.

He knocked it away, then slapped me full on across the face. My eyes watered and my head rocked against the floor. I squinted up at his ugly face as he levelled the gun right at me.

This was it.

All the fighting. All the running. All the hiding… It all led to this.

"Say bye-bye." He grinned, blood dripping into his mouth and giving his teeth a sickly outline.

And then he shot me.

42

Liam

Outside, a blizzard was raging. Inside me was far much worse. I shoved out the back door, letting the weather pummel my clothes, body, and skin.

All I could think of was Bellamy, praying I wasn't too late.

My snowmobile was parked near the building, the snow coming down so fast it was partially covered. I didn't feel the icy cold penetrate into my bare hands or the moisture from the snow soaking through my jeans.

Snow flew up behind me as I gunned the sled forward, bursting through the small bank that formed while it was parked.

The headlights barely cut through the arctic blast.

It didn't matter.

I would drive across this resort blind and still get there. I didn't have a choice.

43

Bellamy

I waited for the pain. For the blinding white light everyone says offers you a welcome into eternity.

None came.

I lay there cringing and anticipating.

The weight of the intruder's body was no longer over me, and I couldn't understand. Terrified to lie there, terrified to get up, I made a choice.

Squinting open one eye, I peered up. The only thing I noted was the crackling of the fire and the sounds of the vicious blizzard raging outside.

Sitting up, I pressed a hand to my head, fighting back a wave of dizziness. A weight across my legs sent fear shooting up my spine. I gasped and looked down.

My killer was sprawled there, half of him still on me, the other half bleeding out all over the floor. I stared numbly… So much blood. The thick, sticky substance spread toward me, offering me a taste of death.

Shuddering, I lunged back, near hysterical, trying to shove him off my lower half.

He shot me.

I saw the gun. I heard it explode.

So why was I still here and he the one bleeding?

Movement near the back door finally caught my notice. Spidey was standing there, menacing and undisguised, a large black gun gripped tightly in his hand. I swear it was still smoking from the shot he'd just taken.

"You." I gasped, scrambling backward, finally free of the dead body. "Y-you, don't you work for the same side?" I stuttered, glancing at the man he just killed.

He smirked, barely even flicking a glance at the life he'd just robbed. "The only person killing you is me."

"Well, that's not a healthy thing to be obsessed over," I blurted out.

Oh my God. I was losing my mind.

He threw back his head and laughed. It was a sound that would haunt my days and nights. As if to punctuate his vileness, a large gust sent more snow into my kitchen, the white powder creating a cloud at his back.

A horrible cracking sound cut through all the terror and demise in the room, and the house nearly shook when a huge branch outside the living room window broke off a tree and dropped to the ground. A few of the small branches growing off the side scratched the window on the way down, making an eerie sort of scream.

"Must have been the weight of all that snow," I mumbled as if somehow that was relevant or even mattered to what was happening.

"It was fun to play, but the games are over," Spidey intoned and took a step closer.

I sprang into action toward the closet and my gun. I slipped in the pooling blood and fell hard, shrieking because the sticky, metallic liquid seeped into my clothes and clung to me as if it too was trying to pull me into death.

I forced my way up, a strange sucking sound following, and dove into the closet. My hand closed around the case, and hope surged inside me. Spidey chose that second to haul me back, one arm wrapped around my middle.

I clung to the case, but the gun fell out as I moved, leaving me with a useless hunk of plastic. Feeling like I had a second chance here, I swung the case back and hit him in the side of the head. I fell onto the floor, but he instantly gripped me again.

I struggled still, but the sound of an engine cut through.

Both Spidey and I paused, listening to the noise as it grew closer and closer.

I knew the sound. It was Liam's snowmobile. The one he drove to the resort just this morning. Somehow he knew I was home. Somehow he knew I was in trouble.

But, oh my God, now he would be in trouble, too.

"No!" I screamed and kicked, getting loose and diving for the gun.

I picked it up and stood, pointing it right at the man who had caused me hell for so long.

He chuckled. "You even know how to use that?"

I didn't take my eyes off him when I removed the safety and cocked it.

"Touché."

I flicked a glance at the large scar on the side of his neck from when I stabbed him with the pen. I'd say my choice in weapon was much better this time.

"Bellamy!" Liam yelled. His voice carried through the wind and inside the house. He burst through right after. I couldn't see him from my position, but I heard.

Spidey glanced at me and smirked. The gun he had pointed directly at me swung away. "No!" I roared and threw myself at him.

The gun went off right before I slammed into him, and we both went down. He started to laugh, a sound that could melt the blizzard.

I shoved off him and turned to see Liam on the ground, flat on his back, unmoving.

44

Liam

Well, that fucking hurt.

Still, I'd take another and another of those damn flesh-ripping bullets if that meant they stayed out of Bells.

"Liam!" she cried. I could hear her scuffle with Spidey. "Liam!"

The raw fear and grief in her voice was enough to mute the pain and allow me to sit up.

"Bells," I rasped, putting a hand to my shoulder where the bullet cut through me on its way out the door. "I'm okay."

She cried and started toward me.

Behind her, Spidey rose like some kind of phoenix from the ashes.

"No!" I roared and leapt up.

Bellamy spun and fired off a shot, knocking the bastard onto his ass. He sprawled out on the living room floor, and Bellamy rushed to my side.

"You're shot!" She gasped, her hand hovering over me.

"What the hell happened?" I asked as blood leaked through my fingers.

"Sit down!" She fretted. "Sit down!"

I dropped onto a nearby barstool. "Cops are on the way."

"How did you know?" she asked, rushing to get a tea towel from beside the sink.

"Charlie."

"He's okay?" She whimpered. Her face was swollen, and there was a bruise forming on her temple.

"He's okay." I assured her, trying to pull her into my arms.

She resisted and pushed the towel into my shoulder, making me wince.

"They're dead," she murmured. "They're dead." It was almost as though she were reassuring herself.

"They're…?"

Bellamy stepped out from in front of me, glancing across the room. I saw the second body then, and my heart nearly stopped.

"Liam?" a familiar voice called. Stomping up the deck stairs drew my attention. I glanced out the wide-open door and squinted through the angry falling snow.

"Dad!"

"I saw you racing out of the resort and heard you yell for the police." He stormed inside, his eyes widening when he saw Bellamy holding a towel against my shoulder.

"You're shot!"

"He needs a hospital!" Bellamy fussed, swaying on her feet.

"Dear God!" Dad swore, reaching for her. "What the hell has happened?"

A wheeze brought all our heads around. Spidey was on his feet, looking like the walking dead with a literal hole in his chest and blood pouring out by the second. He swayed, his eyes glazed over. But he smiled.

And lifted the gun.

"No!" I yelled, reaching for Bellamy.

"No!" she screamed and pushed me back so hard that I slid backward off the fucking barstool.

The gun went off, and my life condensed into painfully slow seconds.

I hit the ground as Bells spun toward my father, trying to shove him back, too. He evaded her hands and leapt in front of us both.

"Dad!" The sound was deep and drawn out as I screamed his name, almost as if I were underwater.

The second the bullet slammed into him, he dropped to the floor, partially on top of me and Bellamy.

Catapulting up, I bent over him, pressing my hands against his chest wound, tears already filling my eyes as he gasped and gurgled for breath.

Sirens echoed outside, and bright emergency lights shone off the snow.

"Hang on, Dad. Help is here. Don't you die on me!" I screamed.

His hand covered mine where I was pressing as hard as I could against his wound. "Son," he rasped, barely audible.

"Don't talk. Save your strength." I urged.

"Bel-Bell—"

I realized what he was trying to tell me. In my haste to make sure he was okay, I'd lost track of Bells.

Another gun went off. It fired until the sounds of an empty clip echoed through the house.

Bellamy

I tried to protect them, both of them.

Both of them had bullet holes. Both of them were weeping blood. I stood there staring down at the man I loved more than life as he pled with his father not to die. I thought of the baby growing inside me who almost had no chance at life.

The grief and horror was so overwhelming I felt a part of me completely shut down. Sound dimmed out, leaving the humming echo of silence everywhere around me.

I turned, staring at where Spidey had fallen to his knees, gasping for breath as blood dripped from his lips. He raised his weapon one more time, pointing it at me...

I snapped.

Marching forward, I stared down the barrel of his pistol as a cough wracked his body. I kicked the gun out of his hand, and it skittered across the floor. My weapon was lying near my feet, right where it had fallen when I tackled him.

We both saw it at the same time, but I was faster.

I picked it up and took aim.

Spidey smiled.

I shot him over and over. I shot him until there were no bullets left, but I kept on pulling that trigger.

If I could, I would kill him a thousand times over.

Warmth I didn't even know existed anymore enveloped my side. A hand much larger than my own wrapped around and pulled the gun from my grasp. My arm fell as though it weighed a hundred pounds, and I stared down at the man I'd known as Spidey.

He was dead.

Riddled with bullet holes.

Eyes wide open, glassy and empty. Blood everywhere. On him. On me. All over this house.

It wasn't good enough. It would never be good enough. I lunged for the gun again, a cry ripping from my throat.

"No." Liam's voice wrapped around me, reminding me there was more than just thick silence.

I glanced over at him, taking in his jaw, his scruff, and the hair falling into his eyes. "Liam?"

"He's dead, sweetheart. You killed him."

"I killed him," I repeated.

He nodded.

I collapsed against him, and it was as if the world resumed in fast-forward around us.

I gasped, pulling out of his arms. "Ren!"

"He's being taken to the hospital. We've got to go," Liam replied, gently wrapping an arm around me. He handed the gun off to an officer standing by warily.

"She needs to come with us," he said, taking the weapon I'd used to kill Spidey.

"She's coming with me, and if you don't want a scene and a lawsuit that will shut your precinct down, you won't get in my way," Liam intoned, and I shivered. "Call the police chief and have him meet me at the hospital. Call Agent Frost of the FBI, too."

I don't know if the officer replied, but the next thing I knew, I was being lifted into the back of an ambulance, my eyes fastened on the pallid face of Renshaw Mattison as the paramedics worked to save his life.

Shivers wouldn't leave me be. My entire body shook and trembled, no matter how many scratchy blankets they put around me.

The second we got to the hospital, we were forced apart. Liam had to get stitches, Ren went into emergency surgery, and I… They said I was in shock.

Maybe I was. Maybe I wasn't.

I was clearheaded enough that when they came at me with a shot, I recoiled and told them I was pregnant. That seemed to send them into another flurry of activity, and before I knew it, I was on my back with cold gel being slapped onto my belly.

"Would you like me to go get the father?" the nurse asked kindly.

"No," I said, tears filling my eyes.

The ultrasound confirmed what the blood test would have. I was pregnant. My entire world came rushing back, reality in all its grim glory as I stared, weepy, at the tiny little peanut on the monitor.

"I'd put you at seven to eight weeks," the technician said. "Shall we see if we can hear the heartbeat?"

I stared at the monitor a few moments longer, feeling slightly remorseful that Liam wasn't here to see the first glimpse of his child.

"Miss?" the technician said, glancing at me.

I tore my eyes from the monitor. "Can we hear it?"

"Usually, you can hear the heartbeat around eight weeks. We can try."

I nodded. "Okay."

Again, I felt guilty for doing this without Liam. But at the same time, I wanted to hear. I needed proof that the baby inside me was okay after everything that happened.

It seemed to take forever. The silence stretched throughout the room as the wand moved around my belly. Anxiety started to fill my lungs and tighten my chest.

What if something is wrong?

Just as I was about to ask why there was no sound, I heard it.

I gasped and glanced at the technician with wide, questioning eyes.

He smiled. "There's your baby."

"That's my baby?" I repeated, awed.

Whoosh-whoosh-whoosh. It was kind of like an echo but consistent and strong.

Tears burned the backs of my eyes. Seeing the blob on the monitor had been amazing. But hearing it? Having tangible proof that a piece of Liam was growing inside me?

It was incredible.

"How is he?" I worried. "Is the heartbeat okay?"

The tech nodded. "Baby is just fine. Nice strong heartbeat. I'd say you're definitely at least eight weeks."

"Can you print out a picture?" I asked, swiping the tears off my cheeks.

A few seconds later, I was handed a black-and-white image filled with blobs. I wanted to be happy, so happy... but how I could I be?

Minutes later, Liam's angry snarl came from outside the partition, and in seconds, the curtain was ripped back to reveal his naked torso and glittering eyes.

"Bells," he rumbled, a great deal of tension visibly leaving him when his eyes found mine. "Are you okay?"

I nodded, slyly sliding the sonogram behind me.

Liam glanced at the ultrasound equipment parked nearby. "What the fuck is all this? What's wrong?" He rushed toward me, sweeping me against his chest.

"I'm fine." I assured him. "That was already here when I got here."

Behind him, the nurse made a face, and I prayed she wouldn't rat me out.

"Can you give us a minute?" Liam said, kind of snappy.

She left without a backward glance.

Liam grasped me gently, his eyes stoic and concerned. "I'm so glad you're okay," he murmured, pulling me against him.

My cheek pillowed against the warm flesh of his chest. The steady, strong beat of his heart reduced me to tears.

Hearing me sniffle, Liam drew back, swiping the tears away, and kissed my hairline. "What is it, baby?"

I stared at the giant white bandage taped across his shoulder. "He shot you," I murmured, grazing unsteady fingers over the edge.

He caught my hand and kissed the fingers. "Bullet went clear through. It's nothing serious."

"Ren?" I asked, my eyes seeking his.

The gray dulled, and worry filled his face. "He's still in surgery."

I started to cry. I thought I was numb, cried out even, but I guess I was wrong. Liam held me close while I washed his torso with tears and muffled my cries of grief with his strength.

"Let me see you," he murmured after a while, pulling me back and holding my face in his hands. "I need to look at you."

The gentle way his fingertips perused my face, grazing gently over the bruising, made me feel as if everything might actually be okay.

"Liam?" I tipped my chin back, seeking his gaze.

"Hmm?" He dropped a tender kiss against my lips.

"Do you think it's over?" I hated the way my voice wobbled.

He gathered me close again. "Don't worry about that right now."

"I killed a man."

"He wasn't a man. He was an animal."

"Liam?" A woman's frantic voice echoed nearby. "Liam Mattison?"

"Mom," he said, instantly rushing around the curtain. "Mom, I'm here."

"Oh, honey, what on earth is going on? They say your father is in surgery!"

Liam wrapped an arm around his mother and glanced at me from the hall.

Go, I mouthed, gesturing that he should be with her.

He hesitated, clearly unsure what to do.

She pulled back and gasped, seeing the bandage on his shoulder. "You're hurt!"

"I'm fine."

"Where's Bellamy?"

"I'm here," I said, seeing the absolute way her life was crumbling around her just then, her son, her husband.

All because of me.

"Go see if there's word on Ren." I urged. "I'll get dressed and join you."

Gripping Liam like a lifeline, his mother went off, frantic to find out how her lifelong love was faring.

When they were gone, I pulled the curtain back around and ignored the protests in my body as I glanced around for my clothes.

They were saturated with blood.

I didn't even have shoes.

Leaving the clothes where they lay, I picked up the sonogram, eyes roaming over it. Carefully, I tucked it into my panties beneath the hospital gown because there was nowhere else to put it and left the cubicle in search of Liam.

"Oh, Mrs. Mattison," a nurse said as I walked by. She called out again, and I turned, no idea that she'd been talking to me.

She must have thought Liam and I were married.

"Yes?"

"Your father-in-law has just been moved to a private room. They sent us to tell the family."

Already?

I glanced at the doctor standing a few feet behind her, a surgical mask pulled below his chin.

"How is he?"

"I'd rather talk to everyone at once," the doctor said.

I heard what he didn't say. I felt the dread surrounding us all and pushed a hand over my mouth, swaying.

"Oh!" The nurse caught me, offering a steadying hand. "Honey, he's still alive. He's in his room."

"I need to see him," I begged. "Please."

"Where is his wife and son?" the doctor asked. I didn't know how he could stand there so calmly while everything fell apart.

"They went that way, trying to find answers," I said, motioning down the hall.

He started that way, and the nurse pulled me along.

I grabbed her hand and squeezed. "I need to see him. Now."

She glanced back toward the doctor, unsure.

I squeezed her hand again. "He saved my life."

She nodded once and led me to his room. Hesitating at the door, she said, "He needs rest. Don't upset him."

I nodded emphatically and stepped inside.

The sound of monitors beeping filled the tomb-like room. The bed was in the center of the space, the curtains drawn, only the light of the hallway illuminating him. Ren looked small and ghostly against the hospital sheets. I was overcome with confusion and despair at how a man like him could look so... frail.

My steps slowed to a near crawl, even though I felt like running to his side. I glanced back at the door, suddenly feeling as though this wasn't my place. The first to see him should be his wife and son. I shouldn't be here without them.

I started back toward the door, planning to wait in the hall.

A sound came from the vicinity of the bed, and I stopped, turning back.

He made the sound again, and one of his fingers moved.

"Ren?" I said. "Ren, can you hear me?"

He made a sound again, and I rushed to his side. Carefully, I took his hand, wrapping both of mine around it. His skin was cold, his fingers bony.

"Holly and Liam are on their way up. They'll be here in just a minute."

His eyes blinked open, and he focused on me.

I couldn't keep the tears at bay. They slid one after another down my cheeks, and I pretended they weren't even there. "You saved my life," I said, unable to keep the words in. "You jumped in front of a bullet meant for me."

He made another sound.

I squeezed his hand gently. "I wish you wouldn't have done that. But thank you. Thank you so much for saving my life."

"Son… l-loves you," he rasped, each word a struggle.

I swallowed and leaned down to kiss his head, then lay my cheek against his. "I'm pregnant," I confided.

A sound of surprise but also of joy erupted out of him. I pulled back and gazed down at him. His eyes sought mine.

I nodded. "You didn't save me today. You saved your grandchild."

A tear slipped out of the corner of his eye, and I brushed it away. "You're the first to know," I whispered.

He glanced down toward my stomach, so I stepped back a little so he could see. "It's still early." I cautioned. "I'm not showing yet."

He lifted his hand, shaking with the effort.

Knowing what he intended, I lifted it and pressed it against my stomach.

"Love," he said, his eyes bright as he looked at where his hand lay.

I nodded.

"Take care… of… them."

I leaned forward over him. "I will, but you will, too. It's not your time yet." My chest began squeezing, closing off like it was being crushed.

"Dad?" Liam said from the doorway.

"Ren!" Holly cried and rushed through the door to his side. He turned his head toward her, a smile on his lips.

I stepped away from the bed and felt Liam's stare. "The nurse led me here," I explained. "I was going to wait for you, but he was awake…" I gazed back at the man who'd saved my life. "I didn't want him to be alone."

On his way past me, Liam linked our hands. "Thank you."

Holly was crying, and Ren was trying to reassure her. Liam stood stoically at his side. I could feel the tension and grief wave off him like a tsunami.

I slinked back into the curtain, wanting to give this family time to grieve, time to say good-bye.

46

Liam

We saw the doctor coming before he even looked in our direction. Mom would have fallen in her haste to get to him had it not been for the hold I kept on her.

"How is he?" she asked, pleading for good news.

"Mrs. Mattison?"

"Yes," Mom said impatiently. "How is my husband?"

"There is no easy way to say this." He began, and Mom nearly collapsed right there.

"No," she keened, and it was the most helpless I'd felt in my entire life. My throat was bone dry, my eyes gritty with sand and regret. The only thing that kept me on my feet was sheer will.

"He's still alive," the doctor hastened to say.

Mom perked up. The horrible sounds she was making ceased. I didn't feel any better because I knew. I knew deep down in my gut that this man had no good news.

"He is?"

The doctor nodded once. "Unfortunately, we weren't able to go ahead with the surgery," he explained and glanced at his clipboard. "The patient—"

"His name is Renshaw," I growled.

My father was more than a patient. More than a piece of paper. *More.*

The doctor cleared his throat. "Renshaw. I see he is terminally ill… the cancer having spread quite widely throughout his body."

I swallowed.

"Given that and the recent loss of blood, he wouldn't survive the kind of operation he requires."

"So we wait?" Mom said. "Until he's stronger?"

The doctor cleared his throat again, and for a nanosecond, I felt bad for the man. "I'm afraid he doesn't have much time. We've moved him into a room and are keeping him comfortable. But I would recommend going and saying your good-byes."

The doctor's words hit like being shot all over again. I'd known my father was living on borrowed time. I just had no idea that it would run out this fast.

"I want to see him!" my mother demanded. "Right now!"

A nurse came forward and led the way. The entire time we followed, I felt I was being brought to a firing squad. I had no idea what I would see when we walked into his room. I had no idea how I would hold it together.

I didn't expect him to be awake. I didn't expect Bells to be standing there holding his hand. Seeing them like that, seeing him living in the moment, gave me a spark of hope.

I didn't know which was worse. A spark of hope or the darkness that followed when the spark burned out.

Mom rushed into the room, right to his side, and as I watched her, my heart deflated.

"I love you," she whispered, kissing him on the cheek.

"My love," Dad answered, his voice so incredibly weak.

Mom climbed onto the bed, fitting herself alongside him, gently draping her arm over his middle. I almost turned away. It felt invasive to be here. It felt way too hard.

"Son," Dad mumbled, and I let go of the hold I had on Bellamy.

"Right here, Dad." I promised, leaning close so he could see me.

"Too hard on you," he said, pausing to take a breath between each word.

"Never." I assured him, suddenly feeling overwhelming regret our "last" talk had been sort of an argument. "You have always been exactly what I needed," I said, hoping to put his mind at ease, wanting him to know I respected him.

"Live... your... dreams," Dad implored.

The grit in my eyes washed away as tears flooded them. "I will. I swear."

Dad lifted his hand, and I went down, hugging both him and my mother for what would become the last family embrace we would ever have.

"No regrets," Dad whispered. "Bell—"

I reached out behind me, motioning for Bells. She came, and I pulled her down to be part of the embrace.

"I love you all," he whispered, his eyes fluttering closed.

"Ren!" Mom worried, lifting her head.

He smiled. "Just resting, love."

I listened to the sound of his labored breathing for a while, none of us daring to move an inch.

I sensed my father's eyes fluttering open and lifted my head.

His stare was slightly unfocused and sort of glassy, but I could have sworn he looked into mine. "Take care of them... especially him."

Him? Did he mean her? Mom?

"I promise." I vowed.

A look of pure peace came over him, and his eyes flickered closed.

They didn't reopen.

Bellamy

We stayed with the body until the staff ordered us out.

It was hard to walk away, hard to say good-bye, even harder to see how completely shattered Liam and his mother were.

This was my fault.

He won't look at me.

I was no longer his second chance, the girl who got away. I was the woman who came back and shattered his world, bringing death and pain.

I should have run. I never should have promised to stay. I thought about the duffle out in the hallway. I doubted he would even try and stop me if I tried to leave.

I was nothing but a painful memory now, a visual reminder that his father was dead.

I knew all too well what it was like to lose a father. It was something you never quite healed from.

I shouldn't stay.

I couldn't go.

My body wasn't just mine any longer. It was Liam's, too.

How was I going to tell him? What on earth would he say?

I was the woman who killed his father—but also the woman who would make him one.

48

Liam

How could I look at her?

I'd failed my family in the worst possible way a man could.

I heard her moving quietly around in our bedroom. Numbly, I wondered if I would ever be welcome there again. Bellamy almost got killed tonight. My father did.

My father did.

I will never see him again. Never hear his laugh, never again feel that bond between father and son.

He said he didn't have regrets.

I did. *I do.*

Large, gaping, ugly regrets that would leave even uglier scars.

Outside the window, the landscape was black. That color called to me, welcomed me, begged to swallow me. I fought it back because this wasn't over. I couldn't succumb to the demons inside me. I might have fucked this shit up profoundly, but I would die before I let anyone else I loved die.

Almost as if conjured, there was a sudden light rap on the back door. Every muscle inside me tightened so tautly I hummed. As I moved rapidly toward the door, adrenaline surged through my limbs, offering feeling to my otherwise numb form.

Fight and anger, which I feared I'd lost, rose inside me. Resolve and determination rooted deep down and bloomed fast. I glanced down the hallway as I went, a pinched feeling coming over my heart when I saw the closed bedroom door.

I continued on and yanked open the door with so much force the curtains slapped against the window. Winter swirled up around me, almost like armor, reminding me that I was *made* of snow.

Light powder gusted in, sprinkling my legs and feet. I barely noticed because I was too focused on who was there.

No one.

But a note. Dangling on a string from the top of the doorframe.

The white envelope waved around in the wind, the paper already damp from the snow.

I snatched it down, glanced around the empty yard, and shut the door. I didn't bother throwing the lock. If someone came at me right now, I'd smile and kill them with my bare hands.

As I stalked back to my position in front of the living room window, the cold stayed pressed against my skin. The envelope was sealed with old-school wax, the color blood red, the symbol one that made my upper lip curl.

I plucked it off and tossed it down without another glance, pulling open the single sheet of paper that was folded in half.

William…

The letter began. He thought he was clever, using a name on my birth certificate, a name barely anyone realized was mine. His knowledge didn't make him intimidating. It made him a nuisance.

My deepest regrets on the death of your father. The loss of anyone close to us leaves wounds that will never heal. As it is, I've considered your request of a trade. Perhaps this jail cell is making me soft, or perhaps I feel sorry for you. In any case, I have decided that the debt is paid.

You killed one of my men, and I killed one of yours.

It's rather poetic that you will have to live knowing you sacrificed your father for a woman. And she will have to live with knowing you will blame her for that for the rest of her days.

The bounty I put on Bellamy is void.

Congratulations on the fulfillment of the debt.

Sincerely,

PC

I crumpled the paper in one hand, squeezing until my knuckles popped and ached. Dropping it at my feet, I glanced back out the window, back into the darkness.

You killed one of my men, and I killed one of yours.

He thought I killed Spidey. He was taking credit for the death of my father.

Perry Crone thought that made us even. He thought this was over.

He was wrong. I was just getting started.

Crone was a man who usually did the chasing. I wondered how he'd react when it was his turn to run.

THE END

—for now—

AUTHOR'S NOTE

This book has no cliffhanger at all. I'm expecting everyone to be super thrilled about it.

Don't you just love when a book wraps up and there are no loose ends, nothing to wonder about?

Me, too!

But seriously, I didn't really plan for Blizzard to end this way, but here we are. I gotta say this wasn't an easy write. There were more twists and turns than I expected. In the end, I like how this story came out. I like the growth of the characters and the way the plot was propelled forward. I never really intended for this series to be quite as dark as it's become or for Liam to be as flawed. It's definitely got some suspense thrown in with the romance, but hopefully you will find a good mix of both.

I really debated on Ren... his cancer, his death... everything.

I have *never* wanted to write cancer. It's touched my life far too many times. So when this was whispered in my head by the characters, I searched for other plots. I searched for anything different. But some characters won't be swayed, and so Ren revealed he was terminally ill. I know the end of this book is sad, but to be honest, it was almost a relief for me. I'd rather Ren die saving the life of people he loves than wasting away in a bitter battle with a disease that would win out in the end.

I want to thank you for reading this one and for being patient while I completed it. I hope it was worth the wait and that you will continue on with book three.

Without you, the reader, I wouldn't be able to do what I love. Your support is invaluable in so many ways.

See you next book (which hopefully won't have a cliffhanger)!

XOXO,
Cambria

ABOUT CAMBRIA HEBERT

Cambria Hebert is an award-winning, bestselling novelist of more than forty books. She went to college for a bachelor's degree, couldn't pick a major, and ended up with a degree in cosmetology. So rest assured her characters will always have good hair.

Besides writing, Cambria loves a caramel latte, staying up late, sleeping in, and watching movies. She considers math human torture and has an irrational fear of birds (including chickens). You can often find her painting her toenails (because she bites her fingernails) or walking her Chihuahuas (the real rulers of the house).

Cambria has written within the young adult and new adult genres, penning many paranormal and contemporary titles. She has also written romantic suspense, science fiction, and most recently, male/male romance. Her favorite genre to read and write is contemporary romance. A few of her most recognized titles are: *The Hashtag Series, GearShark Series, Text, Amnesia,* and *Butterfly*.

Recent awards include: Author of the Year, Best Contemporary Series (*The Hashtag Series*), Best Contemporary Book of the Year, Best Book Trailer of the Year, Best Contemporary Lead, Best Contemporary Book Cover of the Year. In addition, her most recognized title, *#Nerd*, was listed at Buzzfeed.com as a top fifty summer romance read.

Cambria Hebert owns and operates Cambria Hebert Books, LLC.

You can find out more about Cambria and her titles by visiting her website: http://www.cambriahebert.com.
Please sign up for my newsletter to stay in the know about all my cover reveals, releases and more:
http://eepurl.com/bUL5_5.